"I have rage,"

"So much rage. I don't know what to do with it. I don't want it and yet it just...sits there." Her breath emerged on another sob. "This is why you work alone, isn't it? If you don't let anyone in, if you don't trust, then you can't feel...this."

"The flip side is there's the risk I'll stop feeling anything," he admitted as he eased his hold and set her back so he could look down at her. Something he didn't often get to do when she was wearing those heels of hers. He held her face in his hands, stroked his thumbs down the sides of her face, which contained no trace of the tears he expected to find.

Her hands gently clasped his wrists, holding him in place as she looked up at him. Her dark eyes shimmered with the only thing he ever wanted to see in their depths: hope. And promise.

Dear Reader,

From the moment Howell McKenna walked on the page of *Arctic Pursuit*, I looked forward to writing his story and finding the perfect woman for his HEA. Enter Kara Gallagher, federal prosecutor and the woman responsible for Howell's former partner losing his job. To say sparks fly between these two from the start is an understatement. Trust isn't easy for either of them, and their differences are many. One thing they agree on? The need for and the importance of justice.

Kara has spent most of her life dedicated to making the man responsible for her father's death pay. If there's one thing Howell understands, it's the importance of family. But Howell also sees her desire for justice might be clouded by a desire for revenge, and after falling fast for this headstrong, determined single mother, he's willing to do anything to ensure she doesn't cross the line.

I hope you enjoy Kara and Howell's search for justice... and their winding road to happily-ever-after.

Happy reading,

Anna J

UNDER THE MARSHAL'S PROTECTION

ANNA J. STEWART

ROMANTIC SUSPENSE

If you purchased this book without a cover you should be aware that this book is stolen property. It was reported as "unsold and destroyed" to the publisher, and neither the author nor the publisher has received any payment for this "stripped book."

Harlequin ROMANTIC SUSPENSE

Recycling programs for this product may not exist in your area.

ISBN-13: 978-1-335-47170-3

Under the Marshal's Protection

Copyright © 2025 by Anna J. Stewart

All rights reserved. No part of this book may be used or reproduced in any manner whatsoever without written permission.

Without limiting the author's and publisher's exclusive rights, any unauthorized use of this publication to train generative artificial intelligence (AI) technologies is expressly prohibited.

This is a work of fiction. Names, characters, places and incidents are either the product of the author's imagination or are used fictitiously. Any resemblance to actual persons, living or dead, businesses, companies, events or locales is entirely coincidental.

For questions and comments about the quality of this book, please contact us at CustomerService@Harlequin.com.

TM and ® are trademarks of Harlequin Enterprises ULC.

 Harlequin Enterprises ULC
22 Adelaide St. West, 41st Floor
Toronto, Ontario M5H 4E3, Canada
www.Harlequin.com

MIX
Paper | Supporting responsible forestry
FSC® C021394

Printed in Lithuania

Bestselling author **Anna J. Stewart** honestly believes she was born with a book in her hand. After growing up devouring every story she could get her hands on, now she gets to make her living making up stories and fulfilling happily-ever-afters of her own. Her dreams have most definitely come true. Anna lives in Northern California (only a ninety-minute flight from Disneyland, her favorite place on earth) with two monstrous, devious, adorable cats named Sherlock and Rosie.

Books by Anna J. Stewart

Harlequin Romantic Suspense

The McKenna Code

Arctic Pursuit
Under the Marshal's Protection

The Coltons of Roaring Springs

Colton on the Run

Colton 911: Chicago

Undercover Heat

The Coltons of Owl Creek

Hunting Colton's Witness

Visit the Author Profile page
at Harlequin.com for more titles.

For Cari. Thanks for walking me through this one.

Chapter 1

United States Marshal Howell McKenna shoved out of the chartered helicopter before it fully touched down. Ducking to keep his six-foot-three-inch frame out of the whipping blades, he circled around the front of the aircraft, moving quickly toward the spinning lights of the local sheriff's SUV parked nearby. Twenty-three miles from his destination, this was the only clearing large enough this deep in the southern Virginia woods for the chopper to land. He had time and ground to make up. Fast. He wanted this over and done before the sun came up.

"Sheriff Hayes?" He shouted as the chopper took off again and drifted into the pitch black of a cold February night.

The middle-aged man holding on to his wide brimmed hat extended his hand. "Yes, sir, Marshal." The khaki uniform he wore looked as if it had been passed down through generations of local law enforcement.

"Howell's fine." He inclined his head and tried to get his ears to stop buzzing as he strode to the lead car. "You get eyes on Blevins?"

"Not...exactly."

Howell stopped and turned, the adrenaline that had been coursing through his system coming to a similar halt. The hope he'd carried with him from his bedroom in Camden, New Jersey, fizzled as he stared the sheriff down. "I was told—"

"Well, you see..." Now that the chopper was out of range, silence descended with surprising force. Sheriff Hayes scrubbed a hand across his weary brow. "It was one of our gals down at Grumpy's who sounded the alarm and called the toll-free number. Abby Monroe. See, she watches all of those true crime shows—"

"Grumpy's?"

"Local market. Only market in town actually. We're pretty small." Sheriff Hayes seemed suddenly uncertain. "Last count we only have three hundred..." he broke off at Howell's steely look. "Sorry. Anyway, so before Abby calls that number, she convinces her coworker to follow the guy after he leaves."

This was sounding worse by the second. "Her coworker."

"Yes, sir. Eli Carter. Good kid. Bit lovesick over Abby so it never occurred to him to say no. Next thing I know, Eli's running into the station saying he followed this guy all the way out to the old Westcott place about twenty minutes out of town. Place has been abandoned for almost a year. Kid said the guy gave him the creeps. Said he kept looking over his shoulder as if afraid someone was following him."

Someone *was* following him but Howell bit that remark back. "Is this Abby an alarmist?" When the sheriff blinked at him, Howell clarified. "Does she ever cry wolf? Imagine stuff?"

"Abby? No, sir." Sheriff Hayes shook his head. "She's pretty solid, in fact. Stays calm in a crisis. Must be all those crime shows she watches. I believed her. If I didn't, I would have said something when I got the call you'd be coming."

Howell prided himself on being able to read people. It was one reason he was so good at his job. Growing up with three siblings in a law enforcement house tended to make one both observant and cautious. He was a talk-less-think-more kind of person. It was a good quality for a US marshal primarily in charge of providing protection and relocation to important witnesses entering the WITSEC program. The quality came in very handy with fugitive catching as well.

That said? The only off thing he got about Sheriff Hayes was that the guy was...for want of a better word, scared.

"Let's get out there. See what we can see." Howell motioned to the SUV and the two of them climbed inside.

He adjusted the paddle holster at his waist before securing his seat belt. His US Marshal windbreaker did little to keep the chill of winter off, but the bracing cold kept him awake. That and the coffee he'd drunk while waiting for the chopper the Service had ordered for him. The forty-five minute flight to the southernmost part of Virginia had given him time to review the few reported sightings of Roy Blevins. There hadn't been many. The suspected killer had disappeared pretty quickly, which told Howell he'd had a plan.

"So this guy Blevins," the sheriff hedged. "He's dangerous?"

Howell heard the hope in the sheriff's voice. Hope that Howell would tell him not to worry. "He's the prime suspect in the disappearance of at least eight young women in four states." That they knew of. "One of the assistants in the federal prosecutor's office got chatty at a bar, didn't realize the woman was a reporter. Story broke about the suspect and Blevins bolted before he could be arrested." Howell stared out into the pitch black of the wooded road. "Figured he'd disappear into a remote area. You have any reported disappearances around here?"

"No, sir." Hayes shook his head. "I even called the sheriff in Crowder County, asked him for his advice and to see what he might know about this guy. His town's a lot bigger than mine and he's got more experience with this sort of stuff." Hayes glanced over. "I, uh, noticed you came alone." He winced. "That normal for you marshals?"

"It's normal for me." Now at least. Howell was a solo kind of guy and not particularly trusting these days. Working with a partner, heck, working with anyone for that matter, offered more problems than benefits in his opinion. That did not mean he wasn't a team player. He did whatever it took to get the job done. That mind-set had cost him a lot over the years: his marriage, time with his kids, more time away from his family. But what he did mattered. He made a difference. And if there was one thing the McKenna family was known for, aside from blanketing the entirety of federal law enforcement, it was making a difference.

"Remote out here." Howell's musing was more for himself. It made sense Blevins would have chosen a place like this to vanish. Low population, mountainous region. Lots of forest and woods. It made Virginia an excellent place to get lost in. Howell would bet a good part of his pension that Roy Blevins had debated for days whether to take the chance of going into town. Desperation had brought more than one fugitive to justice in Howell's experience. "About three hundred people live around here you said?"

"Three hundred and two," Sheriff Hayes said with a bit of pride. "The Fullers had twins last month, which got us over the hump. Sorry." He winced again. "Seems strange to feel proud about that when we've got this fugitive hanging over our heads."

"He won't be there much longer." Provided this guy really was Roy Blevins. Howell trusted his gut and so far, it wasn't giving him cause to doubt. True crime watchers like Grumpy's Abby Monroe tended to be very attentive to detail. The fact she'd called the 800 number rather than a reporter told Howell she wasn't interested in publicity or notoriety. Unusual these days to the point of being refreshing. "Tell me about your deputies."

"Ah. Right. Chuck Roberts and Shep Marcus. Chuck's ex-army. I hired him when he got back from his second tour in Afghanistan. Good guy. Saw some stuff over there, but he's got his head on right."

Howell nodded in approval. "And Shep?"

"Shep's dad was my best friend and my lead deputy until he passed last year. Shep stepped right in despite the big shoes to fill. He takes care of his mother and younger sister. He's a little green, but he's solid. You can trust him. You can trust all of us."

"I don't have any intention of putting any of you at more risk than necessary," Howell told him. His plan was simple. Approach Blevins on the sly and get him to open the door. Making it more complicated than that would just ask for trouble.

The rest of the drive was made in silence. Howell's spine stiffened as they turned off the road and Sheriff

Hayes killed the head lamps. When the car stopped, Howell's eyes adjusted and he saw the outline of the two men and the distinctive law enforcement vehicle parked well away from the narrow, overgrown road Howell assumed led to the house in question.

"Got us a special delivery from the US Marshal Service." Sheriff Hayes closed the door and walked around to make the introductions.

To Howell's eyes, the sheriff's assessment of his deputies was right on target. There was no mistaking which was the former soldier and which was the probie. The latter wore an expression of determined bravado while Chuck seemed relatively unfazed by the situation. Both men's breaths turned to mist as they hit the icy predawn air.

"Appreciate you coming out." Chuck's gloved hand shot out in greeting.

"Not as much as I appreciate the call," Howell said. It never ceased to impress him how welcoming most local law enforcement tended to be. Not at all like TV and movies played it out—as if conflict and ego were the most important aspects of their job. No. This was what was important. Joining forces to get the right people behind bars and protecting the rest. Nothing else, as far as Howell was concerned, mattered. "Any sight of Blevins?"

Shep elbowed Chuck in the ribs.

"What?" Howell asked Chuck when he glared at his coworker. "Now's not the time to hold anything back."

Shep shook his head, as if understanding the transgression of tattling.

"I took a walk about an hour ago," Chuck admitted

through gritted teeth. "Just wanted to see if I could get a look inside the house."

Howell swallowed the criticism that wanted to spill out, but once a soldier, always a soldier. No way Chuck would have found it easy to sit back and wait. "And?"

"I looked in through the window on the east side of the house," Chuck's voice grew more confident. "Electricity's been off since the owner died. Guy inside's got a bunch of candles going in the bedroom." He reached into his pocket, then pulled out a scrunched piece of paper. "Shep printed a picture of him from the Marshals' website. I got a good enough look. It's him."

Relief surged through Howell. Not so much because this wasn't going to be a wasted trip, but because in a matter of minutes he would have Roy Blevins in custody. He unzipped his jacket, tossed it onto the hood of Sheriff Hayes's SUV and removed his hip holster. He untucked his shirt and wedged his Glock 22 into the back of his waistband. He messed up his hair, bent down to scrub some dirt over his shirt and jeans.

"Going for the stranded driver look," Howell said at their curious expressions. "Do you know anything about the house? Any way out other than the front door, Sheriff?"

"Place was built more than fifty years ago. Creativity didn't enter into it," Chuck said. "One way in, one way out."

"Good for us." Howell quickly put a plan in place. "Chuck, since you've already been around the house, I'm going to have you go to where you were, but stay low and away from the windows. Sheriff, you're going to take the other side. You see any weapons inside?" He shifted back to Chuck who shook his head.

"Unknown. Not enough light to see."

"We've got a lot of gun owners in these parts. I drove out here after the old man who owned it died," Sheriff Hayes said. "I confiscated all the weapons I could find. If Blevins has a gun, he brought it with him."

Howell nodded. Blevins was more known for using a knife rather than a firearm. When his place had been tossed by the Feds after he'd bolted, they hadn't found any guns. But they'd found a collection of hunting knives that, according to the lab results, had been used more on human beings than animals.

"Shep, I want you staying back—out of sight near the front of the house. Just in case."

The kid nodded and rested a hand on the butt of his holstered gun. "Understood."

"Good." Feeling confident in his backup, Howell stood and motioned for the deputies and sheriff to take up their positions. When they were out of sight, he slowly walked down the narrow lane. Trees had overgrown to the point of arching and completely blocking any moonlight overhead. It was like a tunnel leading to the property line and, when he'd reached it, Howell took a moment to breathe.

Candlelight flickered in the slight crack in the shutters covering the front window. The front door was warped and sagged a bit. No doubt those porch planks were going to creak and whine the second Howell stepped on one.

The cold had already seeped into Howell's bones. Growing up in Boston had prepared him for colder climates, but it still took some getting used to. The wind barely blew, but it was enough to make Howell's teeth chatter a bit. The adrenaline surged again. That would warm him up.

An owl hooted overhead, followed by another. The rustling of leaves and debris sounded in the distance. Foxes, Howell thought. Or a restless deer taking a moonlit stroll. Only the insects were smart enough to go dormant this time of year.

Howell stopped at the edge of the porch and leaned around to see what, if anything, he could see inside. He lifted one foot, set it carefully on the bottom step.

The wood creaked.

The crack in the door went wider. Heart hammering, Howell held up both hands. "Hello?" He tried to add desperation to his voice, but that was not a setting he was overly familiar with. "Hey, is anyone in there? My car broke down about a mile back down the road and my cell's not working."

The door opened slightly more. The barrel of a shotgun emerged, poking out just enough for Howell to see it in the barely-there light Blevins's eyes struggled to adjust to.

"I'm harmless, man." Howell forced a laugh. "Honest, I'm just looking for a phone."

The gun moved, not out, but to the side. The faint candlelight burned inside until the man stepped out into full view.

The relief Howell had felt earlier solidified.

Chuck had been right. Definitely Roy Blevins.

"You aren't going to shoot me, are you?" Howell tried to laugh again.

"Haven't decided." The smoker's voice vibrated against the cold.

"Oh." Howell's voice shook. "Do you mind if I put my

hands down? Or can I come inside? I'm freezing, man. That walk from the car nearly killed me."

Blevins stuck his dark head out the door, scanned the area, before he stepped back and waved Howell inside. He wore torn, ragged jeans that were caked in mud and dirt. The soiled white T-shirt clinging to his anemic frame was evidence he'd lost considerable weight since being on the run. Twenty, maybe thirty pounds. An unhealthy amount at that speed, which meant Blevins's strength would be diminished.

One thing Howell wasn't worried about was becoming Blevins's next victim. He wasn't Blevins's type and from what he knew of Blevins's background, Howell was the same age the man's younger brother would have been had he lived.

It was the smell that hit Howell square in the face when he entered the cabin. "Nice place." He swallowed hard around the stench of rotting food, dirt and body odor and tried to breathe through his mouth. If the electricity didn't work, chances are the water and septic system didn't, either. Obviously showers weren't on Blevins's to-do list. "Um, the phone?"

"There's a cell." Blevins pointed the gun toward the cluttered table near the kitchen. "Not sure how much charge it's got."

"Hopefully just enough." Howell walked carefully, doing his best to remain facing Blevins. He found the cell beneath a pile of half-empty cans of beans. A rat scurried across the kitchen floor near the refrigerator. Beyond Blevins, Howell saw a shadow move by the window.

Chuck.

Blevins shifted, frowning at Howell before he turned

to see what Howell had been looking at. The second he did, Howell moved in. He grabbed the barrel of the shotgun and yanked hard, pulling it clean out of Blevins's grip. He bent down to set it on the ground.

A shocked gasp erupted from Blevins's mouth. His eyes spun as if his brain were trying to process what was happening. Howell stood up to his full height, reached into his back pocket for his badge.

"US Marshal Howell McKenna. Roy Blevins, you're under arrest for the murder of—"

Blevins charged. Howell took one step to the side and whipped his right arm straight out. He caught Blevins in the throat and sent him flying to the ground. The resulting crash had the front door busting open.

Sheriff Hayes entered, gun drawn.

Blevins clutched at his throat, dragging in ragged breaths. "Can't...breathe."

"It'll come back to you," Howell said. "You got cuffs? Left mine with my jacket." He bent down and held out his hand to the sheriff. Shep and Chuck stepped out of the dimming shadow of the night.

"Is it over?" Shep asked.

"Yep." Howell shoved Blevins over onto his stomach and cuffed him. He would have taken a deep breath but the stench would have suffocated him. "Got him. Thanks for the assist."

The deputies and sheriff looked a bit shell-shocked.

Howell's phone rang in his back pocket. The distinctive tone assigned to the office of the deputy director of the US Marshal Service chimed through the cabin. Surprise had him pulling out his phone, checking the screen. It was almost four in the morning. Apparently he wasn't the only one who didn't sleep much. "Watch him for me, will you?" He pointed to Blevins, then to the shotgun. "And get that for evidence." He stepped outside and answered before his voice mail engaged. "This is McKenna."

"Marshal McKenna, this is Deputy Director Lance Coleson."

Feeling a bit off-kilter, Howell's mind raced. "If you're looking for an update on Roy Blevins, Deputy Director, I can report he's been taken into custody. I'll arrange transport over to—"

"I'm sending the chopper back for you as we speak."

Howell frowned. That didn't make any sense. "Sir, how did you know I'd already...?"

"Because you're you," Coleson stated. "Good work. Nabbing him will definitely look good on that application you've put in for head of the Investigative Operations Division."

"Ah, thank you, sir. But—"

"I need you at headquarters in Arlington this morning. First thing."

Howell checked his watch. "All right."

"The Service has had a special request from a federal prosecutor. Your expertise in prisoner transfers and witness protection is required."

Dread pooled in his gut. He was so ready to put that part of his job behind him. "I thought my transfer out of WITSEC was a done deal."

"It is. Consider this one last hurrah," Coleson said. "You're the best we've got and that's what this prosecutor needs and she called in a big favor to make it happen. She won't take no for an answer. From either of us."

Something in the way Coleson spoke had Howell's insides pitching like a tugboat in a hurricane. "She, sir?"

"Kara Gallagher. She has a skittish witness she needs your help with."

Howell blinked. "Kara Gallagher requested me?"

"I understand why this would come as a surprise—"

Anger bubbled and nearly overrode reason. "Her questioning of me at the Fielding trial left a lot to be desired, sir. For me and the Marshal Service." Not to mention his former partner.

"Ms. Gallagher's technique with witnesses in the courtroom is definitely an acquired taste," Coleson said. "And I get why you'd be leery—"

"Leery?" Howell actually laughed. Last year Kara Gallagher had preemptively exposed a series of serious mistakes and unfortunate miscalculations on the part of Howell's partner during a domestic terrorism case. Kara Gallagher had been in charge of the prosecution and thrown them all under the bus to protect her securing a conviction.

He didn't resent the job she had to do. But he didn't appreciate being used not only to get her points across, but to call out—on the stand—mistakes that could have been addressed more discreetly. Her questioning had blindsided him and Howell's resulting testimony ended up being partially responsible for ending the career of a good marshal. And an even better friend. "Ms. Gallagher is no friend of the Marshals," was all Howell could think to add without sounding insubordinate.

"Yes, well, the request for us to take the meeting comes from high up in the DOJ. Which should tell you she's either desperate or determined. Regardless, we're caught in the middle. That said, if we go along, it could put her in our debt for helping her."

Huh. Howell's frown disappeared. That actually wasn't a horrible idea.

"The chopper will be back to your location within the hour. Two of your fellow marshals will meet you at the airport in Arlington to take Blevins into custody and transfer him to Pennsylvania. Ms. Gallagher is known for being early, so I suggest you get here as soon as you can."

"Yes, sir. Of course." Even if it was a problem, there wasn't any other answer for Howell to give. He clicked off as Chuck and Shep dragged a still whining Blevins out of the cabin.

"Need you to drop us off where you picked me up. Doable?" Howell called to Sheriff Hayes.

"Sure thing!"

"Congratulations, Blevins," Howell called. "You're getting an expedited transfer back home. If you're lucky, you'll be processed into lockup in time for breakfast."

Blevins tried to spit at him as he passed, but he tripped and ended up on his knees before the deputies hauled him back up. Howell was tempted to remind Blevins what was bound to happen to him once he hit general population, but why ruin the surprise. The hierarchy of prisoners based on the crimes they committed put Blevins pretty far down on the food chain.

It was a bit like wrangling an untamed cat into a carrier, but the deputies managed to get Blevins strapped into the back seat of their vehicle.

"Thanks again for your help," Howell told the others as Sheriff Hayes headed for his SUV. "I'll be sure to mention all of you in my report. As well as Abby Monroe and Eli Carter."

"You remember their names?" Shep sounded impressed.

"I remember everyone's names." Names. Faces. Connections. It was a talent he'd honed over the years. He flashed a smile and waved before he climbed into the sheriff's SUV. He made it a point to remember everyone he came in contact with. Sometimes out of respect.

Other times, like in the case of Kara Gallagher, he remembered out of self-preservation.

Chapter 2

"Ms. Gallagher?"

"Yes." Kara barely stepped off the elevator onto the main floor of the US Marshals headquarters in Arlington, Virginia, before she was greeted by a middle-aged bespectacled man in an impressive dark suit.

Her hand tightened around the handle of her soft-sided briefcase, chin tilting up as it tended to do when she was taken by surprise. She was thirty minutes early, mainly in the hope of finding coffee so she could get her thoughts together for her meeting with the deputy director. And Howell McKenna. Her blood raced. She couldn't forget Marshal McKenna.

"Deputy Director Coleson is expecting you, ma'am," the man told her. "If you'll please come with me."

Kara forced a smile. "Of course." She followed him down the silvery gray carpeted hallway, through the thick glass doors emblazoned with the distinctive US Marshal badge icon. Unzipping her long down parka, she blew out the last of the winter chill that had filled her lungs outside.

She'd been to Washington often enough that it took a lot to impress her. This office managed to with its pristine presentation and efficient design.

Her stomach growled at the same level of irritation

as her nerves jangled. She'd been up for thirty-six hours straight, dotting every *I* and crossing every *T* she could. Kara had waited years, dug for years, obsessing about the possibility of bringing a case against the Alessi crime family that would actually stick. Now, finally, she had the evidence she'd been searching for.

Nothing, not warnings from her boss at the Connecticut attorney general's office, not even the entirety of the US Marshal Service was going to stand in Kara's way of taking Salvatore Alessi to trial. Unfortunately for Kara, her main—and only—witness was well aware of Kara's single-minded determination not to mention her borderline obsession with the Alessis, neither of which left Kara in as powerful a position as she was used to. Or would have liked.

Thus, her appointment with the US Marshals.

Bringing the Marshals on board, to her mind at least, would prove she was focused on the merits of the case rather than any perceived personal vendetta. And, maybe, she had to admit, to act as a check for those teeny, unidentifiable doubts she couldn't shake.

Kara's cell phone buzzed. She lifted her arm to check the alert on her watch, familiar irritation sliding through her at the sight of her ex-husband's number. The litany of annoyances that came to mind got pushed aside as she focused on the task at hand. Tick tock. Concentrate on the case. That's all that mattered.

At times like this Kara wondered what on earth she'd been thinking marrying Garrett Gallagher in the first place. First year law school naivety she supposed. What she wouldn't do to go back in time and talk some sense into the young woman who'd had far too many stars in her eyes to pay attention to reality.

As usual, the irritation didn't last longer than a moment. She'd gotten two incredible kids out of her time with Garrett so she couldn't regret the marriage too much. Nine-year-old Mia and eight-year-old Jonah were capable of turning on the light in Kara's darkest days. Her ex, on the other hand, possessed the extraordinary ability to transform into a black cloud promising torrential rains and, if the mood suited him, a hurricane-sized hissy fit. Heaven only knew what had triggered him this morning.

She'd find out. Eventually. She tapped her watch to decline the call.

Kara followed her escort through the empty, quiet hallways. She caught sight of a few people in their cubicles, behind desks or even milling about the coffee room, but at just after six thirty on a Thursday morning, she was surprised even by that.

She stopped when her guide paused to speak to a young woman sitting behind a desk in a spacious waiting area for what was clearly designated as the deputy director's office.

Kara scrunched her toes in her heeled boots and shifted her briefcase in front of her.

"Thanks, Cliff. Ms. Gallagher." The woman rose and motioned to the wide double doors to her left. She knocked once, then opened the right one and stepped back. "Please. Deputy Director? Ms. Gallagher is here."

"Thank you." Kara caught the scent of lavender and orange as she walked past. "Is that Luna Aura?" she asked the assistant.

"Yes." The other woman smiled and her passive dark eyes brightened. "My mother buys it for me every Christmas."

"It's one my mother's favorites as well."

"Ms. Gallagher." Deputy Director Lance Coleson stood up from behind his desk and walked around, hand outstretched. "Pleasure to meet you in person."

Kara bit the inside of her cheek. She'd bet that was a straight up lie. "Appreciate you seeing me on short notice."

Her fingers went numb before she shook his hand. He was tall and slender with the appearance of a man used to politicking. The easy smile, the guarded expression in his dark eyes. The pristine gray suit and stark red tie. The man exuded confidence and experience evidenced by the slight graying at his temples.

"I don't recall the deputy attorney general giving me the option to decline your request."

She wasn't about to apologize for playing the biggest card in her hand. "Uncle James knows I wouldn't have asked for this meeting if it wasn't important."

Coleson's left eyebrow arched. "*Uncle* James?"

"James Ashton, yes." Kara tightened her grip on her briefcase. "He's my godfather."

"I see."

She doubted that, but he would by the time their conversation concluded. She didn't like the idea of being thought of as some kind of prosecutorial bully, or that she liked using her personal connections for professional clout, but if either helped her get what she wanted, so be it.

"Please." He gestured to one of the two chairs in front of his desk as she shrugged out of her jacket and hung it on one of the hooks by the door.

Before she turned, she took a moment, pressed two

fingers against the infinity charm she wore at her throat and let out a slow, controlled, calming breath.

"Rita, would you mind running down to the cafeteria and grabbing—"

"Oh, please, not on my account," Kara said as she noticed the coffee machine on the side shelf. As hungry as she was, her stomach was pitching like a schooner caught in a summer storm.

"That'll be all then, Rita. Thanks again for coming in early this morning."

"Of course, sir." Rita backed out of the room and closed the door with barely a click.

"Marshal McKenna is on his way," Deputy Director Coleson informed her.

Kara's uneasy stomach knotted hard. "I'm sure he's as thrilled to be meeting with me as you are."

Coleson's smile was a mere flash, as was the glint in his eyes. "I believe he indicated as much. Help yourself to coffee." He pointed to the setup she'd noticed immediately upon entering.

"Thanks." She set her briefcase down and barely blinked at the sophisticated coffee machine. A few minutes later she turned, mug in hand, and took her first swallow of the morning.

Ahhhh. Finally.

"I'm impressed," Deputy Director Coleson said. "That machine confuses the heck out of most people, my assistant included."

"I worked as a barista in both college and law school." She sipped again and resisted the urge to sigh. It was a family trait—caffeine addiction. She knew for certain her mother had it. No doubt it was a matter of time before Mia and Jonah developed an affection for it as well. "I've yet to encounter a machine I can't figure out."

She wandered the office, too nervous to sit. Besides, between the predawn flight from Connecticut and the ride from the Arlington airport, she needed to keep moving. She found the deputy director's office to be as practical and uncluttered as she imagined. A person didn't reach this level of service by being an unorganized slob. The narrow table behind where he sat at his desk displayed the photos of his family—wife, three teenage boys and then another photo of who Kara assumed were his parents.

"I apologize Marshal McKenna isn't here yet." Deputy Coleson said. "I reminded him you tend to run on the early side."

"It's fine," Kara said and meant it. "Contrary to popular belief, I am aware I'm not the only person in the world." She didn't expect anyone to be at her beck and call. Most of the time.

"Well, I assure you he has a good reason. We got word in the middle of the night that Roy Blevins was spotted in southern Virginia. Howell went out to make the arrest personally."

"Roy Blevins." The name was more than familiar and sent a chill racing down Kara's spine. "He's the primary suspect in those young women's deaths." Was it seven... no, eight victims who had met a violent and unnecessary end. Killing like that would never make sense to her—one reason she preferred organized crime, domestic terrorism and white-collar cases over murder. She understood how those types of criminals thought and operated. Serial killers? Not so much. "I take it Blevins's apprehension was successful?"

"Marshal McKenna always gets the job done." Deputy Director Coleson rose to prepare his own coffee.

"Yes, I know." She didn't mean to sound smug. "That's why I've requested him." She was unashamed to admit she needed help if it meant getting this case locked down and if she was going to ask for assistance, she was darn well going to make certain she got the best.

It wasn't just Howell McKenna's sterling reputation as a US marshal that put him at the top of her list; she'd read his file. She knew his record. She'd questioned him under oath and knew him to be a principled man. She needed someone as dedicated to the rule of law as she was.

Whether they liked each other or not was beside the point.

Still, Kara held no illusions as to her own reputation, especially with the Marshal Service. She'd put them through the wringer last year in a way that led to an internal investigation resulting in a number of firings, suspensions and reassignments. She wasn't about to apologize for what she'd done. Her questioning had uncovered dubious actions on the part of a handful of employees in the agency. Was she sorry she'd done it? No. Did she regret the fallout? Maybe. A little.

Surely a man who possessed as much integrity as Howell McKenna would understand that.

She was halfway through her second cup of coffee when the knock on the door came.

"Come in."

US Marshal Howell McKenna strode into the room with purpose and a presence that even from her seat Kara found powerful. She remembered him from his testimony. How could she forget him given the cool stare he'd locked on her while she'd questioned him? He was tall, strongly built, with a physique that said he could more than hold himself in any kind of fight or altercation.

But it was that face of his that at times still haunted her dreams. A face that belonged more on a big cinema screen rather than on the ID badge of law enforcement. Clean cut with his dark blond hair at what she assumed was regulation length. A hint of stubble covered his chin and sent him over the edge into ruggedly handsome territory. Those all-seeing blue eyes of his were something else and, as she shifted in her chair, she saw they were currently pinned on her.

"Marshal McKenna." She offered a smile before drinking more coffee, then set the mug down before he noticed her hands were trembling.

"Sorry to have kept you waiting." His deep voice carried that ever-so-slightly irritated tone that confirmed her suspicion that he was definitely not happy about being summoned.

"Everything handled with Blevins?" Deputy Coleson rose and gestured to the empty chair beside Kara. "Coffee?"

"No, thanks. The handoff went smoothly enough. The helicopter ride, not so much." He grimaced. "Blevins bashed his head into his window to try to make like a flying squirrel as we were coming in to land. Guess the idea of prison really doesn't appeal to him." He touched a hand to the rip in his jacket and indicated the dirt and mud smeared on his shirt. "Apologies for my appearance." He shifted his gaze back to Kara. "I didn't have time to change."

"Not a problem." Still, Kara swallowed hard. The man

was alpha-male appealing in a way that disturbed her. She liked brains, not brawn. But Howell McKenna was the kind of man who had and used both easily and, surprisingly, without arrogance. Confidence on the other hand... he had that to spare. "Thank you for making the time."

Howell's eyes filled with doubt, as if he didn't believe she was being sincere. She couldn't blame him. Her cutthroat reputation preceded her and, more times than not, alienated those who worked beside her on the right side of justice. Likability was overrated as far as she was concerned and completely paled in comparison to effectiveness and results. She'd take being disliked if it meant more bad guys got convicted.

"This is your show, Ms. Gallagher." Deputy Director Coleson motioned to her. "Let's have it."

She took a deep breath and, before the panic could set in, plunged ahead. "A little over two weeks ago I was approached by a former employee from Briarwood Construction in Connecticut. This person told me that during the time they worked in Briarwood's accounting department, they came across evidence of the company being used as a front for various criminal activities. Money laundering primarily. Bribery, kickbacks. You get the idea."

"Briarwood." Coleson frowned. "I've heard of them, but I can't..." He looked to Howell. "Why have I heard of them?"

"Briarwood is one of the numerous companies and businesses run and owned by the Alessi family," Howell said in a way that told Kara she had their attention.

"Yes!" Coleson snapped his fingers. "Thank you. Sorry. Go on," he urged Kara.

"My witness's name is Juliet Unger. She's twenty-six, single, and has her certification for record keeping and computer science from a business college." She leaned down, unzipped her briefcase and withdrew the copies she'd made of the summary file she'd put together. "Her mother died when she was young and she moved to New York to live with her grandmother Estelle. Her grandmother's now in a care facility for dementia patients. Juliet bounced around from job to job after college, eventually landing at Briarwood—first as an office assistant, before she began working in the accounting department. The way she tells it, it was the perfect job. She double-checked accounting entries, maintained the computer server room, simple nine to five. It was good pay with excellent benefits. Turnover was rare according to her. Employees are very loyal to the Alessis."

"Best way to stay alive, I imagine," Howell murmured.

"According to Juliet." Kara wasn't about to get sidetracked by his sarcasm. "Sal Alessi's health has been on the decline since he suffered a massive coronary eighteen months ago." Difficult to believe considering most people who came into contact with Sal weren't sure whether he even had a heart. "Since then Sal's been relinquishing control of the family businesses. His son Rafael runs Briarwood now. Along with the family's trucking company and strip...er, gentlemen's clubs. The transfer of control is not common knowledge apparently."

"I shouldn't think so," Howell said. "Other families and organizations would be circling like sharks if they even suspected a shift in leadership at the top. The Alessis will work hard to keep it quiet until they can't."

Kara nodded, bolstered by his understanding of the situation.

"What evidence did Juliet find exactly?" Coleson pressed.

"Pages nine through fifteen in your folders," she told them and waited for them to flip over. "These are copies of a portion of the accounting records for Briarwood, along with invoices and work orders that were sent to companies that don't seem to exist except on paper. But there're also invoices for Hudson Bay Logistics—"

"Rafael's trucking company," Howell clarified.

"Yes, and Sutton Ridge Financial." When the men didn't respond, she added, "That's Elena Alessi, Sal's daughter's financial firm. Her business is listed as a primary consultant for Briarwood. Everything seems to run through Briarwood."

"He's using his own kids' companies to launder the money," Coleson chuffed and shook his head. "That's gutsy."

"It's arrogance," Kara tried not to snap. "Sal assumes he's covered and up until now he's been untouchable. Elena's a shark of a defense attorney. The family fixer. Everyone, from Sal's most trusted advisors to the busboys at the clubs, if they get in trouble, she's their first call. She's smart and worse," Kara added, "she's really, really good at her job."

"Is that admiration?" Howell asked. "Or concern?"

She looked at him, met his gaze with what she hoped was an unflinching one. "Yes. To both."

Coleson scowled. "Are these dates correct?"

Kara had to force herself to break eye contact with

Howell. The man may as well have a pair of tractor beams shooting out of his eyes the way he drew her in.

"The dates—" she cleared her throat and refocused "—for these pages, yes, they're correct." She took a steeling breath. "I know. We can't use them as they're outside the statute of limitations, which is what I told Julia at our first meeting. But at our next meeting, she brought me more. If you turn the page—" she braced herself "—these include at least half a dozen more businesses. Most importantly, the dates are current. But we have to move fast."

"Speed of light fast." Deputy Director Coleson looked across the desk at her. "I'm doing the math. You've got what? Two, maybe three months before these expire as well?"

"Three months isn't enough time to get you on the court schedule," Howell said.

"I'm confident I can make it happen," she assured them. "It'll be a challenge, but it's worth it. Connecticut doesn't have a grand jury we need to go through, so as soon as I can lock down the evidence and witnesses, I can file. That'll freeze the time and give me leeway with court dates. But I can't do any of that until I've got the complete files off the hard drive Juliet claims she has."

"What hard drive?" Howell asked in a way that set her nerves on edge.

Here's where Juliet didn't come off so well. "Before she left Briarwood, she was, well, a bit on the angry side. She admits she did something without thinking it through." Kara shrugged. "She made a copy of Briarwood's server hard drive. Once she turns it over to me, I'm going to use that to bring a—"

"RICO case," Howell said almost to himself. He looked up again. "Sorry. You were saving that as your punch line, weren't you?"

"It's fine." She tried not to feel robbed after the buildup. "You're right, of course. Once Juliet gives me all of the records, , I can start to build a case for racketeering, money laundering, and fraud against the Alessis in Connecticut. I'm hopeful that will lead to additional charges in other states."

"Reasonable hope," Howell said.

"Even one case is a big ask," Coleson said. "The Alessis have been around since the sixties when Sal's father Alphonse ran casinos in Atlantic City."

"Ah, the good old days," Howell said as he scanned more of her notes. "When criminals were gentlemen and lived by a code."

"Yeah, well, that code died with Alphonse Alessi." Kara crossed her legs, then rested her still shaking hands on her knee. The adrenaline still hadn't worn off but that was because she still didn't have what she'd come for. "The old man liked sticking a finger in the eye of law enforcement and they let him get away with it because for the most part he kept the reprobates in line. Some have gone so far as to say Atlantic City was a safer place with Alphonse running it. He wasn't a man anyone wanted to cross. On either side of the law."

"Sometimes it takes a criminal to control criminals." Howell glanced up when she didn't respond. "Again, sorry. Mulling. You know your organized crime history."

"It's a hobby," she said simply. "There's nothing the Alessis don't have their hands in, but change is coming.

We have to stop them now, before they regroup and become untouchable."

"Some would argue they already are," Coleson said. "You don't go to war with a family like the Alessis unless you're very sure you're going to win."

"Anyone who argues we've already lost shouldn't be working in the judicial system." Kara had to force herself not to say more. Some things she took very personally. "The second we give up because going after someone because it's too hard or too dangerous, we've already lost."

"I'll second that." Howell continued flipping through the pages of his file. "Correct me if I'm wrong, but I seem to remember a case being brought against Sal, filed by a New York prosecutor about what? Twenty, twenty-five years ago?"

"Twenty-one, actually." Kara cleared her throat and focused on keeping her voice even. Her heart beat faster. "Sal was charged with the murder of a low-level drug dealer in Queens who was skimming profits from the heroin the Alessis were bringing in." She narrowed her eyes and avoided Howell's probing gaze. "A witness was willing to testify Sal Alessi pulled the trigger himself."

"I don't see any mention of that case in your file," the deputy director said. "What happened with it?"

"The prosecuting attorney was killed." Kara's stomach pitched when Howell reached for his cell phone. She knew what he was ready to do. What she'd be doing in his place—looking up the details she'd purposely left out of her report. Stupid, now that she thought about it. Of course they'd notice what wasn't there. "It was a car bomb. Planted overnight when the vehicle was parked in the driveway of the family home. The explosion tore the entire front face of the house off its foundation." Kara clenched her fists and hoped neither would notice. "Any hope of someone else picking up the case ended shortly after when the primary witness committed suicide. Since then no one has been willing to take on the Alessis. Add to that the continuing rumors that the Alessis have their hooks into people in all kinds of law enforcement agencies—"

"That's never been proven." Coleson cut her off.

Kara frowned. "It would explain why no agency has been willing to dedicate the resources it would take to bring them down."

"She's right." Howell looked up and his eyes met hers for a brief moment. "I don't like the idea any more than you do, Deputy Director, but it would be arrogant of us or any other agency to think any department was insulated from that kind of infiltration. Organizations like the Alessis have a long reach and even deeper pockets. Plus, they excel at finding the right buttons to push. They exploit weaknesses like most of us breathe air. All the more reason to keep this conversation amongst ourselves moving forward."

He met Kara's surprised gaze.

Kara chewed on the inside of her cheek. *Interesting.* They were on the same side within moments of being in the same room. Maybe this was going better than she'd anticipated.

"I apologize," Howell said to her. "You were about to share why you didn't include the former case against Sal Alessi in your file."

She felt both hot and cold at the same time. "I didn't mention it because I wanted to keep my presentation as clean as possible." She needed to get all of this out, laid out in front of them so they couldn't deny her request. "My case has nothing to do with the previous one, but in my opinion this has more teeth. Finances always trick people up, as evidenced by what Juliet's uncovered. It's what brought down Capone."

"Why do people always say that?" Coleson asked rhetorically.

"Because in the end, Capone was held to account," Howell said. "For most people that was enough."

"I'm under no illusion this case will be easy," Kara veered them back on topic. "But I can't move forward without the help of the Marshal Service. I need Juliet protected. I've done my best up until now, but this isn't my area of expertise, and I do not want to get this woman killed."

Howell's expression gave no indication whether her plea had landed or not.

She needed one more show of good faith. One she had been holding in reserve just in case she hadn't been convincing. "I need to be honest with you both," she began. "This isn't the first time I've considered bringing charges against Sal Alessi."

Both men looked at her. She swallowed hard.

"The first time I had something, it was extortion against local businesses. I couldn't convince anyone to actually testify." It had been one of her earliest and hardest lessons when she'd first started in the federal prosecutor's office. "The second case revolved around the prosecution of Mayor William Shelton."

"He was convicted of taking kickbacks from various businesses in exchange for contracts being awarded," Coleson said. "You were in on that case?"

"I was second chair." But as second chair, she hadn't had the voice to be able to push harder for an investigation into those businesses—two of which had been run by the Alessis. Her second strike. She had no intention of striking out a third time. "I'm going to do this but I'd prefer to do it with competent, reliable backup." Her gaze flickered to Howell who tapped his phone awake and sat forward before typing. "No one else is willing to, but someone has to take a stand."

"No one else wants to get blown to smithereens like that New York prosecutor," Coleson muttered under his breath.

Kara's ears began to ring. "I would not be here if I didn't think I had a solid case. I can absolutely build one. Juliet Unger and the evidence she's got is the ticket to taking the Alessis down once and for all."

"You sound suspiciously like an optimist," Howell said with something she thought sounded like admiration.

"Where this opportunity is concerned? Absolutely," she agreed. "A determined one."

"Kara's right in that the Alessis have been a thorn in law enforcement's side for decades," Deputy Director Coleson stated. "What makes you think you can succeed where others, or rather one other, failed?"

"I'm properly motivated." She set her jaw. "I'm not doing this on a whim," she insisted. "I've done my due diligence and confirmed as much of Juliet's story as I could. She's definitely not perfect." Understatement, Kara thought. In the few times they'd met, she'd found Juliet to be slightly erratic and impatient. Hence those doubts Kara couldn't shake. Or define. But now wasn't the moment to voice those concerns. "Juliet's history is colorful to be sure. Nothing serious. Vandalism, trespassing. Stupid kid stuff. I'd do a deeper dive, but I don't have the capability of doing that without alerting a number of other people about what I'm working on. Keeping this on the q.t. for as long as we can is the only way it'll succeed. With a little more investigating and research, I should have enough for an electronic records warrant for their business and personal devices. That'll help to corroborate whatever information is on that drive. Add to that a surveillance warrant, but I'm trying not to get ahead of myself. It's going to take time, time we don't really have, so it all needs to start happening now." She hesitated, flinching before she thought to catch herself.

"Here it comes." Howell smirked.

"I've had this happen in the past. You know, where witnesses get...hinky." It was the only word she could come up with. "Juliet's had just enough time with all this to get spooked. At first she seemed really solid, like she was okay with how coming forward was going to change her life." Kara flexed her fingers to prevent twisting her hands together. "Now I think she's realized there's no going back to whatever she had before."

"She wants protection," Howell guessed. "And a place in witness protection."

Coleson tapped a finger against his lips. "I think we—"

"Hold on." Howell held up a finger, eyes glued to his phone. "Before we get to that, back up." He inclined his head and finally looked to Kara. "I think you left out an important detail, Kara." He turned his phone toward her so she could see the picture from the article he'd found online. "That's you, isn't it?"

She thought she'd prepared herself for it but nevertheless her blood ran cold. "I don't see what that—"

"Yes, you do." The edge of hostility she'd heard earlier was gone, but she couldn't define what had replaced it. Or maybe she didn't want to. "Otherwise you wouldn't have left this detail out of your report."

"What detail?" Deputy Coleson asked. "What am I missing?"

"The New York prosecutor who was murdered? The one who brought the murder case against Sal Alessi twenty-one years ago? His name was Patrick Hewitt."

Kara's mouth went dry. She could all but feel her chances for help slipping out of her grasp. Trust was tantamount to success, but she just hadn't been able to take hers that far.

"Do you want to tell him or should I?" Howell asked her.

Every cell in Kara's body went cold when the two men turned their attention on her. Trapped, she surrendered. There wasn't any other choice but to come clean.

"Patrick Hewitt was my father."

Chapter 3

Howell remained in his chair, staring down at the image of Kara Gallagher, barely a teenager, standing in her mother's arms. Both of their faces were stained with tears and soot—remnants of the smoke and fire from the bomb that had blown the front of their house apart, along with their lives.

He recognized that look in Kara's young, dazed eyes. The shock, the anger. Utter despair at having lost someone she cared about in such a horrific, violent way. An experience like that, it shaped a person's life from that moment forward. Whoever Kara had been before the day, before that bomb went off, died alongside her father. A new Kara had been born.

A Kara Gallagher who made so much more sense to him now. So much more that it shook him.

"Sorry about that." Deputy Director Coleson hung up his phone. "Are we waiting for Ms. Gallagher to come back?"

"I suggested she wait outside while the two of us speak in private," Howell said. All the fight and resentment he'd come in with had vanished. It couldn't hold strong with what he'd learned—what he now knew—let alone with the possibilities right in front of all of them.

"Let me guess. You want me to cut her loose."

"No." Howell shifted in his seat, clasped hands dangling between his knees as his mind raced. "Quite the contrary. I'm willing to help her. I think she's onto something."

Deputy Director Coleson's eyes went wide before he sighed. "Okay."

"You're surprised."

"Yes and no." Coleson's lips twitched. "She knows who she's dealing with. She wants help with her witness, and she knew the right card to play in order to get it. At least where you're concerned."

"What card is that?"

"Family." His boss shrugged. "It's your weak spot. Or as weak a spot as you possess."

Howell couldn't argue with that. Honor. Duty. Family. It was the McKenna motto and not one Howell or any of his siblings would ever shirk. "She needs help." Probably more than she realized. Despite her confidence, the Alessis weren't to be messed with and he'd bet big bucks the crime family was well aware of her investigation. "She's convincing. That said, there's no doubt in my mind she's too close to this case to see the Alessis clearly." But right now it wasn't Sal Alessi that concerned him.

"No one sees them clearly enough to prosecute," Coleson said. "Probably the reason they've remained unchecked for this long. Would be nice, though. To bring them down and off the board completely."

Howell couldn't disagree. "If she's come to us that tells me she's been hanging out on this ledge alone. I'd be interested to see what her backup consists of in the prosecutor's office. And who all she's talked to about this."

"I can make some discreet calls," Deputy Director Coleson said. "Find out what else she might have left out of that perfectly put together dossier."

Howell nodded. "In the meantime, I'll extend an olive branch and get more details about this witness of hers and what she's specifically asking for. Maybe talk to Juliet Unger myself." He stood, straightened his jacket, frowned and shook his head. There was this...niggling. This voice that wouldn't stop yapping at him. "Something about this entire situation isn't sitting right with me."

"You think she's overestimating her case?" Coleson asked. "Or that her witness is lying?"

"I'm not taking anything off the table. But I'd be the one lying if I said I didn't think it's going to require more than one witness to bring the Alessis down." Why had Juliet come to Kara, of all people, with this information? It was the one question no one had asked and yet it was the one that Howell couldn't get out of his head. He couldn't imagine Kara hadn't asked it herself. But that was the problem when emotions got involved. Sometimes you stopped looking for certain answers.

"You've got carte blanche to handle this as you see fit," his boss told Howell. "You've earned enough trust for me to say that. Keep Kara on track, but most of all, keep this from blowing up in her face—and the justice department's for that matter."

"Understood."

"And keep me in the loop!" Coleson called after him as Howell headed toward the door. "I can't help protect either one of you if I'm in the dark."

"Copy that."

The second Howell pulled open the door, Kara shot

to her feet from where she'd been sitting on a cushioned bench in the waiting area.

There was so much in her expression that struck a chord with him. Hope. Anticipation. Doubt. Skepticism. Fear. All of it was painted on her face like well-applied makeup, of which she wore little. She had an oval face with strikingly sharp cheekbones. She wore her brown hair loose around her shoulders with amber highlights accenting the gold flecks in her soft brown eyes and the tan hue to her skin.

She was shorter than he remembered but then, the last time he'd seen her she'd been looming over him in the witness box. The last thing he'd been paying attention to was whether the top of her head reached his chin. It did, mostly because of the insanely high spiked heels she wore. The black of her boots was so shiny he could see his reflection in the pointed toes. She presented a powerful picture. A pretty, powerful picture. Pretty enough he could almost, *almost* see past their previous interaction.

She was here for a purpose. He had to remember that, especially since he was probably about to get caught in some kind of professional and dangerous wringer. She had an agenda. His purpose was to make sure she didn't create more problems than she was trying to solve.

He wondered at the practicality of her shoes, particularly since it was still winter in Virginia. Now that he thought about it, every time he'd seen her she'd been wearing similar heels. She didn't strike him as a woman out to make a fashion statement, but what statement she was trying to make with what had to be torture devices escaped him.

She wasn't the least bit slight and wore her curves elegantly displayed in a sharp skirt and blouse the color of peak season cranberries. The jacket he'd seen hanging in his boss's office lay draped over her briefcase that sat on the floor beside her.

Taken a bit off guard by her snap to attention, he found it was her determined attitude and take-no-prisoners posture that had him looking beyond—at least for now—the damage she was capable of inflicting on anyone standing between her and a guilty verdict.

The elevator in the distance was dinging frequently now. Employees had begun to fill the halls and offices. The muted rumblings of conversations and clicking computer keys filled the air. Someone had burned the coffee again in the break room, but also added the fresh baked aroma of donuts destined to curb morning sugar cravings.

"Are you going to escort me out and tell me to get lost?" The challenge was implicit in Kara's voice, as was the worry in her eyes.

He could play with her, he realized. Lean into her supposition that he and his boss had decided to walk away from her Captain Ahab tendencies where the Alessi family was concerned. Or.

Yeah, he liked his *or* idea better.

"You hungry?" He'd heard her stomach rumbling the entire time they'd been sitting next to one another in the office. "There's a diner a few blocks from here. I tend to make at least one visit when I'm in town. We can relax and talk a bit more about your case and what your witness is asking of you."

"Thanks." The relief on her face was almost comical. At least before she covered. "I'm starving, actually." She grabbed her jacket and slipped it on.

"After you." He motioned for her to head on out while he double-checked his phone for messages. The only one he'd been waiting for had come through. Blevins had been booked and processed just, as Howell had predicted, in time for inmate breakfast. He mentally closed the book on that case while opening the cover of another.

"You're being nice to me," she said once they exited the lobby downstairs and he held the door open for her. "Why? Trying to put me off guard?"

"I'm being polite," he corrected and steered her toward the garage. "I'm polite to everyone. Until I'm not." And then he simply got arctic cool. It was one of those talents he'd learned from his mother. A woman didn't make it to the position of Boston police commissioner without learning how to work people. "I'm parked in the lot."

"How far is it to the diner?"

"Three blocks that way." He pointed down the road. The area was peppered with mid-range hotels and services like dry cleaners and real estate offices. Traffic, pedestrian and automobile alike, began to pick up as the day got started. Cabs and rideshare services deposited their passengers practically on a conveyer belt. Charlie's Diner had become a favorite for business workers and tourists alike, attracting customers from all over the Arlington region.

"I can walk."

It was on the tip of his tongue to argue, but who was he to challenge a woman's ability to walk in skyscraper stilts? "All right." They fell into step side by side.

"I met your sister a while back," she said in a decent attempt at small talk.

"Which one?" He had two, both younger.

"Wren. She came to speak to a group of us at the justice department about her and her partner's role in taking down Ambrose Treyhern last year."

"They're getting a lot of mileage out of that case." Howell ducked his head, smiling to himself. He'd had a small, unofficial hand in the capture when he'd headed up to the small Alaska town where Wren and her partner Ty Savakis had gone to help protect a former witness of Ty's. The fact Howell had been stuck in town during a megastorm while the two of them had headed up the mountain in a tram still didn't sit well with him. He'd missed most of the action.

"They've earned bragging rights," Kara said with admiration. "Granted their methods might have been a bit unorthodox."

"Is that what you call going off book and pretending your phone doesn't ring when your FBI boss calls?" Howell said. "Kidding. Ty had some ghosts to put to rest where Ambrose was concerned. I'm trying not to hold it against him that he nearly got my sister killed in the process."

Kara glanced at him, her brow furrowed. "That's not how she tells it."

"She wouldn't." They crossed the street once the light turned. "They're getting married this summer. Did she mention that?"

"She did not." Pleasure filled her eyes. "Do you disapprove?"

"Absolutely not." Not only because Ty had gone old school and spoken with their parents before he'd proposed to Wren, but he'd been stand up enough to talk to Howell and Aiden about it as well. The big brother check, he'd called it. Admirable had been Howell's word. But then he'd always liked Ty. Thankfully. "I don't think I've ever seen two people who fit so well together," he told Kara. "Most of the family is wondering what took them so long to finally realize they had feelings for one another. But the job gets in the way." He shrugged. "It won't anymore. They won't let it."

"Nice to hear some people can manage to make a marriage work." The sarcasm rang loudly in his ears. "I wasn't so lucky."

"Me, either." Divorce wasn't an odd thing to have in common. Not these days. "My marriage lasted for six years. You?"

"About the same." Her flash of a smile was far from amused. "Ridiculous thing is I think we both realized about a year in we'd made a mistake but by then I was pregnant with Mia and then Jonah came along. We tried to make it work for their sake, but there wasn't anything left to cling to. In the end, splitting up set a better example for them."

"You two are cordial then?"

She nodded. "I guess you could say—" Her cell phone rang, playing the familiar tune of a women's anthem about surviving. "I swear the man knows when I'm talking about him." She stopped walking, dug into her bag for her cell. "This is the second time he's called this morning. Do you mind?"

"Not at all." He slowed his pace, catching a very distant glimpse of Charlie's distinctive neon yellow and blue sign.

"Garrett, sorry I wasn't able to talk earlier. I was in a—" Kara turned away, lowered her voice. "Something going on?"

Howell wished there was something to look at as a

distraction. A storefront, even a going-out-of-business sign. Rather than lingering and eavesdropping, he kept walking, putting some distance between them as she finished her call.

"Everything okay?" he asked when she disconnected and headed his way.

"You're law enforcement," she said sharply. "If I tell you the truth you might have to arrest me for premeditated murder." She blew out a long breath, then lifted both hands as if in surrender. "Sorry. Garrett, my ex... He's always doing this last minute, switching up the weekends when he wants the kids. Like there's a chance I'll say no."

Howell's brows knitted. "Why not?"

She smirked. "He likes to threaten me with a custody suit. Goes back to one of the main issues in our marriage. I work too much. I'm gone too much. Never mind that our kids are thriving and doing just fine. If I'm not with them, my mother is." She waved off her tirade. "Sorry. Not what you want to hear about, I'm sure." She checked her watch. "My flight back to New Haven leaves at ten-thirty."

"Plenty of time to get you carb loaded for the day." They fell into step again. "How old are your kids?"

"Mia's about to turn ten and Jonah is eight."

"Fun age. Or so my ex-wife tells me." Howell offered a sympathetic smile. "My son's twelve and my daughter's eleven. They live in Boston where my parents still are but after the divorce I was transferred to Jersey."

"Closer to me than to Boston," she said with a bit of levity in her voice. "How often do you see them?"

"My kids? Every few months. We Zoom most weekends provided I've got good service. Depends on the case I'm working." It wasn't ideal, but he made it a point to be present in their lives. They knew, or at least he hoped they did, that he was there for whatever they needed. "Their stepfather's a good guy. We get along really well. When he and my ex first got together, the kids made several attempts to pit us against each other. We quickly decided to be a united force, the three of us."

"But your work makes things difficult, doesn't it?"

Outside the diner, the air suddenly filled with the enticing aroma of hot butter-grilled pancakes and freshly brewed coffee. Now it was Howell's stomach that growled in anticipation. "Especially as they get older." He reached for the metal handle of the glass door and pulled it open. "One reason I'm anxious for my promotion to come through. It'll take me out of the field for the most part and give me a more predictable schedule so I can get more time with them."

"That'll be nice for all of you." The smile she offered him as she entered the diner felt genuine this time and he took that as a win.

They were early enough to get one of Charlie's coveted black vinyl booths. He asked for the one in the back corner, then slid onto the bench seat that gave him a view of the door. One lesson he'd learned early on working as a marshal—never keep your back to the door and always keep a line of sight for the entire area.

"What are you kids' names?" Kara flipped open the menu and began to scan the multitude of offerings. East Coast diners were a unique experience. Especially the twenty-four hour ones. The menus were vast and varied, from homemade waffles and massive omelets to pastrami sandwiches stacked practically to the ceiling.

"Logan and Zoe." Pride filled his chest and his voice.

"Logan's an artist. Has his sights set on a career in comics or manga. At least this month. Zoe's the athlete. If there's a sport to be played, she's on the team."

"Sounds like my Mia. She's on countdown to soccer season."

"And Jonah?"

She closed her menu, apparently having made her decision. "Jonah will probably end up as a scientist of some kind. Or an engineer. All those left-brained subjects he scores off the charts in aptitude. He loves school, loves learning in general. Never gives me or his grandmother grief about his homework. He practically has it done before he's in the door after school."

Howell chuckled and smiled up at their server when she arrived at their table. "Hey, Claudia." The middle-aged woman wore snug jeans and a T-shirt that depicted a black cat wearing a Sherlock Holmes cap. Her pale blond hair was pulled back from her face, the white apron around her waist stained with remnants of early morning orders. "How've you been?"

"Doing okay, Howell, thanks." She eyed Kara. "First time you've brought a date."

"Not a date," Kara and Howell said at the same time. Claudia merely arched a brow. "This is a business breakfast," Kara added.

"If you say so." Claudia shrugged. "You want your usual, Howell?"

"Please. And a tankard of coffee."

"I'll bring you a carafe," Claudia said as she scribbled on her notepad. "How about you, business acquaintance?"

"Banana waffles with a side of bacon, extra crispy.

And a second carafe of coffee." She shot Howell a look. "Trust me, one is not going to be enough for the table."

"You got it." Claudia moved off.

Howell glanced around the diner and made note of the four individuals sitting at the counter, plus the six other booths currently occupied. His eyes narrowed at the newest arrivals, both young men looking a bit on the scraggly side, but the cook's wave and shouted greeting told him they'd been here before.

"Is it habit or the job that has you doing that?" Kara asked.

"What?" He turned his attention back to her.

"The surveilling."

She'd noticed. "Just like being aware of my surroundings." But that didn't answer the question, did it? "Both." He leaned his arms on the table. "Tell me about your case against Sal Alessi."

"Funny." She sat back as their carafes of coffee and two mugs were delivered to the table. "I thought for sure this was going to start with you asking for an apology for my questioning of you on the stand last year."

"Are you sorry about that?"

"No."

"Then what would be the point?" He had to give her credit. There was no hesitation or regret in her expression and he had to admit that he didn't feel as bitter as he had only hours ago. "You did your job. I might not be happy about the end result. Craig Masters was a good friend and a good agent for a lot of years."

"Until he wasn't," she countered.

There was no arguing when she was right. Craig had fallen seriously out of touch with his oath to the Service, going so far as to begin a personal relationship with a confidential informant. Once Howell's former partner had started down that slippery slope, there'd been no stopping his descent. And there hadn't been anything Howell could or would do to stop his fall. Lying, dishonesty, flat out betrayal was unforgivable in Howell's line of work. Once someone lost his trust, there was no getting it back.

"How did you find Juliet Unger?"

"I didn't. She found me, remember?" She started to reach into her briefcase. Howell's hand shot out and caught her arm.

His fingers tingled where he touched her and, given the surprise that jumped into her eyes, she felt it, too.

"I don't want to read any more reports, Kara. Tell me." He needed to start puzzling her out and conversation, he'd learned years ago, was the best way to get a read on people. Especially when their guard was down. "I want to hear the details from you, not whatever you edited as you typed."

He could feel the tension in her arm, sense her temptation to look down to where they touched, but he pulled away before she had to make that final decision.

He asked, "What do you mean she found you?"

She tucked her hair behind her ears, focused on pouring herself coffee, which she drank straight without cream or sugar. "She approached me at my usual coffee stop. Said she'd read an online article about me being on the previous two Alessi-focused cases." Kara shrugged. "I was skeptical at first."

"Glad to hear it."

"I get it. Her contacting me was...convenient. But my eyes are wide open. I see the blatant coincidences," Kara said easily. "I've also been made aware by my boss that I have a severe conflict of interest where the case is concerned. Enough that I accepted a sort of check and balance on myself."

Howell's eyebrow arched. "Is that what I am?"

"You're a lot of things," she said with a bit of a quirk to her lips. "The bottom line is, even if no one else is willing to carry the torch to the finish line, where the Alessis are concerned, someone at least has to pick it up." She shrugged.

"Still surprises me your boss is letting you run with this."

She smirked. "Like I said, it helps when no one else wants to take a turn at bat. If I get taken off the case for trial, I'll deal with that then. Being the one to hold Alessi responsible for his decades of criminal activity will just have to be enough."

He could see the truth in her hooded gaze. She was clinging to the hope she'd be the one to prosecute, but there was something admirable, he thought, in her being realistic about the justice system, which she'd put all her faith in, limiting her involvement with the case down the road.

"About one of those coincidences. Why do you think Juliet chose you specifically when it came to surrendering the evidence she found?"

She pursed her lips. "I have a bit of a reputation when it comes to the Alessis. Those two previous cases I couldn't make stick? They put me in a bit of a spotlight. If she found me because of it and this leads to finally finishing the job, then maybe they weren't a waste of time after all."

"So the Alessis know who you are." He inclined his head. "Do they know the entirety of who you are?"

"You mean, do they know who my father was?" She shifted in her seat as if suddenly uncomfortable. "We moved to Connecticut a few months after my father was killed. No one was ever arrested for his death. The case went cold."

"You're not naïve or foolish, Kara," Howell said. "Neither are the Alessis. You can't honestly believe you haven't been on their radar in some capacity since your father's death. Especially after you became a prosecutor."

"I'm negligible," Kara said, but her weak smile spoke of irritation. "That's what Elena told me after a meeting with one of her clients a few years back. She paid me as much mind as a bug headed toward a windshield. As long as they keep thinking that, I've got an advantage."

Not if that windshield belonged to a semi-truck.

"You and I have worked in this arena long enough to know cases like this don't go well when revenge is the primary motive."

"Who says that's what this is?" Kara's eyes sparked like a lit match against the night.

"Don't even try to play me, Kara." There were few certainties in life, but Howell would bet everything he had and everything he was that avenging her father's murder had been the primary motivation for whatever she'd done since the day his car blew up in their driveway. "If I'm going to be a part of this, I want it understood that I'm not going to pull punches when I think you're about to cross a line. I need to trust—I need to believe—that the case is what matters. Not your vendetta."

"Fine." She straightened her knife and fork. "I'm all

about checks and balances." She said it with such confidence he had to wonder if she'd expected his comments. "I won't lie. I've been imagining the Alessi family tied up and roasting on a spit since I was thirteen years old. I'd have been perfectly happy if someone else got the fire started, but since no one has, it's left to me."

Again, there was no apology in her tone. Only a cool statement of fact. One that left Howell shivering. "Revenge rarely serves anyone well, Kara."

"I'm not looking for revenge. I'm looking for justice."

For some, Howell thought, they were often the same thing.

"Let's take what happened to my father out of the equation," Kara said with exaggerated patience. "Suppose I was just a federal prosecutor without my history who had been approached by a witness who could potentially bring down the Alessis. They've gotten away with horrific crimes for decades. They hurt innocent people and don't care about collateral damage just so they can increase their profit margins. And again, we aren't including my father, for the moment," she insisted when he opened his mouth to respond. "I'm talking about years upon years of flaunting and flouting the law to the point where they think they're invincible. Where they think they're untouchable. Don't tell me you aren't inclined to want to take them down, too."

Being understood so well didn't come as a surprise considering Howell wore his reputation—and his badge—on his sleeve. "Everything you've just said illustrates you know how dangerous they are. And yet..." He let the thought dangle in the air.

"I know who I'm dealing with."

"Do you?" Near as he could tell, she was taking Sal Alessi's conviction as a given. "You know what they're capable of?"

"Better than anyone." There was a spark of something in her eyes. Something intense and, if he wasn't mistaken, painful.

"A case like this will make them only more determined to keep a hold of their status." More inclined to get rid of anyone who gets in their way. "The second they know about your witness, they're going to come after her. And you."

"All the more reason to do what you suggested earlier and keep our information within a close circle of need-to-knows. The bottom line is that I'm tired," she whispered with a vehemence that he'd never forget. "I'm tired of the entitlement and the blatant disregard of the law. The smug, preening expressions and attitude that just begs someone to do something." She met his gaze. "I meant what I said back in Deputy Director Coleson's office. I'm going to do this. With or without help. That isn't a threat or ultimatum," she added quickly. "It's just a statement of fact. And so is this. Let's say they try to take me out just like they did to my father. Given the history, wouldn't that make them the main suspects?"

"Do you really think they'd care?" Howell asked, disgusted at the idea she'd put herself at risk like this. "You believe in your witness so much, you're willing to risk your life? Your kids' lives? Your mother's?" It wasn't the tactic he'd planned to, or even wanted to, use. But he'd promised to be honest with her. The way she sat back when their breakfast was delivered, the way she focused so completely on their plates, tightened a new knot in his stomach. "Ah, man." He shook his head. "Your mother doesn't know about any of this, does she? You haven't told her."

Her gaze skittered nervously. "I don't want her to worry."

"About what?" Howell shot back. "I thought you just said you're insignificant to them."

She narrowed her eyes as if she didn't appreciate him actually paying attention to what she'd said.

"The word I used was negligent and she wouldn't understand."

"Don't ever underestimate mothers." But the fact she hadn't shared with her family what she was doing was something he could pocket for later. "They always know far more than we give them credit for." They went silent as they ate their breakfast. He refilled both their coffees.

"I would think the fact that I came to the Marshals would show I'm taking this seriously," Kara said as she slathered the oversize toasty banana waffle with butter around the huge dollop of whipped cream and toasted walnuts. "I'm not taking unnecessary risks. I'm doing things by the book and asking for help. So, are you?" she demanded.

"Am I what?" he asked, knowing full well what the question was.

"Are you going to help me or not?"

Her right eye twitched slightly, just enough to show her tell when she was irritated. He'd noticed it when he'd testified last year, when he'd attempted to evade her questions.

"Well?" she prodded.

Of course he was going to help her. But he still had misgivings. And doubts. "I want to talk to your witness." Howell paid careful attention to his veggie omelet that was filled with a double serving of spinach, tomatoes and mushrooms. "That's nonnegotiable, by the way," he added when she eyed him and stabbed her empty fork in his direction. "You and I might be getting along, but I think we can both admit we have trust issues when it comes to working with other people. I need to be convinced, by her, that this is a viable prosecution with a reliable witness who, so long as we can keep her alive, will be of benefit to the case. I need to understand where she's coming from. That's my price," he added when her eyes narrowed. "Take it or leave it. And before you think about calling your DOJ godfather or my boss, know that Deputy Director Coleson gave me the final say-so on whether the Marshal Service goes along with you or not."

She ate more waffle and nibbled on bacon with such delicacy and attention that he had to stop himself from grinning. Try as he might, he couldn't for the life of him recall a woman who had fascinated and appealed to him as much as Kara Gallagher did. Even as she frustrated him. It was…disconcerting at best.

"All right."

Despite the wait, her agreement seemed easy. Too easy. "You knew I'd ask."

She shrugged, that wry quirk of a smile curving her lush lips. "I studied up on you before I had you on the witness stand. Trust me when I say I know you better than you'd be comfortable with. Plus, and don't take this the wrong way, but it's what I would have done."

"Now why would I take that the wrong way?"

"Juliet's skittish at the moment, but considering what she's asked for, she won't say no to meeting with anyone who can get her a deal." She took another bite of her breakfast, chewed while she thought. She set her fork down, reached into her bag for her cell. "Give me your number."

It was, he thought, the sexiest way a woman had ever asked for his information. He rattled it off, watching as she typed it in, and then his phone chimed.

"Add me to your contact list." She started to eat again. "Don't look so worried, McKenna." Only then did he realize she had yet to use his first name. "We'll make a great team and bring down the Alessi family together." Her smile was tempting, as was the rest of her. "Trust me. Everything is going to go perfectly fine."

Chapter 4

"Yes, it's just this one conversation you need to have with him, Juliet." Kara waved off the plate of scrambled eggs and toast her mother tried to push in front of her as she tried to focus on her witness. Sunday had dawned slightly overcast and promised to be a snuggle in front of the fire with a good stack of criminal cases kind of day. If only. Her mind was still reeling a bit after her initial meeting with Howell McKenna two days before. "Not hungry," she mouthed and earned an irritated rolling of the eyes as a response. "Don't worry. Things are falling into place." She glanced at her watch. "We should be there this afternoon." After a few more reassurances Kara hung up and resisted the urge to bang her head on the counter. "Sundays are meant to be days of rest."

"You haven't rested a day since you were born." Pamela Hewitt sipped her coffee, the resignation in her voice all too familiar.

Kara's mother was tall, with a little extra weight clinging to her midsection, and a heart twice as big as the ordinary person's. She tended toward comfortable, casual clothing that made going about her day-to-day activities efficient and unencumbered.

The bond Kara and her mother shared was unlike what

most other children shared with their parents. But then most mothers and daughters hadn't faced what they had.

"I'm doing the grocery shopping later this morning," her mother said. "Anything else you want to add to the list? I've already got down that brand of white wine you like."

"How about another me?"

"I can barely handle one of you," her mother teased with her usual good humor.

Pamela turned off the oven when the timer buzzed and pulled out her usual duo sheets of fresh-baked cookies. This batch was German chocolate chunk cookies with a healthy amount of toasted coconut. Like anyone wanted eggs after smelling those!

"Drink your coffee," her mother said. "And at least eat your toast."

"Then can I have a cookie?"

"Once they've cooled a bit." It was a frequent exchange between them, mostly because her mother's happy place was baking for her family. One of the few traditions from Kara's childhood that Pamela had clung to.

"Why do you fix me eggs when you know I hate them?" At least the bread was sourdough, one of her major nutritional weaknesses. Especially when it was slathered with butter.

"Because eggs are a good protein source and I'm an eternal optimist."

She was that, Kara thought, while Kara had taken after her father in the "trust but verify" mode of thinking. Even now Kara could feel the adrenaline attempting to surge, but the exhaustion she felt after two sleepless nights kept it under control. It was one thing to worry about what would have happened if Howell McKenna had shut her down completely regarding her request. But it was another, completely unexpected, thing to know he was this close to being on board and that she'd have to...

Her face warmed and she blew out a slow, deliberate breath. She'd have to deal with him on a daily basis for the foreseeable future.

The mere mental image of US Marshal McKenna sent her long dormant system into overdrive. Handsome, considerate, respectful. Nice to be reminded men like him existed. That said, she found him irritating. And seriously sexy. Even more so out of the witness box. Funny. She'd locked down not only her libido but any interest in the male species after divorcing Garrett. Of course it would reawaken in regards to the most inconvenient male possible.

Her ex-husband had depleted her relationship and intimacy cells to the point she hadn't even thought about dating since the divorce. Not that she was thinking about *dating* Howell McKenna.

Oh, no. Her mind had leaped straight into far more intimate activities over the past few days since meeting at his boss's office.

Even the text message he'd sent last night in response to her setting up a meeting between him and Juliet this afternoon had sent her hormones into overdrive.

"You need a vacation." Her mother grabbed the butter out of the fridge for her own toast while Kara pressed her hands against her cheeks. "I can't even remember the last time you took a break."

"You are not alone." One of the down sides to being effective at her job—when things blew up at work, she was the one called in to contain the fallout. Made it a little difficult to step away from the office.

"Anything else on your agenda today other than shopping?" The sooner Kara changed the topic, the happier they'd both be.

"Peggy is hosting a bridge brunch."

"You hate bridge."

"But I like mimosas," Pamela said. "What time is Garrett bringing the kids home?"

"He said around five." Kara glanced up at the brass kitchen clock. "His firm rented out one of the local rinks for some big office get-together this morning. Garrett's bucking for partner, so he needed to make an appearance." No doubt wanting his children this particular weekend in an attempt to up his family profile, but at least skating would be fun for the kids.

"Man never met a ladder he didn't try to climb," Pam said. "You found that attractive at one time I believe."

"I found *him* attractive," Kara corrected. "His ambition, not so much." Her ex-husband could charm the socks off a frozen cadaver, which explained why she'd fallen for him. That said, Garrett and an ability to execute a plan didn't exist in the same universe. The man was all promise, no follow-through in just about every aspect of his life. It had taken her far too long to realize that while he liked the idea of working his way to the top of the professional food chain, doing the work it took to make that climb did not appeal. If there was a shortcut to be taken, he found it without fail.

Kara, on the other hand, shot up any ladder she came across, before she'd even gotten into law school. And there'd been no stopping her since entering the front doors of the Connecticut federal prosecutors office. She'd done it the old school way with hard work, sacrifice and one justified guilty verdict at a time. That success, however, had been a big part of the resentment that led to the end of her marriage. Garrett's ego was as fragile as tissue paper beneath a cat's claw.

"I should be home by the time the kids get back," Kara told her mother as she walked over to refill her coffee, a half-eaten piece of toast in hand. "I'll call if I'm going to be—"

The distinctive sound of the front door being suddenly slammed open interrupted her, followed by high-pitched voices.

"It's not my fault!" Mia's exclamation erupted from beyond the kitchen. "He started it!"

"You didn't have to finish it!" Garrett yelled back and instantly set Kara's teeth on edge.

"It's so not five o'clock," she muttered to her mother before heading out into the hall where Mia dumped her overnight backpack on the polished hardwood floor. Garrett stood just inside the door, hands on his hips. His pressed dark chinos and equally dark V-neck sweater made him look as if he was trying too hard to fit into the world of the high-priced legal firm he currently worked for.

"You're early." Kara did her best to smile at the kids, then sent a warning glare to her ex. "How did the ice skating party go?"

"Dad yelled at me in front of everyone." Mia glared at her father as she toed off her sneakers. "Some kid was picking on Jonah because he didn't want to skate. Then *he*..." She pointed at her father. "Gets all mad at *me* because the stupid kid couldn't keep his balance when I shoved him."

Oh, boy. Kara pressed her lips together, torn between fierce, protective pride and love for her warrior child and parental responsibility. "You shouldn't have pushed him, Mia. You know better."

Mia gaped at her. "He took Jonah's book away and threw it onto the ice. I told him to go pick it up and he wouldn't. So I made him. It's not my fault he lost his balance and landed on his—"

"She acted like a feral cat," Garrett cut in.

"She acted like a big sister. Okay, shoving the kid was a step too far, but—"

"That kid is the son of one of the senior partners," Garrett seethed. "Imagine how this makes me look!"

Like an inept father who has no concept of how to parent his children? She didn't say it, but the urge left her vibrating with irritation. What did Garrett expect? He disappointed their children time after time by blowing off his weekend visitation and then when he did show up, he demanded they acted like...well, like something other than normal, temperamental kids who pushed boundaries every chance they got.

"I don't need that kind of reputation when I'm up for promotion," Garrett snapped in that petulant tone he used when things weren't going his way.

"You're always up for promotion."

"Well, Blair was mortified." And Garrett looked disgusted.

"Blair called us monsters." Jonah entered the house, ducked into the corner opposite his father. "She's mean."

No, Kara thought. Blair Wyndham was the boss's

daughter and Garrett's latest third-class ticket to partner. Blair was also twenty-five going on sixteen with an unrivaled attitude of self-importance. Personally, Kara would bet good money Blair couldn't even spell *mean*.

"You okay, Jonah?" She reached for her son as he approached, his arms wrapped tightly around a book that had clearly spent too much time on the ice. Jonah's eyes were red-rimmed and swimming with tears. He'd gotten Garrett's dark curly hair and Kara's eyes, but that dimple in his left cheek was utterly unique.

"That Barton kid ruined my book. I'm sorry, Mom." Jonah's chin wobbled. "I know it was hard for you to find."

"Don't worry about that," Kara said around a suddenly tight throat. It was true, she had pulled some strings to get an autographed copy of one of his favorite fantasy author's books, but she wasn't going to lament that now. She caught Jonah's face in her hands and looked into his eyes. "Are you okay?" she asked again.

He shrugged. "I tried to warn him. I said my sister doesn't like it when someone picks on me."

"Great," Garrett muttered. "This has happened before."

Kara silenced her ex with a look that had him setting his jaw and avoiding her gaze. "We'll talk about this in a bit," she told the kids. "Mia—"

"I know." Mia rolled her eyes and heaved a sigh. "I'm grounded. No television, no tablet, and I'll take out the trash even though there are probably raccoons out there waiting to eat my face."

Kara wanted to laugh but she didn't dare. "I was going to say Nana made cookies and they should be cool by now but if you want to add some extra punishment—"

"Never mind!" Mia yelled. "I'm good. Come on, Jonah!"

Kara touched her son's head, her heart breaking for him. He tried so hard when it came to his father and Garrett never seemed to see that.

"They're becoming brats," Garrett said when they were supposedly out of earshot. Kara glanced back in time to see Mia lean out far enough to meet Kara's gaze. She wanted to ease the hurt she saw in her child's eyes, but there were no words that would suffice. "And you're giving them cookies."

"Let's take this outside, shall we?" Kara pointed to the porch. She pulled the door closed behind her, doing her best to maintain her temper. "If your intention was to parade your kids around in front of your bosses to show them what a great family man you are, I'd say you got what you deserved. They aren't toys in a toy box for you to pull out and play with when you're in the mood or there's something in it for you."

"Well, clearly you aren't doing a great parenting job yourself if our daughter is assaulting other kids!"

"I will talk to her about that, believe me." She walked down the steps, drawing him away from the house. Normally the 1920s colonial style home was a sanctuary for her and her family, but Garrett had a way of tainting everything he looked at and touched. "But if you don't see the value in a sister standing up for her brother, then you're even more lost than I thought you were."

"And maybe if you weren't at work all the time you might be able to exert some control over her," he seethed.

"Exert some..." She blinked, shocked such a thing would come out of Garrett's mouth. "Say that again, Garrett." Recognition over having gone too far rose in his eyes faster than an evening tide. "Say our daughter needs to be *controlled*. I dare you."

He blustered for a moment, then shoved his hands in his pockets and grimaced at her. "Blair suggested I sue you for custody."

The words hit their target and had her hesitating, but only for a moment. Only for as long as it took for her well-practiced defense to kick in. "Go ahead." She tilted her chin up. Her sickly sweet smile could have attracted an entire hive of bees. Once upon a time a threat like that would have had panic coiling inside of her to the point she'd practically cower. The first promise she'd made to herself when she'd filed for divorce was that her days of appeasing his fragile ego were over.

"Blair and I are leaving for the Bahamas this evening." Garrett straightened as if he'd suddenly located his spine. "Trust me, as soon as I get back, I'm going to speak with someone about our custody arrangement. After the show our daughter put on, someone is certain to agree she isn't in the best home environment."

"First, I stopped trusting you around affair number four. Second, and more importantly, you're free to speak to whomever you like." He was a coward at heart. The fact he was willing to use their children against her proved that. After all these years, however, his threats were as exhausting as they were pathetic. "Just keep in mind, suing me for custody would mean I'd have to take the stand and talk about our marriage." She took a step that had him tilting back on his heels. "More specifically, I'd talk about the end of our marriage. You wouldn't want that on the official court record, would you? You certainly wouldn't want Blair to hear those details." In the distance, she heard a car door slam. "I've been more than lenient with your visitation, if that's what you want to call it." A weekend every four or five months hardly seemed like parental responsibility. "That said, you might want to remember I've worked with the best civil attorneys in the country, including some at your firm." Her smile remained in place as she spoke each word with deliberate care. "Trust me when I say they like me a lot better than they like you. In fact, they'd probably pay me to let them drop kick you to the moon."

His Adam's apple bounced in his throat, almost to the same beat of the alarm pulsing in his eyes. "You need to spend more time at home," he muttered. "Maybe if you got your nose out of those cases of yours and interacted with people other than convicted felons or suspects, you might see just how—"

Someone nearby cleared their throat. "Hope I'm not interrupting something."

Kara's temper drained. She closed her eyes, willing the anger and panic to subside. Her cheeks went wildfire hot at the sound of Howell's voice. But that blush was nothing compared to the full body flush she felt the instant he slipped an arm around her waist and pulled her against his side.

In that instant, every bit of anger and worry disappeared, leaving in its wake an odd and frustrating sense of relief, gratitude and, dare she admit it, desire.

"Sorry I'm late." Howell pressed his lips to hers so quickly she wondered if she'd imagined it. The way her mouth tingled when he smiled down at her said otherwise. She blinked up at him, eyes wide. "The drive in from Jersey was rough. You must be the ex I've heard so much about." Howell extended his hand and tightened his grip on her hip when she tried to shift away. "Gavin, isn't it?"

Kara choked back a laugh. "Uh, actually, it's—"

"Garrett," her ex said, flinching when Howell's hand squeezed his. "Garrett Gallagher."

"US Marshal Howell McKenna." Howell moved his jacket aside to show off his badge and gun. Normally the macho flex would have made Kara roll her eyes, but instead she couldn't help but think it was one of the sexiest things she'd seen a man do in a good long while. She rested a hand on his chest and enjoyed the spark against her fingertips. "Good to meet you, Gordon."

Kara pressed her lips into a tight line. The man had impeccable timing and, it seemed, a stellar sense of humor.

"Do I smell cookies?" Howell asked Kara.

"My, um." She pointed back to the house. "Mom bakes them every Sunday morning."

"Then I've timed my arrival perfectly. You two discussing something important?" He looked at Kara, his intense gaze melting away the last of her anxiety. "Anything I can help with?"

"No," Garrett ground out. "We were just working some things out about our children. I meant what I said, Kara." He backed away, turned to his sparkling new Jaguar while Kara had been driving the same beat-up SUV for the past six years.

"So did I!" she called to him. "Have a nice trip." She didn't let herself think about the fact she was clinging to Howell as if he were a life raft in a shark-infested ocean.

She started to turn and head back inside, but Howell held her firm. "Hang on," he said easily, squeezing her again. "Let's give him an image to burn into his brain." When Garrett slid into his seat and slammed his door, Howell bent down and kissed her again.

She had no doubt he'd meant the kiss to be quick and cursory, another symbolic gesture to Garrett as his tires spun before he sped away. But the instant his mouth was on hers, she reached up to touch his face. He'd shaved. His skin was smooth and made her fingertips tingle as he took the kiss deeper and pressed into her.

She lost her breath. Her head spun and she felt herself melting into him in a way she'd never experienced before. He just felt, smelled, tasted so absolutely, perfectly…right.

"Mom!" Mia banged on the living room window.

Kara jumped back as Howell simply stared at her, his expression unreadable.

"I need to get inside," she whispered. Jonah. She needed to check on Jonah. And Mia.

"Didn't mean to overstep with Gregory."

"Garrett." She laughed, but quickly sobered. "Thank you."

"Not a problem. Guy gave off seriously bad vibes from blocks away."

"And no doubt makes you doubt my ability to judge people's character, considering I married the guy." Sometimes she wondered herself. "Don't worry, you made my week and it's only Sunday." Her brain clicked back to business, but she was still a bit foggy. This man's kiss could short-circuit a small city. "Juliet's expecting us, but we've got a little time. Do you, um…" She stepped back, feeling oddly off-kilter being out of his arms. "So you like cookies?"

"Depends." He grinned. "What kind?"

"My mom's famous German chocolate chunk."

"They sound delicious. And for the record, I like moms, too."

"And I bet they love you." She shook her head, motioned him to follow and wondered how much trouble she'd just walked into.

"Who even names their kid Barton?" Howell polished off his third cookie as Jonah sat beside him at the breakfast counter. The kitchen was welcoming and spacious and was definitely made for a cook, which apparently Kara's mother Pamela was. Personally, he was grateful for the distraction. He'd practically forgotten his own name by kissing Kara Gallagher. He wasn't entirely convinced he could still spell it correctly, he'd been so caught off guard by the effect of their kiss. "I mean, even if he does share it with a certain arrow-wielding superhero. Thanks, Pamela." He accepted the refill of coffee and toasted her with it. "You could make a fortune selling these cookies online you know."

"It's not fun when it's work." But Pamela beamed at him.

With her graying brown hair and thoughtful eyes, he could see Kara in her mother. She didn't give off that grandmother vibe but rather seemed more like an elderly wise woman who didn't miss a trick. He also noticed she wore a wedding set on her left hand. Had she gotten married again, he wondered? Or had she never stopped loving her late husband? No doubt it was the latter.

He'd spent the time since his and Kara's meeting gathering information and giving serious thought to her case against the Alessis. He'd stayed up until three this morning reading over all the files on Kara's father's death as well as the case Patrick Hewitt had been building against Sal Alessi. When he'd finally gotten some sleep, it hadn't been more than a few hours before his boss had called confirming at least one positive thing: Kara's investigation into Sal Alessi's financial crimes had, near as anyone could tell him, gone completely under the radar. That had been the good news.

The bad?

Howell wasn't convinced Kara's case was as bulletproof as she believed. He'd meant it when he'd told his boss the case couldn't be made on the shoulders of one witness, no matter what evidence Juliet Unger might have. But Kara had convinced herself, which meant he had no doubt she was leading with her heart and not her head.

He had questions. Lots of questions.

Primarily for the witness who had oh-so-conveniently dropped into Kara's lap.

Sometimes he detested his distrustful nature. Even so, it had never steered him wrong.

Howell reached over and picked up the waterlogged book sitting on the counter. The dejected, sad expression on Jonah's face had Howell imagining how he might have dealt with the kid who'd been bullying him. "Sorry about your book, Jonah."

"Me, too." The boy pushed his wire-rimmed glasses higher up his short nose and heaved a sad sigh that cracked Howell's heart.

Jonah's resemblance to his father was obvious, but Howell could also pick out hints of Kara. Mia, on the other hand, was a billboard example of the tenacity she shared with her mother. Jonah appeared to be more subdued and thoughtful. Given what Howell had heard about the events at the ice rink, his own annoyance was directed squarely at their father, as well as the creep kid who had instigated the whole thing.

"Mia, you know what you did was wrong, don't you?" Kara rested a hand on her daughter's shoulder. "You should never put hands on anyone."

"Sounds to me like the kid got what was coming to him," Pamela said, then immediately held up both hands in surrender. "I seem to recall an altercation you had, Kara, in fourth grade with a girl named Tammy... Sorry," she said quickly before she turned away. "Not my place, I know."

Howell plucked up another cookie, then a second and held it out for Jonah. "Chocolate makes everything better."

Jonah smiled, the happiness finally breaking through as he accepted the treat.

Mia tried again. "But, Mom—"

"There are ways to handle bullies without being physical," Kara said.

"My brother, Aiden, stuffed my bully into a school garbage can at lunch one day," Howell said without thinking. "Mac and cheese day. Totally gross."

Mia giggled.

"Please don't give her ideas." The warning was in Kara's eyes, but instead of feeling remorseful, he grinned.

"Sorry." He shrugged. "There was also the time my sister Wren—"

"Not helping," Kara cut him off in a way that had him grinning even wider. There was something so pleasurable about bantering with her.

"Are you really a US marshal? Like the ones on TV?" Jonah asked with suspicion. "Can I see your badge?"

"We need to find a new show for you to watch," Kara muttered.

Howell pulled back the side of his blazer, revealing where his weapon was holstered on his hip. Then from his back pocket, he produced his badge and ID. He flipped it open, then handed it to Kara's son. "Legal and everything." The encircled gold star always brought him a sense of pride. He'd worked hard to earn it and he planned to wear it until...well. Until it was time to give it up.

"Wow." Jonah traced his finger over the star. "This is so cool."

"I wanna see!" Mia leaned over the counter, held out her hand.

"I just got it!"

"You can see it when he's done, Mia," Kara said. "And you just changed the subject," she accused her son.

"Uh-huh." He grinned, cast what Howell could only describe as a hero-worshipping smile at his sister. "She took care of me, Mom. That's what we're supposed to do, right?"

They both looked to her for confirmation while Howell felt his heart actually melt a little. The love for her children was written all over her pretty face. The smile on her full lips was entirely for them. Lips that had been entirely for him not so long ago. He couldn't wait to find the opportunity to kiss her again. And that, he told himself firmly, was a thought he could not entertain.

"Fine." Kara sighed. "I know when I'm beat. Just do me a favor, please?" She tilted Mia's chin up. "Don't do anything like this again. I don't want to have to come talk to your principal. *Again.* And about your dad—"

At the mention of her father, Mia's eyes narrowed. "I don't want to see him anymore."

"Me, either," Jonah said. "He scared me and yelled. He wasn't nice."

Howell met Kara's suddenly concerned gaze. "Okay," she said slowly, as if choosing her words carefully. "I'll take care of that. I know you're hurting right now, but you only get one father. Just something to think about moving forward."

Mia scowled. Behind her daughter, Pamela rolled her eyes and shook her head. Jonah finally handed Howell's badge over to Mia, who looked at it almost with as much adoration as Howell did.

Howell ate his cookie, feeling more than a little regret over how long it had been since he'd seen his own children. "I hate to cut this short, but what time are we meeting your friend?" he asked Kara as Mia passed his badge back to him.

"Right." Kara looked at the cartoon mouse clock on the wall. "Mom, I'm sorry. I know you had your mimosa brunch—"

"Bridge," Pamela corrected her with a nervous smile aimed at Howell. "I was going to play bridge."

Mia spun around. "You hate bridge."

Pamela laughed, grabbed her granddaughter and twirled her out of the room. "Go put your shoes on. We're going grocery shopping." She stopped beside Howell, touched a hand to his arm. "It was lovely to meet you, Marshal McKenna."

"Howell, please." He covered her hand. "Thank you for the cookies. And the hospitality."

"Come back anytime," she said and eyed her daughter in a way that Howell found hilarious. "I mean that." She walked out of the kitchen with a wide smile on her face.

"Bye." Jonah slid off his chair, then stopped, tilted his head back to look up at Howell. "Could you teach me how to shoot a gun?"

Howell held up a hand, knowing Kara was about to respond without him even looking at her. "I can talk to your mom about it, but shooting a weapon isn't fun and games. It's a very serious responsibility."

"Okay." But there was still hope in his eyes when he glanced at his mother.

"I'd be happy to talk to you about gun safety and how a gun works." Now he did look at Kara. "If that's something that interests you."

Jonah's eyes went wide and he nodded. "That would be cool. Would that be okay, Mom? Can we talk about it?"

"Maybe," Kara said in a way that told Howell he might be in trouble himself. "Go on and get ready to go with Nana." She waited until they were alone before speaking again. "You're good with them."

"Kids are just little adults." He shrugged and eyed the last of the cookies on a plate behind her. "This morning during our chat, Zoe informed me she's making a list of colleges with good sports programs and scholarships. At eleven she makes me feel like a slacker, but they're fun, too. And again, I'm sorry if I overstepped out on the front porch." He stood up as she walked around the island. "I don't go around kissing women like that."

"Their loss," she said as if she hadn't meant to. Embarrassed by the admission, she quickly clarified. "I mean, no apology necessary." She turned and caught him grabbing another handful of cookies. Laughing, she shook her head. "You want to know the truth? I should thank you. You kissing me finally answered a question I've had for a good many years."

"Oh?" He slipped the cookies into his pocket. "What question is that?"

"Whether Garrett was right when he defended his affairs by saying our lack of chemistry was my fault." She turned on a smile that lit parts of his heart he didn't know he had. "Turns out I've got plenty of chemistry left in me."

Yes, she did. He'd barely had to touch his mouth to hers to know that was true. Howell kept his smile to himself as he followed her outside, a bit flummoxed and more than a little intrigued. She definitely had chemistry to spare.

Chapter 5

"The hotel isn't too far away." It had taken fifteen minutes of the almost half-hour drive—to the small ocean side Connecticut town of Stratford—for Kara to get her nerves under control. Nerves that had absolutely nothing to do with her job and everything to do with the man in the driver's seat beside her.

Howell McKenna was meant to be a means to an end not... She exhaled slowly. Not a distraction. She'd witnessed enough workplace relationships imploding to know getting involved with someone she was working with was a bad idea.

Not that they were involved.

A solitary kiss, one that was meant to disarm and irritate her ex-husband, wasn't even on the list of ways to start a relationship. She was being ridiculous to think otherwise. Howell had done what his record showed he always did: he'd seen a potentially not great situation and put a stop to it. Just so happened that meant giving her what amounted to the best kiss of her life. The kind of kiss she thought was relegated to romance novels and fairy-tale movies. For anyone other than her. She'd never felt so confused to be wrong.

Still, she had one responsibility at the moment and that

was keeping her witness content, motivated and, most importantly, alive. Kara was running on borrowed time. Howell was right in that it was a given the Alessis would eventually know what Kara was working on—that is, if they didn't already. Whatever Juliet wanted, Juliet was going to get. Even if what she wanted made Howell less than happy.

That meant that Kara and Howell needed to stay in this odd, for want of a better word, honeymoon phase of their... She glared out the window and rolled her eyes. *Relationship.*

"What's your take on Juliet?" Howell asked. "Gut reaction."

"Determined." There was no hesitation in her answer. She prided herself on getting an instant and accurate read on people. Her gut was never wrong and she trusted it implicitly. "But she's also still a bit hesitant. The Alessis have always treated her well so she's got some guilt—regardless of what they've done to others. She's also been steadfast in her belief that she's doing the right thing. I think it's the unknown of what comes next that's got her spooked. I think once she knows the Marshal Service is involved—"

"She doesn't know?" Howell frowned.

"I told her I was looking into protection options for her. I never mentioned any specifics. For the record, I don't like the idea of you having power over *my* case. You aren't going to threaten to pull your support if things don't go your way, are you?"

"I don't go back on my word, Kara. Once I'm in, I'm in." She could feel the heat of his gaze from where he was sitting. "But I'm not looking for an excuse to say no. If that's what you're afraid of."

"Maybe it is." That was a lie. Part of the reason she'd requested him was because of his honorable reputation.

"Cards on the table, Kara." His voice gentled. "I can't judge what you've done on this case because it wasn't and isn't my case. And I certainly can never understand your specific and personal perspective. But I'm not searching for an escape route from the chance at having a hand in the outcome. There aren't many things that can unify all law enforcement agencies, but I feel safe in saying the Alessi family is one of them. I'm in this until the end, Kara, and that means I'm going to have to defer to your expertise when it comes to building and prosecuting this case. That includes how you handle your witness so long as what you want doesn't interfere with how the Marshals operate. And despite my and the Marshal Service's involvement, she is *your* witness."

Kara unclenched and relaxed a little. "I appreciate that."

"The flip side is that you're going to have to admit I know more about keeping your witness out of harm's way than you do."

She scrunched her mouth. True enough.

"And just a reminder," he continued in a tone that had her bristling. "You came to us. Maybe because it's best for your witness, or maybe, just maybe, you're worried you're out of your depth."

Kara straightened. "I'm out of my element, not depth."

"Noted." He nodded. "Seems as though we've accepted one another's strengths, but we share one common weakness. An inability, or perhaps a better word is reluctance, to acknowledge the other might have important insights at times. As much as we are loathe to acknowledge it, we're going to have to learn to work together."

She actually laughed a little. "That's a diplomatic way of telling me to be prepared to accept when I'm wrong."

"What can I say?" He shrugged. "Growing up with three siblings meant diplomacy at times dictated survival. I'm not about to shirk the responsibility or discount the respect you've offered by coming to me. All I ask is you grant me the same. Respect is a shortcut to success and we both know you'll only accept one outcome for this situation."

She shouldn't have been surprised that he'd already learned what buttons of hers to push to make a point. When in doubt, remind her of the endgame: bringing down the Alessis. Maybe, hopefully, hold them to some accountability for killing her father. Howell was right. She was willing to do, accept and tolerate just about anything if it meant Sal Alessi ended up behind bars.

"So. Back to my question regarding Juliet Unger," Howell said. "Other than determined, scared and apparently smart, what are your other impressions about her?"

"Clever." Kara sorted through her memories of that first meeting with the younger woman. "I probably didn't wear the best mask of indifference when she first came to me. She knows the information she has is important, but my reaction—the fact I didn't jump at the evidence right away—told her I wasn't going to buy what she was selling simply because it dealt with the Alessis. I'll admit, when she asked about witness protection that added a bit more weight to what she was offering."

"Or maybe someone's been whispering in her ear,"

Howell suggested. "Because we're keeping the case as quiet as possible, I couldn't instigate a deep dive into her through my usual channels. What's her life like? You said her mother died a while ago and she then lived with her grandmother. What about friends? Roommates? Boyfriend? Girlfriend? Has she mentioned anyone?"

"No." Kara shook her head. "Other than the preliminary check I ran on her, nothing popped up. Nothing raised any alarms anywhere, so there was enough to convince me that what she'd told me rang true. See? I didn't jump the gun and give credence to everything she said because of who her evidence is against. I did my job. Same as I would for any other witness."

"Okay." It at least sounded as if he believed her. "What exactly did you tell her about me?"

"Just that I was bringing someone whose help we needed to secure her testimony." She hesitated. "But like I said, she's smart. And she's the one who brought up the Marshal Service when she asked about protection and relocation."

"Good to know." Howell nodded again. "Is there anything..." He trailed off, his gaze darting from the rearview mirror to his side one, then back again.

She shifted in her seat and frowned at his suddenly intense expression. "Something wrong?"

"Not sure. Maybe nothing." He glanced at the overpass signs indicating an upcoming exit ramp a good five miles from their destination. "Or maybe we've got a tail."

"What?" Kara turned all the way around to stare out the back window. "Which car?" The highway was at its usual level of busy, meaning there were countless cars all around them.

"Dark blue SUV, two cars back."

Her eyes found the car instantly. Her stomach dropped. "Howell—"

He sped up, changed over one lane to the right without signaling, then moved over one more toward the off-ramp.

Kara watched in growing dread as the SUV followed, triggering a blare of horns in response.

"Thought so." Howell kept to the speed limit, watching to make sure he drew them along.

Kara caught her lower lip in her teeth. "Howell, this isn't what you think."

His hands tightened on the wheel. "Given what you believe the Alessis did to your father, forgive me if I don't feel like taking any chances." The SUV followed but kept a respectable distance away.

"No, seriously," she tried again. "I think—"

He shot her with a look. Feeling a bit like Mia had when she'd been scolded by Garrett, Kara turned back around and slumped in her seat. "You're making a mistake," she whispered and kept her eyes on her own mirror.

When Howell pulled into the parking lot of a fast food restaurant, the SUV followed and parked a few spots away. Howell unsnapped his belt and shoved open the door.

Kara grabbed for him but thought better of it at the last second. Best she not touch him if she could help it. The man made her heartbeat run wild. "Wait, Howell, honestly, you need to—"

"This isn't the first time I've seen that car, Kara." Howell pulled the key out of the ignition and climbed out. "It was parked half a block from your house."

"Yes," she said calmly, despite her pulse kicking into overdrive as she met his gaze. "I know."

"You...know?" He stood for a moment and simply stared at her. "Explain, please."

"I shouldn't have to." She attempted to make light of the situation. "At the diner I told you I knew who I was dealing with where the Alessis are concerned. Do you really think I'd have taken this case on without protecting myself and my family? Like you keep saying, I know what they're capable of."

Anger sparked in his eyes and she wondered if it was aimed at himself or at her. Either way she couldn't help but think this incident wasn't going to improve their tenuous professional relationship.

"Those men work for you," Howell accused in a very deliberate and slow tone.

"From a personal security company I hired, yes." She shrugged and added, "They were in my budget."

"They're inept, so you got what you paid for," Howell muttered. "I'll be right back."

"But—"

"Are you a thousand percent sure these are the guys you hired,"

Her hesitating for a second was all he needed to know it seemed.

"Stay here." He got out and slammed the door. A heartbeat later the locks engaged.

Kara unbuckled her belt so she could watch out the back window. Her mind raced with the situation unfolding in the parking lot. Two men climbed out of the SUV as Howell approached. He held up his badge and immediately the other two raised their hands and moved backward toward their vehicle.

Whatever confidence she'd been clinging to faded when she realized they'd backed off way too quickly to be effective protection. The smell of hot oil and overly grilled hamburgers didn't do her rolling stomach any good as doubt and dread crept in.

The two men looked as shaken as she felt, another not-so-great indicator that they didn't exactly excel at their jobs. In that moment she suspected coming face to face with US Marshal Howell McKenna could very well be more dangerous than dealing with an Alessi henchman.

Kara heard them speaking, but only barely. There was no making out the words exchanged, but the intensity was unmistakable. Howell was ticked and that energy vibrated all the way through the car. Her heart pounded so loud she couldn't hear herself breathe. But still she watched as, first, the two men and then Howell gestured toward the car she currently occupied.

A few moments later the two security men climbed back into the car and drove off, triggering another bout of panic for Kara. She cringed, watching as Howell made a phone call, then she twisted forward in her seat when he started to make his way back to the car. The locks disengaged. Nibbling on her thumbnail—something she only did when she was seriously stressed—she waited for him to open his door. One minute. Two. Three...

She jumped when Howell yanked open her door. She didn't bother with a greeting. "I know I probably should have told you about them before." Her voice actually broke a bit when she spoke. "Honestly, I didn't anticipate you noticing them."

"Then you underestimated me as much as you overestimated them," Howell said with what sounded and felt like forced patience. "For the record, if you've been paying them ten cents an hour, it's been far too much. I've never even heard of McClarren Security and if I've never heard—"

She scoffed. "Like you know every security firm operating on the East Coast." She knew the instant she met his gaze again that he had exactly that information. She cleared her throat and tried to stop the angry frustrated flush creeping up her neck. "I hired them as soon as I realized the Alessi case was serious. My boss and I discussed an official protective detail, but that would have meant bringing other people in and we didn't want to do that. This was all arranged well before I spoke with you in Virginia. And, in case you didn't notice, I'm still alive."

"Proving that miracles do happen. I've fired them, by the way." He inclined his head as if to make certain she heard him. "All of them."

"You can't do that!" Her frustration boiled over. "I've got—"

"A second surveillance team on the house to watch over your mom and kids, yeah. They told me." He nodded once before letting out a long breath. "It's being taken care of."

"Taken care of? How exactly?" she demanded.

"The McKenna way. Effectively and efficiently." He closed her door and walked around the vehicle to climb into the driver's seat.

"They're doing their best," Kara told Howell as he started the car up again. "You're trained to spot tails," she tried to reason as they headed back to the highway.

"Not everyone can live up to the standards of a US marshal." *Or a McKenna.*

"You know who else is trained to spot tails?" He made quick work of the on-ramp. "The Alessis and everyone who works for them. Tell me something."

She had a feeling she wasn't going to like this. "What?"

"Did you let McClarren Security know who they were protecting you from? Specifically. Did you tell them you were taking on the Alessis?"

"I...had to." Her stomach dropped as realization dawned. As careful and smart as she thought she'd been, now she understood how wrong she'd been. "That was a mistake, wasn't it?" She'd have been better off with a detail organized through her office.

"Only because more people are aware of your investigation than we thought. People outside the investigation." He swore, but she recognized it as the pressure release it was. "The plan was to keep this quiet. Between you, your boss and assistant, me and my boss." He shook his head as he merged onto the freeway. "That's been blown sky-high. There's no telling who's in the loop now."

"I know saying sorry won't fix anything, but for what it's worth, I am." She paused. "I should have told you."

"This is why working alone like this is a bad idea." His voice quieted. "You don't have anyone stopping you before you mess up. That won't be a problem now."

Because she had him. She swallowed hard. He would be there, watching her back, standing beside her. Working with her.

Kara blew out a long, slow breath as a headache tugged between her eyes.

Things were getting better with each passing minute.

* * *

"It's just up there on the right."

"Yeah, thanks." Howell had heard the tension in Kara's voice as he stopped at a red light two blocks from the Tidal Cove Lodge. "I see it."

"I just noticed you weren't using—" she said almost defensively as she gestured to his blank dashboard screen. "Are you GPS adverse?"

"When I'm on a case like this? Yes," Howell told her, grateful to finally fill the car with something other than silent tension. "GPS systems can be hacked." He wasn't entirely certain how that worked, but his brother, Aiden—a former secret service agent—assured him it was possible. Howell might not be trusting enough to work with a partner, but when Aiden said something, he listened and paid attention.

"You're still angry, aren't you?"

"I wasn't angry, Kara." He turned into the lodge's parking lot and slowed, gauging his options. The lot wasn't huge, but it was mostly empty, which gave him less to worry about. "I was frustrated, yes. And irritated. Believe me, you'll know when I'm mad." Out of the corner of his eye, he saw the distrust on her face, just before she turned away. He'd taken enough psychology classes and had enough on the job experience to recognize it when he saw it and felt compelled to add "I'm not a violent man."

She snorted. "You carry a gun for a living and deal with human predators. That's overqualified for violence if you ask me."

"Clarification," he said because it seemed needed. "I'm not violent unless the situation calls for it." He chose a parking space at the back of the lot near the entrance to a footpath to the beach. He turned off the car and faced her. Ahead of them, the waves tumbled and crashed onto the shore as the late morning mist and fog broke apart. "Was that a problem with Garrett? Was he angry a lot?"

"Sometimes," she said. "It certainly never helped things. And when I got to the final straw, I was glad I wouldn't have to deal with his temper anymore."

He caught her hand, threaded his fingers through hers and squeezed. When she looked at him, he saw a bit of the bone-tired woman she must have been at the time, instantly shielded by the strong woman she'd become. "That must have been hard. I'm sorry."

She nodded, then offered a small smile. "It was. But he went to anger management therapy. A condition of the divorce in exchange for him not having to pay spousal support. He won't sue me for custody. That's all hot air. Mostly."

"What a prince." Howell knew a lot of men like Garrett Gallagher. They were unhappy bullies who didn't usually know where the boundaries lay until they crossed them.

"I've come across many bullies in various forms. I didn't go along with it then, and I certainly wasn't going to now."

He squeezed her hand again and felt a flash of triumph when she returned the action. He liked touching her. He liked it a lot. Almost as much as he'd liked kissing her. "You're something else, you know that?"

"Noted." And the way she smiled cut through the darkness.

He lifted their joined hands and pressed a kiss to her knuckles. He liked the surprise that jumped into her eyes, along with the faint hint of pink that colored her cheeks. But she still held on. And smiled.

"Does this mean I get to ask you anything I want? Now that you know so much about my personal life?" She teased in that Kara way he was coming to expect and appreciate. "I'm a fan of quid pro quo."

"We'll see how our meeting with Juliet goes." He let go of her hand and climbed out of the car, walked around to meet her as she did the same, hoisting her oversize purse onto her shoulder. "Keeping up appearances," he murmured when he slid an arm around her waist and they walked toward the front entrance of the lodge. Although honestly, he wasn't quite ready to let go of her just yet.

An old sedan rumbled its way into the parking lot, moving past them at a noisy clip. Howell looked behind them as the driver parked beside them.

"Why do people do that?" Kara followed his gaze. "Happens to me all the time. Tons of empty spaces and someone still parks right next to me."

Howell didn't disagree. He kept his eye on the young man who climbed out of the sedan and immediately flipped up the collar of his scarred bomber jacket against the cold, his dark curly hair blowing in the icy wind. He heard the distinctive beep of a car alarm being activated.

He felt Kara shiver despite the down jacket she wore. He picked up the pace to get them inside.

The Tidal Cove Lodge sat back from the road, pushing against the shoreline of the ocean that was having an active day of tumbling and tossing those brave enough to test the chilly waters. The hotel struck Howell as a remnant of the past when hotels were destinations more than conveniences.

"The federal prosecutor's office must have a bigger budget than I realized."

"Actually." She cleared her throat and tightened her hold on her purse. "The location was my choice. I'm picking up the difference. Don't tell me—you disapprove." She rolled her eyes and avoided his gaze.

"Don't put words in my mouth." But she'd just proven, again, how emotionally invested in this case she was. Going out of pocket to cover the witness's lodging? That was above and beyond. "How'd you know about this place, anyway?"

"My parents and I used to stay here for a week in the summer when I was a kid. Before..." Kara blinked away what he decided to interpret as cold-air-induced tears. "It's out of the way and runs special rates during the winter months. Not many customers except for those looking for what's tantamount to a polar bear experience out there." She gestured to the ocean as it continued its wild, misty pitch.

"Which room is she in?" Howell asked as they approached the double doors made of frosted glass and etched with seashells and starfish.

"Two-twelve." She pointed to the second floor of the three-story building.

Winter clung to the facade like barnacles on a ship. Icicles dangled delicately from roof overhangs and edges of balconies. The now constant sound of crashing waves filled the air with the sounds of the ocean that was located steps away. Two dormant fire pits were covered with a light dusting of snow that had fallen earlier this morning but hadn't yet melted away.

With the sun hidden behind a bank of snow clouds,

the air was cold and the sound of Kara's high heels click-clacked against the frozen ground. She huddled against the chill, hands stuffed deep into the pockets of her down jacket.

"It's nice."

"I can't tell if you're being sarcastic or not." The smile she shot him was strained.

"I don't say what I don't mean."

"Good to know." The lines around her eyes eased.

Cozy, comforting vibes welcomed them upon entering. He could hear the crackle and feel the warmth of the flames roaring in the lobby fireplace. His cheeks thawed out with the pinpricks of feeling that returned with the heat.

"So much hasn't changed."

Howell was certain she hadn't meant to say that out loud, but he didn't comment as he looked around for what, if any, security precautions were in place. Finally he spotted a camera aimed at the front door but it looked to be about ten years out of date.

"They've updated the paint color and the accent pieces." Kara pointed to the brass lanterns affixed on either side of the enormous stone fireplace. "Mom and Dad and I would curl up on those sofas, snuggle under the plush throw and drink hot chocolate together."

"Sounds lovely." The memories hurt, though. He could hear it in her voice.

He followed Kara past the old-fashioned registration desk that displayed local tour pamphlets as well as a bowl filled with homemade wrapped caramels. He smiled at the young woman organizing a colorful bouquet of flowers, then pivoted toward the staircase, rather than following Kara, who headed for the pair of elevators.

"I prefer taking the stairs," he said before she could protest.

She frowned at him. "Elevators only have one way in or out."

"Which means someone can be waiting for us when we get out. I don't play sitting duck well."

"Howell, no one knows she's..." She trailed off at his look and sighed as if she'd remembered what he'd said in the car. "This is your show. Lead on."

He was tempted to thank her but worried she might interpret it as sarcasm. He said it anyway. "Thank you."

"For what?"

"For remembering this is why you came to me in the first place. To keep you safe."

"I came to you to keep *Juliet* safe." She stomped her determined feet up the steps.

"I guess you're just a bonus for me then." In more ways than one. It would be interesting, once they were on the other side of this case, to see if the spark remained between them. Or if this was simply adrenaline and conflict induced.

The muted green and blue tones offered a relaxing atmosphere that accented the beauty of the ocean just outside. The decor was caught somewhere between an East Coast seascape and cottage charm.

The vaulted ceilings of the lobby followed them upstairs and led to the second floor with exposed wooden beams, a neutral patterned carpet and room numbers displayed on rustic driftwood above peepholes.

Room 212 was down the hall, well away from the hum

of the ice machine and vending machines providing caffeine and sugar fixes for late-night snackers. The Do Not Disturb sign hung on the handle of the door Kara knocked on. "Juliet? It's me, Kara."

A few moments later, the inside lock released and the door popped open enough for a pair of brown eyes to peer out.

Juliet kept the door fractionally open between them, her narrowed gaze landing first on Howell, then on Kara. "This the guy you needed me to talk to?"

"Yes. US Marshal Howell McKenna."

"A Marshal? Really?" The innocent surprise in her voice didn't quite match the suspicious glint in her eye.

"Ma'am." Howell reached into his inside jacket pocket for his badge. "I'm here to help you. You and Ms. Gallagher."

Juliet eyed him for a moment before she stepped back and unlatched the security bar.

Howell followed Kara inside and waited while Juliet closed the door behind them, snapped the lock and reengaged the security bolt. She hurried past them, her sock-covered feet muted against the carpet. The oversize tightly-knit tunic sweater she wore was in the same blue tone as her snug designer jeans.

The short entryway gave Howell an instant look at the room. It was larger than he expected, with a double bed situated between two whitewashed nightstands. The same brass sconces that decorated the lobby were situated on the wall but the lights remained off. A fluffy white duvet partially covered the tangled sheets. A small suitcase sat open on the luggage rack, clothes neatly arranged inside while one pair of sneakers sat beneath. Simple, tidy, organized.

He stepped back, keeping Kara between them as Juliet instantly dragged shaky hands through her dyed blond hair. Kara offered what he thought was a reassuring smile.

"So, um." Juliet flashed an uneasy grin in Howell's direction. "Kara said I had to talk to you before I could get into witness protection. Sorry." Juliet gestured to the round table beside the television that was covered with books, a hand towel and four plastic containers filled with colorful threads and beads. "After my mother passed my therapist suggested I find something to take my mind off things." She picked up one of a number of hand-knotted beaded bracelets. "It helps with my anxiety, but I think it's become a bit of a compulsion."

It definitely explained the countless bits of thread that clung to her sweater and the carpet.

"I've been telling Juliet she should try selling these online." Kara touched a finger to the pile of half a dozen completed bracelets.

"Nah." Juliet clutched her hands tight and shook her head. "I like giving them away. That reminds me." She plucked up a ziplock plastic bag. "I made this for your daughter." She pulled out a beautifully patterned pink and purple bracelet with bright white square beads that she put into a pink organza drawstring gift bag. "I hope that's okay. You said she likes jewelry."

"Of course it's okay." Kara accepted the bracelet and dropped it into her bag. "I'll be sure to give it to her as soon as I get home. Thank you."

Juliet responded by putting her scissors and stabilizing clips away. "I'll just straighten up."

"Don't worry about it," Kara assured her as Howell continued to scan the room.

"I'm a mess, I know." Juliet tucked her long hair behind her ears. "I think the room service people are taking bets on why I'm here." She turned that still nervous smile on Howell. "I don't know what I'm supposed to do. What do you want me to say?"

There was an odd breathy quality to her voice now, as if she was trying to sound borderline helpless and scared.

"Just relax, Juliet." Howell motioned to the chairs on either side of the table. "I need to ask you some questions before we make anything official."

"But you're going to give me protection, right?" Juliet sat slowly, balancing on the edge of one of the chairs, her fingers clasped between her knees. "That's what the Marshals are supposed to do. Offer people new starts and protect them from the creeps they're testifying against."

"That's part of what we do," Howell confirmed. He agreed with most of Kara's assessment of the young woman. Obviously determined. And smart. "We also work in tandem with other law enforcement agencies who request our assistance. You've got quite a situation you're dealing with at the moment."

"I guess." A helpless shrug accompanied her agreement. "Sometimes it's hard to do the right thing."

"Perfectly said," Howell agreed. "Kara came to us because she wants to ensure your testimony against Sal Alessi, but also keep you safe. You realize that moving forward, chances are you won't be going back to any part of your previous life. Chances are you won't ever see your home again."

She nodded. "Home is just a word."

Not in his experience, but there was no benefit to sharing. "Okay. Let's start at the beginning. Can you tell me how you came to work for the Alessis?"

A defiant spark caught in Juliet's eye. "Kara didn't tell you?"

"I told him you'd worked a number of jobs during school and before you were hired at Briarwood."

Howell didn't like that sudden clarification, as if Kara had purposely left something out of her oh-so-organized background report.

"I would like to hear all the details from you, please, Juliet." Howell stepped back and motioned for Kara to take a seat in the other chair. He walked over and opened the patio door wider, grabbed one of the metal framed chairs in a way that gave him the chance to assess the surrounding areas.

No easy access to the second level, but he wouldn't put it past anyone suitably driven to get to Juliet. The beach lay only steps away from the back entry to the hotel. He leaned out and caught a glimpse of where they'd parked before scanning the rest of their surroundings.

The collection of third-story balconies were staggered overhead, making it a challenge to drop down from one level to another. Doable, though, Howell thought. Still, the hotel wasn't a bad setup for the protection of a witness.

The pages of a word puzzle book on the nightstand rustled in the breeze as he came back inside. He pulled the door closed and silenced the room with a distinctive *wumph*.

"I know it's tiring to go over things again and again." He turned the chair around and sat down. "Consider it rehearsal for when you take the stand in court. Tell me about working for Sal Alessi and his family."

Juliet's gaze dropped immediately.

"It's okay, Juliet." Kara's tone gentled—much the way it did when she spoke to her children. "You already told me—"

"I lied." Juliet lifted her chin, her eyes filled with tears and desperation. "Not about everything, I swear. But about...where I was working when I met Albert."

"Albert Mercer," Howell clarified, recalling the name from Kara's report that he'd basically memorized. "The Alessis' senior accountant."

"Yes. He's worked for them for over thirty years," Juliet confirmed. "I'm so sorry, Kara! I was afraid you wouldn't believe me if you knew what I'd been doing."

Kara sat back, that passive expression blanketing the tension Howell felt rolling off her. "Tell me now," she said slowly. "And we'll go from there."

"I was a dancer," Juliet whispered. "At Velvet and Vice. I started working there while I was still in school. The job wouldn't have popped up on any records. They never wanted our real names. Only a stage one. Protection, I guess," she said with a glance toward the balcony. "In case they got caught for paying their dancers under the table. None of the names on file would connect to anyone. Albert was one of my regular customers."

"What kind of customer?" Howell inclined his head.

"Like I said, I was a dancer." Anger flashed in her eyes that, for an instant, completely changed her face. "That's all I did. That meant my job was to get my admirers to buy a lot of watered down drinks. I didn't do any of the other...stuff. Albert gave me money to sit with him after.

We talked and he asked about me and my plans for the future and…" She shrugged. "He was really nice. When I graduated from business college he talked to Mr. Alessi and got me a job at Briarwood Construction."

"So you stopped working at the club?" Kara asked.

"Mostly." She winced. "Sometimes I'd go back to make some extra cash. My grandmother's been ill for a really long time. She has dementia and I had to put her in a care facility. A few nights every month helped me cover that cost."

"I'm not passing any judgments on you, Juliet," Howell assured her. "Your grandmother's in New York, right? Brookside Court Senior Care?"

"Yes. Her retirement picks up a portion of the costs, but what I make dancing takes care of the rest. I visit her when I'm in the city," Juliet explained. "But she doesn't even recognize me anymore."

"Does Albert know you still work at Velvet and Vice?" Howell asked.

"No," she insisted. "No, he'd be horrified. Part of the reason he helped me get a good job was so I could quit. I didn't have the heart to tell him it wasn't quite enough."

So far, Howell believed her. Especially about the cost of her grandmother's care. His own grandfather had lived in an assisted-living facility the last few years of his life. It hadn't been cheap ten years ago and, since then, costs had only increased. But as for the rest…

His gut wasn't nearly satisfied so far.

"You were never recognized at Briarwood by Sal or Rafael?" Kara asked. "Despite working at the club?"

"Once you're hired at Velvet and Vice, they don't pay much attention to your face." Juliet's gaze shot to Kara's.

"What's going to happen to my grandma if I testify? I'm all she has. I can't leave her behind."

"I'm not going to let anything happen to your grandma, Juliet."

Howell wanted to remind Kara not to make any promises, but that wouldn't play into the united front they needed to present.

"Tell us about Briarwood, Juliet," Howell said. "How involved is Sal these days?"

"His name is on the checks and all the business stuff, but he hasn't come into the office for close to a year now," Juliet said. "He didn't even come in to fire me. I should be grateful for that, I guess. Late last year we were told Rafael was taking over most of the day-to-day operations because of Mr. Alessi's health, but nothing changed really. Briarwood is the second biggest construction firm in Connecticut," Juliet said. "It runs really smoothly. They do a lot of business with foreign companies as well as local government projects. My job was primarily to maintain the filing system, both on paper in the basement file room and with the on-site server. The Alessis don't trust cloud storage. Everything's password encrypted on the system and kept close by."

Howell nodded. "Tell me about the accounting record you gave Kara," Howell said. "How did you come across that information?"

"Albert was having computer issues and he asked if I could help. When I was working on his laptop, I came across the duplicate files. I thought they were part of the problems he was having, but when I looked closer, I realized it was a duplicate set of books." She pulled her feet up, wrapped her arms around her knees. "I'll admit, I was curious, so I did some poking around in the system and when I put everything together, I realized just how much illegal stuff was going on. The fake companies and payments. All the money just siphons through other Alessi businesses. So I, um—" she wrinkled her nose like a toddler who'd gotten caught out of bed after lights out "—I made a copy of the server's hard drive. At first, I was thinking it would be good to have an extra backup, but after I got fired…" she broke off, shrugging again.

Howell had no doubt she'd wondered if that hard drive could equal a huge payday. But accusing her outright wasn't going to help the current situation. Plus, it would probably only tick Kara off and he couldn't risk that at the moment. But.

He did have a question Kara probably wasn't going to be happy about.

"Why Kara?"

Right on schedule, Kara touched his arm. "I don't think—" She broke off when he glanced at her with what he considered his "I'm doing my job" expression.

"Juliet?" Howell prodded. "You could have taken this information to anyone. The Feds, local law enforcement. Instead, you chose Kara."

It wasn't the answer he wanted so much as Juliet's reaction to the question. He'd caught her off guard. She was quick in covering, but there was a flash of annoyance, a flash that shouldn't have been there if she wasn't trying to hide something.

The moment of silence indicated she was attempting to create a fathomable explanation. But why? The truth was so much easier.

"You know about what happened to her father, don't

you?" He pressed. "You know Sal Alessi is suspected of being responsible for his murder."

Juliet's gaze skittered to Kara. "I'm sorry." The tremble in her voice almost made Howell a believer. "I... I knew I couldn't trust just anyone with this. Sal always bragged about how he has eyes and ears everywhere. It's how he stays free. But I figured he had to have enemies, right? So I started digging and I read about your father's death." She flinched. "He'd been investigating Sal, so of course that's who the authorities suspected, but..." She shrugged and settled into her story. "I figured you'd be more inclined to believe me and work to make the case against him than anyone else I could approach. Considering your history with Sal."

"So I was your mark," Kara clarified and earned points in Howell's estimation for the control in her voice. It was, Howell thought, the most precise comment she could have made. Glancing at her, he couldn't help but think this didn't come as a complete surprise to her.

"We have a common interest," Juliet said. "Sal Alessi. He's a bad guy. He's gotten away with a lot and he's hurt many people. Someone needs to stop him. I'm no one, but you..." She gestured almost helplessly, a little too helplessly, Howell thought. "What's that saying, *the enemy of my enemy is my friend*. It made sense to approach someone who wouldn't bend the knee to Sal Alessi."

Howell respected that. Juliet had figured out all the angles. Whether Kara appreciated hearing the truth was, no doubt, going to be a conversation for later.

"Did you print anything out other than what you've given Kara?"

"No." Her eyes were sharp now, any pretense of helplessness all but gone. "I have all the drive's information on a dedicated and secured laptop I built. It's somewhere safe."

"She said she'd turn the laptop over to me once she's approved for witness protection," Kara said quietly. Howell didn't know Kara very well, but he could hear the undertones of doubt and disappointment in her voice.

"Well, then, we've got a problem, Juliet." Howell ignored Kara's glare of irritation. "I can't just admit you into the program until the evidence you have is verified as authentic. Until we're one hundred percent sure everything you've told us is on the up-and-up. Once Kara signs off on all the evidence and she's confident in your testimony and the case is good to go, then we can talk details about your relocation and your grandmother's."

"So you're saying I have to give up everything and trust you'll take care of me?" It wasn't what she said so much as how she said it that raised alarms for Howell. It was as if she was trying too hard to sound...scared.

Howell nodded, playing along. "Just like you trusted Kara enough to want to see this case through."

"I guess I don't really have a choice, do I?"

"We can always choose to do the right thing." But there was a hint of defeat in Kara's voice.

"One last question," Howell said. "What would you have done with that hard drive if she'd said no, Juliet?" He wanted nothing more than to reach out and take Kara's hand. To squeeze and hold it in comfort and silently convey that he knew this information was painful. And that she may have misjudged her golden witness. "What were your plans if she turned you away?"

"I don't know." She avoided his gaze.

"I think you do." Howell had seen this before. Far more times than he cared to admit. People like Juliet, they always had a backup plan. "Kara was your first stop, but your next one was Sal Alessi."

"No!" Genuine fear leaped into her eyes. "No, I'd never... He's terrifying. There's this...thing he has, it's like the second he enters a room, the temperature drops thirty degrees. I wouldn't have..." She wrung her hands. "I was going to tell Albert what I had and ask for money."

"And he'd have paid," Howell confirmed. "Because Albert Mercer wouldn't want Sal to know he'd lost control of the system's server." Howell had to admit. It wasn't bad as far as backup plans went.

"I know that sounds horrible," Juliet whispered in a desperate tone to Kara. "And I'm sorry I didn't tell you everything, Kara. But I have to tell the truth now, otherwise he won't let me into the program."

Kara nodded but still looked detached from the conversation. "Nothing more is going to happen until you give us that drive, Juliet."

Juliet stood, walked over to the glass door, stared out at the ocean waves tumbling onto the shore and breaking against the sand.

Juliet was good, Howell thought. But she also thought loud enough for Sal Alessi himself to hear her from his estate thirty miles away. He had no doubt that the last thing Juliet Unger was was helpless. She was exactly where she wanted to be. That said, she was working through the angles she thought she'd already prepared for. He'd cornered her, which meant the chances of her moving on with the case was currently fifty-fifty.

He'd played worse odds before and won.

He waited, finally giving in to the impulse to hold out his hand to Kara. When Kara took it, when he felt the coolness of her skin and her shaking fingers, he wanted nothing more than to assure her everything was going to be okay. Even if he didn't believe it himself.

When Juliet finally turned around, Kara snatched her hand back.

"Did you decide what you want to do, Juliet?" Howell asked.

"Like I said before, I don't really have a choice?" Juliet's eyes glinted. "I can't go back to my job because I've been gone too long. And I can't go out on my own because, chances are, the Alessis are going to figure out I hacked into their server so..." She motioned to them. "You're my only option. The laptop is with my friend Jazz. We met at Velvet and Vice and she let me crash at her place for a while." Defeat shadowed her gaze. "The evidence you need is in New York."

Chapter 6

"I'll save you the 'I told you so,'" Kara said as she walked out the front door of the lodge ahead of Howell, wincing against the instant whip of cold air assaulting her face. "You were right. I missed something. I felt something was off, I just couldn't…" The knots in her belly had begun to form sometime around Juliet's first apology and had yet to ease. She felt frozen, both mentally and physically. Worse, she felt…duped. And irritated at herself for not following her instincts. At least she'd paid enough attention to bring Howell on board. So far that decision was paying off better than putting her faith in Juliet. "I was too eager to believe her, I didn't ask the right questions."

Howell touched a hand to the small of her back. Immediately that cold enveloping her eased. "I think the woman up there is, like you said, very smart, very clever, and you understood and saw exactly what she wanted you to."

Kara hated the sympathy in his voice. She'd have preferred the "I told you so." Still, it meant a lot that he didn't gloat.

"Whatever else is going on," Howell said. "She was telling the truth about one thing. She's got that hard drive. That's what we turn our attention to right now. We need to find it."

"Before the Alessis do."

"That," Howell agreed. "And before that statute of limitations run out. We've got two ticking clocks running down on us and not a lot of time to waste. You still in?"

Kara scoffed, the blood rushing back into her face. "I want to find out exactly what is going on. You're absolutely right I'm still in."

"Okay." He nodded once and let her go to pull out his phone. "First step is me calling in a pair of marshals to keep an eye on her until we figure out our next move."

"Sounds good." That would give her some peace of mind.

There was no distracting arm around her waist as there had been on the walk inside the lodge. No comforting warmth that seeped through her jacket. Probably for the best, Kara thought and set a new goal of remaining distraction free. She moved away while he talked on the cell, focusing on the new and unexpected puzzle she had to figure out. In her experience, however, puzzles were near impossible when you didn't know what the finished picture was meant to be.

"Kara," Howell called before she nearly skidded off her feet due to the snow covering her high-heeled boots.

"What?" She regained her balance, her frown deepening when she didn't find him looking at her as expected. Instead, his gaze was on the beach. Kara moved closer to him, the tension rising again. He disconnected his call, his jaw tensing. "Is something wrong?"

He shook his head. "Not sure."

Kara followed his line of sight, stepping back to him in the middle of the parking lot. She looked around but didn't notice anything out of the ordinary. The beach was mostly empty save for a few people out for a stroll or taking their dogs for a waterlogged walk. It took her a moment to lock in on who Howell was observing: the young man who had parked beside them.

He stood on the beach, hands pushed deep into the pockets of his jacket, curly hair blowing into his face from the wind tumbling in over the waves behind him.

Kara shivered and stepped even closer to Howell. "Is he watching us?"

"Yes." The instant Howell said it, the man stepped back. Even from a distance there was no mistaking the slow smile that curved his lips. He turned his head away, ever so slightly, and closed his eyes.

Howell whipped his arm up and around her shoulders, pivoting them both away even as he pulled her down. The explosion ripped through the air like a sudden tornado. The impact tossed them both to the ground in a tangled heap.

Kara gasped as heat and noise erupted behind and around her. She sprawled on the asphalt beneath the weight of Howell's body. Her ears rang as she blinked to try to keep her eyes open, dragging impossible, hot air into her straining lungs. Howell shifted, blanketing her from the lick of flames she could feel through the soles of her shoes.

Kara was stunned at first; unable to connect to what was happening. Her ears felt plugged; her lungs empty, and when she tried to breathe, all she caught was gasoline fumes and smoke.

She choked, coughing and shifting, desperate to drag in the smallest amount of oxygen that couldn't be found. Nothing sounded normal. It was as if she'd been thrown into the deepest part of the ocean where the voices and screams and shouts were muffled, unrecognizable. Incomprehensible.

She sobbed, shoved her hands under her chest and tried to push herself up.

"Stay still! Stay down!" Howell yelled as he curled himself over her.

The second explosion robbed her of panic, of thought and nearly of consciousness. Her scream was muffled by the edges of her jacket and the rough ground. The unbelievable pressure that pushed down on them had her sucking and choking once more. She tucked her head in and blinked against the brilliant ball of flame and smoke that billowed up and into the sky directly over Howell's SUV.

Everything moved in fast-forward even as things slowed down. She felt Howell's hands on her arms, hauling her up, propelling her forward toward the lodge as people spilled out of the front door. Kara's eyes watered against the smoke as Howell pushed her into the lobby.

"Kara!" Howell ran his hands down the sides of her head, her face, over her shoulders and along her arms. She could barely feel his touch—could only stare blankly at the fireball burning where Howell's car had been moments before. "Kara." Howell caught her face in his hands, turned her toward him and all but pressed his nose against hers. She saw so much in the flash of a moment: shock, steadfastness. Fear. But the last he blinked away in the next second. The marshal was there. In control. Focused on her. "You okay?"

She nodded even as his hands continued to skim over her body, stopping occasionally, she assumed, to make sure he didn't encounter blood. "Fine," she half whispered, half choked. She drew a hand across her stinging cheek and throbbing forehead. "Are you?" She grabbed hold of him, both to steady herself and to make sure he was still in one piece. With both hands she yanked at him, catching the barest of glimpses of the scorch marks on his back. "You're hurt?"

"I'm okay." He kept one hand on her shoulder and met her gaze with a look that said everything she needed to know.

Howell spoke to someone behind her and it was only then that she noticed the crowd of people that had appeared. She stood close to what remained of the glass doors, staring dazedly at the fire as it continued to burn in the near distance. The air was heavy with the stench of fuel and burning rubber. Beneath her jeans she could feel the scrapes on her knees, feel the bruising begin to take hold. But she couldn't look away.

Not from the flames. Not from the past.

Not from what could have so easily been.

Her mind shifted almost instantly back to twenty-one years ago. Back to the day her father had walked out of the house, only to be killed moments later by the bomb in his car. Back to when she'd been thrown off the stool at their breakfast bar where she'd been eating the cereal she and her mother had argued over. Back to when her life had changed in an instant.

She sobbed, swayed, caught the wave riding the thin line between then and now. Her entire body turned into a block of ice that was incapable of thawing.

She reached out, grabbed hold of the wall. Howell's strong hand was gone and she wished she understood why that bothered her as much as it did. Taking a gulp of air, she tried to recall the moments before the blast, when she seemed capable of standing on her own.

Her head and her ears, pounded as that sound, that explosion, played over and over. She'd heard it all before. Felt it all before. But until this instant she hadn't understood exactly...

She reached for the infinity charm she wore at the base of her throat. It was the charm her mother had given her shortly after her father was killed. The charm that was meant to start the healing but had only served as a reminder of the unending past. It felt hot beneath her trembling fingers even as it cleared the fog and shock from her mind.

"Kara?" Howell's voice sounded faint when he spoke to her. He reached out to her, but it was too late, she'd stepped back outside.

"I'm fine." She didn't care if he heard her. She could only focus on one thing. The fire.

Even with the ringing in her ears she heard the sirens in the distance. She scanned the beach, trying to peer through the smoke and flames to find the man who had stood watching them what felt like hours before.

Everyone else on the beach had come closer, creating the usual human curiosity ring around the scene of destruction. But the man? She looked again. Blinked to clear her vision.

He was gone.

"Juliet." The name shot through her mind like an arrow of clarity. "Juliet." She turned, looking first for Howell, only to find him all but swallowed by the crowd. He'd followed her and had his badge out. He was attempting to keep the crowd back as the fire continued to rage. The wind caught the black smoke and sent it surging toward the street. Kara began to walk. She stumbled at first, nearly tripped and face planted for a second time on the asphalt, but she caught herself on a nearby car.

When she pulled her hand free, it was covered with ash and soot. She scrubbed her palm on her coat and kept moving.

"Kara!"

Her ears may have been tricking her with that desperation she heard in Howell's voice as she pushed her way through the growing crowd toward the front door of the lodge. The beautifully etched glass doors had shattered, as had the plate glass windows that lined one side of the building, all the way up to the second floor. Her heels crunched as she slipped and slid her way back inside, lungs straining as she struggled to breathe.

She didn't feel the warmth when she entered this time and heard the frantic voices of people on their phones, some of them were recording the show of flames arcing into the sky.

"Kara!"

Kara refused to stop. She got to the stairs, grabbed hold of the banister and hauled herself up, her legs threatening to buckle even as she forced them to obey. There wasn't a part of her that didn't hurt, didn't ache, and she could feel the adrenaline surging to take the place of the common sense that told her to stop, to sit. To give in.

She rounded the corner of the second floor with a vehemence she'd only felt a handful of times before, as if her desperation was fuel.

"Juliet!" She meant to yell, to shout, but she found

herself jostled and bumped by a pair of guests emerging from their room.

Dread swirled around her as she saw the door to Juliet's room ajar. Fear and fury mingled as she dived inside and skidded to a stop at the edge of the bed. "Juliet?" Silence.

The room was empty.

The two chairs they'd occupied minutes before were upended. The table tipped over. The curtains on the window ripped and hanging at an odd angle. Juliet's suitcase lay on the floor, its contents spilled everywhere. A whimper of panic lodged in Kara's throat before she swallowed it.

"Kara."

Howell reached her in determined strides, the panic on his face touching. Kara dropped her bag that she'd somehow managed to keep hold of. Every bit of strength that had carried her up the stairs drained out of her when he spun her around.

Tears of defeat pooled in her eyes when she looked up at him.

"She's gone."

Howell clutched his cell phone in one hand, waiting anxiously for the return call from his brother he feared might come too late.

Fear had no place in a case, in an investigation, in any protective detail. And yet, it had lodged in his chest like shrapnel from the exploded car.

Kara.

First responders had the fire under control quickly after arriving on the scene. Around him the chaos had calmed, but the residual tension clung like the ash and smoke from the fire.

It had been over an hour since the first engine arrived. Forty-seven minutes since the first patrol car carrying two uniformed officers parked haphazardly across the way. Forty-one since Detective Hale had shown up as the investigator in charge.

Howell gave a preliminary statement to one officer while Detective Hale went inside to speak with Kara where Howell had left her in the lodge's coffee shop with orders for her not to move.

As much as he'd wanted to stay with her while she gave her own statement, Howell needed the emotional distance both for himself and for the validity of whatever information she was going to impart. Nothing about this incident, nothing about this case, made sense now. It had been hinky from the jump and maybe if he'd said something to Kara earlier…

Stop! He couldn't change things now, only move forward and focus on the information they knew to be true.

That car exploding had blown to smithereens whatever tenuous hold he had on the truth.

Juliet had been right about one thing. Sal Alessi wouldn't have taken kindly to his server being hacked to the point his entire criminal enterprise had been exposed. Kara had been insistent no one knew about her investigation, but clearly someone did, otherwise his vehicle wouldn't have gone up in flames seconds before Kara climbed into it.

Alessi had blown up one prosecutor twenty-five years ago. Pretty risky to attempt to do it again to his previous victim's daughter. Something more was going on with this case, but for the life of him, he couldn't grasp what. The trail of it went in circles and he wouldn't be able to make sense of it until his head was on straight.

The firefighters aimed their sharp streams of water at the shell of Howell's car along with what remained of the nearby vehicles. While the explosive detection unit was on site, so far they'd only been able to confirm what Howell himself suspected: the car that parked beside them had been the actual bomb.

It would take days for the lab to confirm the details unless he called in a massive amount of favors and was granted an equal number of miracles.

They didn't have days to sit around waiting for results. He needed to make them happen ASAP. If only to make sure Kara was safe.

Howell's hand tightened around his cell so hard he had to stop himself from shattering it. He should have seen it sooner. Should have been paying closer attention. He shouldn't have let himself get distracted by...

He shook his head as if he could dislodge the thought. Kara hadn't distracted him. He'd been paying attention. What he had done was what he'd accused her of doing from that first meeting in Deputy Director Coleson's office. He'd underestimated the Alessis. Not in how far they'd go.

But in how fast they'd come after her.

The main question he wanted an answer to right now was *how* did the Alessis know about the investigation?

Guilt eked in around the anger he'd been trained to tamp down. They'd almost died. *Kara* had almost died. A greasy, sick sensation slid through his belly at the thought. It wasn't just that someone would have had to tell Pamela she'd lost her daughter to the same violence, the same criminals that had robbed her of her husband. Or that he'd have had to face Mia and Jonah... He swallowed hard and squeezed his eyes shut in an attempt to reset his mindset.

It was the idea of Kara no longer existing in this world that had him balancing on the precipice of straight up unexpected terror.

He'd promised to protect her, and he had. Barely. But now? He took a deep breath that finally smelled more like ocean than burnt rubber and gasoline. Now he was on a different path when it came to taking the Alessis down once and for all.

Now he had a score to settle.

"Marshal McKenna." Detective Walter Hale appeared at his side, the middle-aged man looking as strained and stressed as Howell felt. "I just finished speaking with Ms. Gallagher."

"How is she?" Howell asked as he continued to watch the water arcing over the carcass of his vehicle.

"Remarkably calm and astute," the detective said. "Shock, probably. She asked about security cameras in the area, suggested we look for signs of an abduction coinciding with the timing of the explosion."

Howell ducked his head, his lips actually twitching. Kara was nothing if not dedicated. "Is that doable?" He had little doubt Kara's attention was going to be solely focused on finding Juliet and not on the fact someone had just tried to blow them up.

"I've already got a pair of officers making the rounds to the local businesses," Detective Hale assured him. "It's an older part of town, so I don't recommend holding out much hope. Ms. Gallagher mentioned the driver of the car that was parked next to you. She's not sure she got a good enough look to work with a sketch artist. Don't suppose you did?"

"It's more likely I could pick him out of a lineup." Finally the lookie-loos were dispersing, but of course they were being replaced by news crews spilling into the lots across the street and spaces lining the road. "I'm going to ask a favor of you, Detective. A professional courtesy." He finally turned all his attention on the man. "As I indicated in my statement, Ms. Gallagher and I are working on a sensitive case at the moment. I'd appreciate it if you and your department would lean away from the explosion being the result of a planted bomb for the time being. At least as far as the press is concerned."

"Word's going to get out eventually," Detective Hale said. "Not that our department leaks, but car bombs aren't exactly the norm around here. People are going to talk. I can give you two, maybe three days before we have to make an official statement. Publicly I can push the faulty fuel line angle for a bit."

"Any time you can give us would be great." And just like that, the clock started ticking. "I'd also like to be copied in on all the reports, including Ms. Gallagher's statement and all photographs that are being taken of the scene. Down here and also up in Juliet Unger's room." Howell caught sight of a dark SUV being stopped at the yellow tape blocking off the parking lot.

"I can do that," Detective Hale said. "I'd be happy for any assistance you and the Marshal Service can provide."

"Thanks." Howell's entire nervous system tensed until he caught the plate reading SAFEGRD. Instantly, he breathed easier as the patrol officers pulled back the caution tape to let the SUV drive in. "You have my number and e-mail if you need to get in touch with either Ms. Gallagher or myself."

"Yes, sir." Detective Hale nodded. "I'll be in touch."

The SUV drove right up to where Howell stood. It took more effort than Howell was comfortable with not to let his relief show as the familiar tall, dark-haired man climbed out of the vehicle. The facade of control, however, broke completely at the sight of the woman who got out of the passenger side and walked around the front of the car.

"Regan." He cleared his throat and managed to smile at his youngest sister as she walked straight at him. She didn't stop until she'd wrapped him in a tight hug. A hug he gratefully returned. "What are you doing here?"

"Just finished a case and had a few days off. Been hanging out with Aiden." ATF Agent Regan McKenna leaned back, her soft brown hair and light green eyes shimmering in the cloud-obscured sunlight. She rubbed his arms, her brow knitting in concern. "You okay?"

"I'm good." He looked over her head to their brother, Aiden. "You got here fast."

"I was in New Rochelle meeting with a potential client." Aiden moved in when Regan stepped aside to offer his own hug. The fact he held on a little longer and a little tighter than usual told Howell his big shot older brother had been digging into Howell's current circumstance and realized he was neck-deep in something serious. "We need to work on you being the expert of understatement," Aiden said when he released him. "I'd call nearly being blown into the afterlife by a car bomb more than a situation."

"It's a kind of situation." They both knew why he hadn't gone into details over the phone after Howell had called about the security detail Kara had hired. Despite Aiden's legendary calm, when it came to family, there were limits to his ability to compartmentalize. While Howell was only two years younger and had stood toe to toe with Aiden for most of their lives—despite being slightly taller—he looked up to his oldest sibling in ways that would probably make the security specialist uncomfortable.

"Kara's inside." Howell jerked a thumb in the direction of the front doors where one of the employees stood just inside sweeping up the shattered glass. "She's probably on her second round of coffee about now."

"A woman after my own heart." Regan's gaze was frozen on the firefighters and burned out cars. "Any idea what explosive was used?"

"Won't have the lab results on that until late tomorrow at the earliest," Howell said. "Want to hazard a guess?" Given her seven plus years as an ATF agent, Regan had more than earned her creds in explosives and weaponry.

She pursed her lips.

"There aren't any toes to step on," Howell assured her. "The locals have been more than happy for any help."

"In that case." Regan cocked her head and seemed to grow a full inch taller before she pivoted and walked over to where the firefighters were extinguishing the water and pulling back from the scene.

"Regan wasn't working with you on something, was she?" Howell asked Aiden.

"She just closed a case she's been focused on for three months." Aiden's stoic expression said a lot. "Domestic terrorist ring down south dealing in ghost guns. She didn't give me any details, but she turned up on my doorstep last night with takeout. Tells me things didn't end particularly well." He turned his eyes on Howell. "Kind of like you calling to say you had a *situation*."

"Like you said," Howell said. "We McKennas are experts of understatement. Is Regan okay?"

"She crashed in my guest room last night after drinking pretty much a whole bottle of wine." Aiden's concern rang loud and clear. "When she was still there this morning, I thought she might be of help here."

Howell winced. Regan wasn't much of a drinker, which meant that whatever did happen had definitely left her shaken. But, like the rest of the McKennas, she'd talk about it when she was ready. One benefit to having siblings who were all in law enforcement—there was always an understanding ear.

Across the way, Regan crouched beside one of the fire investigators and snapped on a pair of gloves. She was nodding and pointing. Then she glanced back at them in a way that had Howell and Aiden walking over.

"You find something?" Howell asked his sister.

"Another bomb." She pointed at the metal tube wedged against the back axel of the undercarriage of the car that had been parked next to his.

Howell's pulse jumped but he kept his feet planted.

"Since you're crouching over it like it's a baby squirrel, I'm going with it's not live." Aiden's comment earned a grin from their sister.

"It's a fake." The thirtysomething fire investigator said before Regan could. "We'll bag it up for evidence but there's no powder inside. See?" He pointed to the end of the pipe without a blasting cap twisted onto it.

"The cap could have gotten dislodged when the first

bomb went off," Regan suggested. "You might still find it in the wreckage."

"We'll watch for it for sure," the investigator said. "Detective Hale said you wanted copies of all our findings, Marshal?"

"Please," Howell said. "Are you sure you're done, Regan? I'd appreciate it if you two took a look at the hotel room upstairs."

"The one belonging to your missing witness?" Regan pushed to her feet, snapped off her gloves and shook the investigator's hand in thanks. "Sure. But why?"

Howell shrugged. "Wouldn't mind having another pair of eyes I trust up there."

"Excellent." Regan slapped her hands together. "Lead on. At some point are you going to tell me who you and the prosecutor ticked off?"

"Sal Alessi."

Regan snorted in disbelief, then nearly choked catching her breath in the cold and stumbled. "You're serious, aren't you?"

"In my defense, Kara's ticked him off more than me." Howell led them back to the hotel. The glass and debris had been cleaned up around the entrance but the smell from the explosion was still in the air. "Did you take care of that issue I asked you about?" he asked Aiden on their way to the stairs.

"It's being taken care of as we speak." Aiden lifted a hand to touch Howell's shoulder but pulled him to a stop instead. "How close were you to that thing when it blew?"

"What?" Howell looked over his shoulder and saw the remnants of his shredded and singed jacket. "Oh. Right. Explains the funny looks." Not to mention the draft. And why his back felt battered and bruised. He moved his badge and wallet into his pants pockets and shrugged out of the blazer. "Guess this is toast."

"You should save that," Regan said when he wadded it up. "Seriously. Wrap it up for Mom at Christmas when she complains you've missed too many family dinners. Might remind her things could be worse."

Not a terrible idea. Howell smirked and tucked it under his arm instead of tossing it. Their family did tend to have a rather macabre sense of humor when it came to the dangers of the job.

They made quick work of the stairs, navigating their way through a trio of lab techs moving in and out of Juliet's room.

"Can we have a few minutes?" Howell asked the one woman he'd seen speaking with Detective Hale previously.

"You can have five." She looked at him over the rims of her cat's-eye glasses. "We just finished taking photos."

"You're bagging everything up for evidence?" Aiden asked.

"As soon as you're done in here," she confirmed. "Five minutes," she added with a steely glare at Howell and held up her hand, fingers splayed. "No more."

"Territorial," Regan muttered as she went into the room first. "Hey, guys." She flashed her badge. "Your boss said we could have a few. Can we get some gloves?"

The younger of the two male techs pointed to the box outside the door on their way out. Aiden grabbed the box and nudged the door closed behind him with his foot. "What is it you want us to see?"

Howell was trying to tamp down on his suspicions.

"There was this...look on Juliet's face when I told her I was with the Marshal Service." He wasn't so confident in his memory to even try to define it. "She sounded surprised, but she didn't look it."

"Yeah, well, that line doesn't impress everyone, Howell," Regan teased as she put on her gloves. She crouched to get a look at the lower part of the room, under the bed. She pivoted easily, those countless ballet lessons she'd taken as a kid still paying off.

"You think Juliet was expecting you?" Aiden asked, handing Howell his own pair of latex gloves.

"I think she not only expected me, I think she planned it." The instant he voiced it, that niggling sensation in the back of his mind eased. "When we got here, Juliet was wearing designer jeans, expensive ones. Like the ones you always asked Mom to buy for you," he told his sister. The kind that were so far out of their family budget that Regan would have had to apply for a student loan to buy a pair. "Sweater was definitely newer. Her hair was dyed, but not in a drugstore kind of way. Highlights. Extensions. Been a few weeks since she's had them done, though. Serious manicure. Nothing about her screamed ordinary. Or struggling. Everything came across as...rehearsed and prepared."

"Look at you, knowing about hair and nails," their sister said while thumbing through the word puzzle books on the nightstand.

Aiden shot him a look. "What's bugging you, Howell?"

"Other than the fact she seemed...made up and rehearsed? This." He crouched, pointed to the upturned table Kara and Juliet had sat at. "Juliet's been making these knotted bead bracelets. Said her therapist suggested she take up the hobby to help with her anxiety."

"Makes sense." Regan stood, walked around the bed and stepped carefully away from the evidence markers on the floor.

"Yeah, well, this table was covered in supplies. All of which are now gone. Not many kidnappers would stop long enough for their target to pack up." He stood, walked over to the sliding glass door. He tried to open it. "I locked this when I was here. No one's gotten in this way, which means—" he pointed to the main door of the room "—that's the only way in or out." He pulled open the nightstand drawer and found a flip phone. He opened it to check the call log. The only number there was Kara's. "Burner," he muttered. One she'd left behind.

"Anyone report sounds of a struggle? Anyone hear her cry out or scream?" Aiden asked.

"Not that's been reported," Howell confirmed. "Of course everyone was distracted by the cars exploding in the parking lot."

The three siblings went silent, each looking at one another.

"Playing devil's advocate," Aiden said. "The puzzle books are still here." He pointed to the cluttered nightstand.

"No reason to take them," Regan told them. "They're all filled in. My gut's siding with Howell. Either Juliet was taken by a very polite, considerate kidnapper," Regan hedged.

"Or Juliet wasn't kidnapped at all," Howell finished, looking at his brother. "She left on her own."

Aiden frowned. "But—"

A knock sounded on the door before the lock disengaged and the lead crime scene tech walked in. "That's five. Detective Hale said you might want to see this." She held out a plastic evidence bag containing what looked like a singed toy key chain. "They found it in the rubble of the bomb car."

Howell accepted the bag that was heavier than expected. The metal car was black beneath the soot and ash. His mind raced, going straight back to the reports he'd read about another car bombing. Twenty-one years ago. "It's an Impala."

"I take it that's significant?" Regan asked.

"Kara's father was a New York City prosecutor," Howell told his sister. "He was building a murder case against Sal Alessi when he was killed." He looked at Regan, feeling a bit detached and more than a little on edge. "A car bomb in their driveway." He held up the evidence bag that now caught against the sun. "He drove a classic black 1967 Impala."

"That's...bold," Regan said. "I mean, bombers frequently sign their work, but that's just..."

"Overkill?" Aiden held up both hands. "Sorry. Unfortunate choice of word."

Unfortunate, perhaps, Howell thought. But accurate nonetheless. "Alessi's not the man he used to be," he told his siblings. "Maybe he's slipping more than anyone realizes."

After taking back the key chain, the lab tech ushered them out of the room and they returned downstairs. But before heading into the restaurant where Kara waited, Howell pulled them into a corner. "I don't want Kara knowing about any of this. Not yet." Hopefully not ever.

"About what exactly?" Regan asked. "The key chain or the missing craft supplies?"

"All of it," Howell clarified. He didn't think she'd appreciate his pressing the point about her witness not being who or what she was presenting herself as. "I'll tell her later, when we've got actual proof this was staged."

"You said before this case has felt off," Aiden said.

"Correct." Howell couldn't help but feel as if the pieces to this strange puzzle that had never fit were suddenly making a macabre kind of sense. "And Kara was just getting on board with that idea when the world blew up. I need to stay close and I'd prefer not to give her an excuse to get rid of me."

"How close?" Regan said with a grin that immediately faded. "Sorry. Coping mechanism. Who else knows about this case she's got against Sal Alessi, anyway?"

"I spoke with the owner of the security firm Kara hired," Aiden told him. "Guy's got a good reputation and his people are solid, even if they aren't up to your exacting standards."

"Okay." That only left people he originally thought were in the know. "That leaves me, my boss, Kara, her boss and her assistant."

"And Juliet Unger," Aiden finished. "I'd look there before you turn your eyes on either the Marshal Service or the prosecutor's office here in Connecticut."

His brother wasn't wrong. "I'll ask Kara for the expanded background reports she put together on Juliet," Howell said. "I'd do a deeper dive if my laptop hadn't gotten blown up along with my car."

"I'll call Jason Sutton out in Sacramento," Aiden offered. "He's working as a counselor these days, helping teens and young offenders, but he's always looking to keep up with his hacking—I mean his *computer* skills." His smile was quick and unforgiving. "I'd have Jason contact the private lab I've been working with the last few months, but we don't have any evidence with DNA or prints on it to run through the systems." He glanced back to the stairs with irritation on his face.

"Good thing I grabbed this then." Regan reached into her jacket pocket and pulled out a white washcloth. She unwrapped it, exposing a toothbrush. "It's yours if you'll just do me a favor." She covered it back up and pushed it into her brother's hand. "And please, please can we go get some coffee?"

Howell and Aiden exchanged unsurprised glances before following their sister into the coffee shop situated in the lobby of the Tidal Cove Lodge. Like the rest of the hotel, it had that homey, seaside feel to it with oak wood tables and upholstered seating in the same fabric as the café curtains draping the windows.

The excitement and shock over the morning's events clearly had not worn off given the frenetic conversation among the patrons and employees. Add to that, rumors of a kidnapping and the flurry of phone activity, no doubt social media was buzzing hotter than a beehive on fire. Many of the customers had gathered together and were talking at warp speed about what they had witnessed both before and after the explosion.

All that noise faded into the background the second Howell spotted Kara in the back booth, facing the entrance of the restaurant. Some of her color had come back, but not all of it. She wore this dazed expression that told him she was struggling not to drop beneath the weight of worry and concern. Anger pitched inside of him at the thought of Juliet being anything other than what Kara believed her to be, but the more he thought about it, the more convinced he became that he was right.

Both of Kara's hands were wrapped tightly around a mug of coffee Howell would bet had stopped steaming ages ago.

"Kara." He slid in next to her while Aiden and Regan sat on the other side. She looked up, that unsettling, dazed expression turning on him. Instantly he slid an arm around her shoulders and drew her close, telling himself she was in need of the comfort he found himself desiring. He took a moment, tightening his hold until he felt her relax. Until he was one hundred percent convinced that she was okay. "You doing better?"

"My ears are still ringing." She frowned and rolled her shoulders, her voice a bit louder than normal. "Where have you been?"

He ignored the raised eyebrows of his siblings when he glanced at them and felt even more comfort when Kara leaned into him and, for a blissful moment, rested her head on his shoulder.

"I was checking on the scene."

"I need to get home." She shivered. "Please, Howell, my family. I need to—"

"I sent two of my people to your house as soon as Howell called to tell me he'd fired your personal protection." Aiden's cell phone went off and he pulled it free of his back pocket. "In fact, this is them right now letting me know they've arrived."

Kara lifted her head and blinked slowly, as if she'd only now noticed Aiden and Regan were there. "You look familiar." She sat back, glared at Howell and in that moment the worry inside of him eased. "Howell, what did you do?"

"I needed reinforcements we can trust." He'd been prepared for this reaction. He'd been so adamant about keeping this case as quiet as possible. Of course she would worry he'd taken things a step too far. "Kara Gallagher, my brother and sister—Aiden and Regan McKenna."

"Pleasure to meet you, Kara," Regan said in that familiar and irritating little sister voice. It's the tone she took whenever she wanted to keep the mood light. "I can't even remember the last time Howell introduced us to someone he was...*working* with."

The glint in his younger sister's eye wasn't dissimilar to the one she'd worn at ten years old when she'd caught him in the family's hall closet making out with Talia Sherman at one of Aiden's birthday parties. Not that Howell was going to share that information with Kara. But he also knew Regan well enough that he understood what she was doing. She was hoping to keep Kara's attention on anything other than Juliet's disappearance.

"I'm going to assume the EMTs took a look at you." Aiden pointed to the scrape on Kara's cheek before quickly texting back whoever had messaged him.

"Yeah, I'm fine." She touched a hand to the bruise forming on her forehead. Probably from where she'd face planted on the cement when he'd knocked her to the ground. Howell flinched inwardly, wishing there had been a gentler way to protect her from the explosion.

"It's nice to meet you both," Kara said quietly. "But like I said, I'd really like to get—"

From the depths of Kara's purse, her phone rang. She moved almost in slow motion to retrieve it while Howell signaled to one of the servers not caught up in the chaos of post-car-bomb frenzy.

"Mom?" Kara tried to keep her voice down while Aiden and Regan each ordered some food and they all asked for more coffee. "What's wrong?"

Howell braced himself.

"No, Mom, um." She glanced up at Aiden. "They're friends of Howell's and his brother. I need you to let them in, okay? Something's happened with work." Tears tainted her voice. She ducked her head and she shifted to a whisper. "No, Mom. Please. I can't argue with you about this right—"

Unable to bear the sight of her crying, Howell plucked the phone out of her hand. "Pamela? It's Howell."

"What on earth is going on?" Kara's mother demanded. "First there was this weird car out in front of the house this morning and now these two are knocking on the door saying they're here to protect us. Protect us from what? Who are these people? What's Kara gotten herself into?"

It wasn't panic he heard over the line but irritation and anger. Not dissimilar to what he'd heard from Kara recently.

Howell looked at his brother. "Who?" He mouthed and when Aiden told him who he'd sent to the house, the knots tightening in Howell's chest eased considerably. "Their names are Lana and Eamon Quinn. They work for my brother who runs a private security firm. Eamon is former FBI and Lana used to be a cop in Seattle. You can trust them, Pamela."

"What on—"

"Pamela, I know this is a lot. This is a precaution only.

I'll bring Kara home in a little while and she'll explain everything then."

Kara dropped her head back and groaned.

"I promise, we'll tell you everything," he added quietly. "But for now, I need you to let Eamon and Lana in."

There was a pause. "I'm doing this with you on the phone," Pamela said finally. "Mia, Jonah, get away from the window right now!" Howell winced at the sharp tone in Kara's mother's voice. He heard her open the door, then some muffled conversation. "What color is Eamon's hair?" Pamela asked when she was back on the line.

"He's a ginger," Howell said. "Red hair. And he likes cookies." He shrugged at Kara's glare.

"He'd better. My daughter's okay?" Pamela's voice dropped as if she was making sure the kids couldn't overhear. "She's done something reckless, hasn't she?"

"She's okay." He wasn't convinced reckless was the right word. "We'll be back in a bit."

"Don't you let her out of your sight," Pamela ordered. "Take care of her. Please. I don't think anyone else can."

"Yes, ma'am." He gave Kara an encouraging nod and she held up her hand to take the phone back. "Would you like to talk to her—"

"No," Pamela said firmly. "Just…get her home safe."

"I'll do that, ma'am." He hung up and handed the phone to Kara. "She's…perturbed."

Kara slid the phone back into her bag and rested her elbows on the table, rubbed both temples in circles. "You told her I'd tell her the truth."

"Yes, I did. Don't make a liar out of me, Kara."

"I won't." Kara dropped her hands and looked among the three of them with something akin to resignation on her face. "I knew I couldn't keep my case against Sal Alessi a secret from her forever. I just didn't think they'd come at me this fast."

Howell glanced at his brother who simply stared back.

Irritation flooded Howell's system. So she had known they'd retaliate despite playing it off. Once again he felt torn between wanting to chastise her and holding her, if only to ease the last of the anxious knots tightening inside of him.

He didn't have to look at his siblings to know they were watching him, no doubt with more curiosity than they had in years. That she'd clung to him told Howell one of two things: either she'd finally realized she wasn't alone in this or she was feeling shaky enough not to care about being in his arms.

He decided both could be true.

He wasn't one for public displays of affection or sharing what meager social life he possessed with his family. But Kara had him throwing all kinds of wrenches into the mechanics of his life it seemed. And holding her, knowing how close they'd both come to dying today, made him feel better than he'd felt in a very, very long time.

"So." Regan cleared her throat and sat back as their coffee was delivered. She waited a beat until Kara was sitting up straight, refilling her mug, before continuing. "You're going after Sal Alessi, huh?" She rested her chin in her hand and batted playfully innocent yet wise-beyond-her-thirty-one-year-old eyes at Kara. "Tell us everything."

Chapter 7

Kara managed to hold it together until Aiden's and Regan's food hit the table. The second she stopped talking and started thinking again, along with the smell of grilled burgers and oily hot fries, her stomach pitched. Hard.

"I need to get out."

Howell moved before she had the chance to push at him. She kept her eyes firmly focused on the restroom sign and did her best to bolt inside as fast as she could. Her knees hit the floor of the first stall almost instantly, and she threw up the previously nerve-calming coffee that had clearly refused to settle.

She couldn't remember the last time she'd been sick. She'd forgotten how instantly draining it tended to be. Her skin went clammy and she trembled as she heaved, barely noticing the sand-and-white-colored tile floor. It wasn't until she felt gentle hands pulling her hair back that she realized she hadn't closed the stall door.

The tears and sobs hit with the same ferocity as her stomach purging itself of the fear and anxiety.

"Take it easy." Regan McKenna's gentle voice brought an unexpected sense of solace. Kara closed her eyes. "Breathe, Kara. Your body needs oxygen. Just breathe."

"If I breathe too deep, I'm going to puke again." She

pushed back a little, her hands clutching the edge of the toilet as she rested on her heels. Her stomach ached beyond the bruises she'd received in the aftermath of the bombs exploding. Throwing up always felt like an obnoxious way to get an ab workout.

"You could have picked a worse bathroom." Regan's voice was filled with that tension-cutting humor Kara recognized from the table. "Seriously. I had this happen at a truck stop near Las Vegas a few years ago. Only the men's room was available." She shuddered, keeping Kara's hair gently in one hand. "That was the night I learned how to say *ick* in twenty-seven languages."

Kara couldn't help it. She laughed. The instant she did, the nausea eased and the tears faded. She reached back, feeling for the wall and sat down before stretching out her legs in front of her. She smiled and let out a long, slow breath.

Regan crouched beside her, let go of her hair, but rested a hand on Kara's shoulder. "There you go. The first of it is gone."

"The first of it?" Kara managed to say as Regan stood to retrieve a handful of paper towels she doused with cool water. "I feel like I just threw up what I ate in fifth grade."

"Trauma. Shock. Terror." Regan flushed the toilet, leaned against the opposite wall and handed her the towels. "Howell filled Aiden in on some of your past. I did a little research on the drive up." She paused, the kindness on her face a recognizable McKenna feature. "I'm so sorry about your father."

Fresh tears burned and Kara quickly pressed the damp towels against her eyes before wiping her face, then her mouth. The pressure built in her chest, demanding to be set free. Even now she could hear that explosion, feel that heat.

"That's what you can't shake, isn't it?" Regan asked gently. "You're thinking of him. Of how he died. How you almost died then. And how you almost died today."

"He got off lucky," Kara whispered brokenly, hating the weepy sensation. She didn't cry! She stood. She fought! She…conquered. She did not cower in the bathroom and puke her guts out. But Regan had opened a floodgate Kara only now realized was there. "There wasn't time for my dad to know what happened," she whispered. "It's the only blessing I've ever found."

"But you remember every second." It wasn't a question, but a clear statement of fact that left Kara, for the first time in her life, feeling completely understood. "There hasn't been a day you haven't thought of that morning. Replayed it in your mind. In your dreams." Regan slid farther down the wall until they sat knee to knee on the floor of the stall. "And now you've got your own nightmare to cope with. A darker, more difficult one. One you're going to need help with."

Kara sniffled, tried to wipe her face. "Are you a therapist as well as an ATF agent?"

"I'm a woman. I can be both." Regan nudged her leg against Kara's. "But seriously," she added on a laugh. "I'm only two units shy of a psychology degree. I spend a lot of time observing and mentally dissecting people. I know, I know." She held up a hand. "It's a quirky habit, but it entertains and educates at the same time. You're human, Kara. What happened when you were a child was horrific but you let it define you in a productive rather than damaging way. That's something to be proud of. Hold on to that. But also be ready. It's not easy—living with the fact that someone wants you dead. It's even harder when you're surrounded by people who care about you. People who might be in danger as well." She leaned out of the stall when the door to the restroom opened. "Occupied! Come back in a few."

The door closed again with a gentle swoosh.

"I'm going to share with you one of the worst kept secrets in the McKenna family, Kara."

"You are?" Her natural skepticism was making a comeback. "Why?"

"Because I saw the way Howell looked at you. How he was with you. You're more than a job to him, Kara."

Kara scoffed, unwilling to believe that was true.

"I say that with much certainty," Regan continued. "I can't even remember the last time he turned up at home with a work partner let alone a woman. And calling the family for help with a case? Please." She rolled her eyes and dismissed the idea with a wave of her hand. "You're different. He cares." She paused. "That bothers you."

Kara frowned. "It surprises me." But how could it bother her knowing how attractive she found him. How appealing. How...incredibly frustrating, enticing and... She sighed. No, no, no. Her brain felt like a broken puzzle she couldn't piece back together. Now was not the time to be admitting she had feelings for a US marshal.

"He's the best of us. Of all of us," Regan continued. "Beyond the code we were raised with, he has his own. He's the most honorable person I've ever known and I work with some pretty amazing people. Whatever else comes at you for the foreseeable future, if Howell's by your side, you're going to be just fine." A minute passed, maybe more before Regan asked, "Feel better?"

About the car bomb? Yes. About Howell? "There's nothing between—"

"Please." Regan snorted and grinned at Kara in a way close friends often did. "You're as bad a liar as he is. He's always our first call. It's as simple as that. But do you know how many times Howell has called on any of the family for help? None. Zero. Not until today. He's usually a one-man show with impeccable trust in himself to get the job done."

"Except with me." Kara made a weak attempt at a laugh.

"Because of you." Regan grabbed hold of her hand and squeezed. "Because you matter. Like you, he might not want to accept that just yet." She shrugged. "But whatever is going on between the two of you, he's on your side and he's willing to bring us in to make sure he succeeds. Knock back those reservations you might have about him, about this situation. Kick them to the curb. You're dealing with the McKennas now. Honor. Family. Duty. That's what we're about. And with Howell, you get a huge helping of nobility on top of that. That's the McKenna code. And none of us, especially Howell, are going to let you down."

In the back seat of Aiden's substantially enhanced bulletproof SUV, Howell kept one eye on the passing suburban scenery and the other—less visibly—on Kara. She sat beside him, nibbling on the thumbnail she'd already gnawed down to nothing, but the color was back in her face. Mostly. The spark in her eyes, on the other hand? That was nowhere to be seen.

It certainly wasn't going to return if Howell shared his suspicions about Juliet with her. He couldn't pinpoint what Kara's witness might be up to, but Juliet obviously believed Kara had a role to play in whatever game the witness was playing. In his business, confusion was the most important ingredient in a recipe for disaster.

As much as he didn't like that idea, he really didn't appreciate the fact that Kara was quickly becoming something more to him than an assignment. Than his job.

Part of him understood why. They set each other off hotter than an accelerant and match and...okay. He winced. Bad example. But he was a realist. Their previous professional combativeness could very well have been camouflage for an attraction neither of them particularly wanted or had time for. Now that their protective shields had all but been blown apart...

He cringed at another all-too-apt analogy. Yeah, this was why he didn't commiserate with others on relationship potential. It would just get him into trouble.

It hadn't dawned on him until after Kara and Regan returned to the table from the bathroom that he understood why Aiden had brought their sister along. He should have realized of course. The family joke for years had been Regan might work for the ATF, but she was the family therapist. Unflappable. Analytical. Observant and patient. She didn't possess the often times bombastic personality so often seen in agents. She could talk to anyone about anything, even if she wasn't an expert on the subject. It made her ideal for undercover work as that mind of hers contained endless and sometimes ridiculous bits of information. That said, the main thing Regan did command was a natural calming influence that at times had been known to tame even the most dangerous of criminals.

Whatever Regan had said to Kara seemed to have taken the edge off of the emotions rioting inside of her.

"You doing okay?" He reached over to tug Kara's thumb away from her mouth and earned a ghost of a smile in return.

"Better. Thanks." She reached for the can of ginger ale he'd gotten at the restaurant on their way out. She emptied the can with a slurp. Her hand only trembled a little now. "We have to find Juliet." The whispered plea sounded like both a prayer for herself and a request for Howell. "Not just because of the case, but I promised her everything would be okay, Howell."

"I know." He was already working on a plan. Maybe not one she'd approve of, but a plan nonetheless. He had no doubt that finding Juliet Unger was the key to sorting out this whole mess. "We'll find her."

"If she's not already dead."

If Regan or Aiden were listening, they didn't give any indication, continuing their yearslong discussion over who ranked on their top ten list of best musicians. Every ride they shared consisted of them each listing their top ten in a variety of arenas ranging from vocalists, to who played bass best and who, if anyone, could ever replace Springsteen in the E Street Band.

It was a coping mechanism for them both, especially when either of them were heading into a situation that could prove stressful, dangerous or deadly. Contrary to recent events, while McKennas didn't purposely court danger, they'd certainly seen their share of it, especially since they were scattered around various branches of law enforcement.

"She's not. Juliet. She's not dead," he said at Kara's quizzical look. "Otherwise they'd have left her body in the hotel room to be found."

"Oh." Kara blinked as if that hadn't occurred to her. "So, good news then." Her smile was tight and there was no sign of humor on her face. "What is the plan exactly?" She leaned forward and touched Aiden's shoulder. "For my family?"

"Minotaur has a couple of safe houses in the Catskill mountains," Aiden told her. "We'll get them to one today."

Howell glanced at his watch. It was already closing in on four. That was going to make for a long day.

"Minotaur is your private security company, correct?" Kara asked him.

"Yes."

That she was asking questions again was another good sign she was on the road to mental recovery, Howell thought. "I told you Aiden's former Secret Service, right? He started his own firm after..." He caught Aiden's sharp look in the rearview mirror. "After he retired." Howell hoped Kara wouldn't notice the sudden tension. Aiden's quick and dramatic separation from the Service, even after all these years, remained a serious sore spot for his brother. "He's got his own fleet of aircraft, too. Private plane, helicopters. Along with protected properties in numerous states."

"I've done okay," Aiden said.

"If they ever discontinue the US Marshal Service," Regan teased. "Aiden can step right in and provide protection and prisoner transport. He'd have to take a substantial pay cut, however."

Aiden knocked his fist into her shoulder with typical sibling playfulness.

Kara's eyes filled with humor when she looked at Howell. "Sibling rivalry?"

"Us? Just a little," Howell admitted. He really liked it when she turned that smile on him.

"I work with a variety of clients all over the world, Kara," Aiden said as if defending himself. "And I treat them all the same."

"Meaning your family will be treated with the same level of protection that the crown Saudi prince received last year when he visited DC." Regan smirked at Aiden's frown. "Like you don't have that detail plastered all over your website."

"It's discreetly placed," Aiden said. "I've got four main branches of Minotaur. Main headquarters is in Boston—"

"He's the child who rarely misses our monthly family dinners," Howell cut in. "Probably explains why he's Mom's favorite."

"I've got another office in Florida," Aiden went on as if Howell hadn't spoken. "One in New Orleans and then the newest in Sacramento."

"Sacramento? California? Really?" Kara sounded baffled. "Why there?"

"Eamon has family there," Aiden said. "And there's stellar law enforcement support for us. There's a PI from the area who I've brought on board as a Minotaur partner and consultant, so we've got a good number of people we can call on. Plus, central California gives us good access up and down the West Coast. Between Vince and

Jason's contacts and ours, we've expanded our reach significantly. Lana, Eamon's wife, is my head of operations out there. Eamon wanted to be a little less responsible and more mobile. So far it's working out well for everyone and sometimes they get to work and travel together, which is why they were out this way this week."

"I look forward to meeting them," Kara said.

"That's code for she's reserving approval until after she's eyed them in person," Howell said and earned a familiar glare from Kara in response. Ah, good. Maybe he could irk her back to normalcy.

"If you have any hesitation about them, I've got plenty of other agents who can step in," Aiden said easily. "But if it was my family that needed guarding, they're who I'd want."

"Good to know. Thanks." Kara sat back and appeared to be breathing a bit easier. "What about Juliet? What are we doing to find her?"

"Detective Hale has put out an all-points on her and we're circulating her picture. Departments up and down the coast will be watching for her."

Regan and Aiden went back to discussing the latest Eurovision competition.

"Do me a favor?" Kara leaned over and whispered in Howell's ear. "When we get home, would you stay with me while I talk to my mom?"

"Sure." There were a lot of jokes he could make, but now wasn't the time. "So long as you know I'm holding you to my promise."

She winced. "Couldn't I just—"

"No. You couldn't." He wasn't about to take any risks with her family and he wanted—no, needed—Pamela to realize how much danger she and her grandchildren could be in. "We can couch the truth for Mia and Jonah, but your mother deserves to know what's going on. If only because it will help to convince her to go with Eamon and Lana to the safe house."

"Right. Yeah, you're right, I guess." She pulled the band out of her hair, which sent it spilling over her shoulders. "Guess that'll make two bombs exploding in my face today."

Howell held out his hand, palm up, and felt a sense of triumph when she slipped her fingers around his. That tingle of excitement shifted into a full-on spark of desire that had him flexing his hand in hers in the hope he could contain the sensation. "You've been keeping a lot of things from her, things she has a vested interest in knowing about. You knew this was coming, Kara."

"I anticipated my confession being motivated by success after the fact rather than...this."

"We'll ease her into it." He reached his other hand across to gently wipe away a smudge of smoke that marred her smooth skin. Every time he touched her it felt like a new experience. One he couldn't wait to have again. "Cards on the table. Your mother deserves the truth, yeah?"

"Yeah." She nodded and settled back for the rest of the drive.

It was the laughter Kara heard first. Laughter so utterly unexpected, jarring and familiar that she had to stop just inside the front door of her house in order to take it in.

The sound of her children's delight broke through the thickest part of the shock she'd carried with her from the lodge. She felt Howell's hand on the base of her spine. Not pushing. Simply supporting. The very idea settled something inside of her she wasn't aware needed calming.

Tears of appreciation threatened to well, but she swallowed them.

Regan had remained outside by the car. Probably, Kara thought, to keep an eye on the street. Aiden closed the door behind them.

Footsteps immediately pounded down the hall toward them.

"Mom!" Mia locked her arms around Kara's waist and squeezed. Kara gasped, the breath nearly driven out of her as the bruises and soreness awoke completely. Mia turned her face up, wrinkled her nose. "You stink."

She barely noticed the smoke any longer—not a topic she wanted to address—but the sight of her oldest child looking as bright and cheery as Christmas morning was another balm against her bruised heart. "Where's your brother?"

"In the kitchen. He's teaching Eamon and Lana how to play Exploding Kittens."

"Ah, irony," Aiden said from behind his brother.

Mia leaned over to peer around Kara. "Who are you?"

"This is my big brother, Aiden." Now Howell nudged Kara toward the living room. "He's Lana and Eamon's boss."

"Really?" Mia's eyes went huge. "Are you a marshal like Howell?"

"No one's a marshal like Howell," Aiden said easily. "I have a very special company that works to keep people safe. Tell me something, Mia."

"Sure." Mia shrugged, her arms tightening even more around Kara.

"Is it true your grandmother bakes amazing cookies?"

"Uh-huh." Mia's smile widened. "She's been baking a ton since she talked to you." Mia tilted her chin up to look at Kara expectantly.

"Awesome." No sooner did the word slip out of her mouth than her mother appeared in the kitchen doorway. The expression on her face told Kara, in no uncertain terms, that she did not appreciate the abrupt conversation they'd shared earlier. Kara swallowed hard. Suddenly, she felt smaller and younger than her own daughter. "Hey, Mom. You baked more cookies, huh?"

"White chocolate macadamia." Pamela's edgy gaze shifted from Kara to Howell to Aiden. "Please, help yourself."

"Sounds good to me." Aiden stepped around Kara and Howell, surprising Kara with a murmured good luck as he passed. "Mia, how do you play Exploding Kittens exactly?" He motioned toward the kitchen and Mia eased away from Kara. "Sounds like an interesting game."

Mia shot a quick look of uncertainty at Kara who simply nodded encouragingly before turning into the living room. Howell's presence behind her added both warmth and pressure. She wanted to believe she'd have handled coming clean with her mother without issue, but yeah. If he wasn't there, she'd probably have chickened out. Not that Pamela would have given her an easy way around any explanation she might have come up with.

Kara padded over to the sofa, shifting the pile of books, baseball glove and in-progress LEGO set out of the way before she sat down. Her body tensed, expecting more pain, but either her body had gotten used to it, or her mother's disapproval overrode Kara's pain sensors.

Pamela pulled the recessed doors closed before she faced the two of them. "What happened?" She stalked over to Kara and stared. "You're hurt."

"I'm okay. Howell was there." It was, she realized, the kindest thing she could have ever said about him. Her heart squeezed in affection and gratitude. "You'd better sit down, Mom." Kara's chest tightened with the buzzing apprehension that appeared whenever an uncomfortable conversation loomed. The last time she'd felt like this was when she'd told Pamela about the divorce. Not that her mother was particularly unhappy about her and Garrett's separation. It was Kara's admission that her mother had been right about him all along that had been difficult to confess.

Pamela turned anxious eyes on Howell, who nodded and motioned to the sofa. He sat in one of the cushioned chairs on the other side of the coffee table.

Pamela sank onto the brown sofa beside Kara as if in slow motion. "Why do you smell like smoke and..." She leaned closer and sniffed. "Gasoline?"

It was on the tip of Kara's tongue to make a joke, but one cautious glare from Howell had her shifting away from her usual defense mechanism. She kept hold of her mother's hand for both stability and comfort.

"I need to tell you about the case I started working on a couple of weeks ago. There's a witness..." she broke off, frowning. No need to get into that many details. They wouldn't matter to her mother. But the truth would. "Mom, I've been building a case against Sal Alessi."

Her mother's hand went ice cold as her eyes went

blank. Just for a moment. Long enough, Kara suspected, to send Pamela straight back to that horrific day twenty-one years ago. The day when both of their lives had been utterly and completely devastated.

"I've got a witness who can put Sal and perhaps his entire family behind bars for a long time," Kara pressed on. "Maybe forever. It's a good case, Mom. A solid one." Or it would be once she got her witness back. The panic and fear over Juliet's disappearance threatened to surge and override the brain power she needed currently. "That's who Howell and I went to see earlier. My witness."

"Sal Alessi." Hearing her mother spew Sal's name like it was the most vulgar profanity had Kara wincing. "You lied to me." Pamela's almost out-of-body voice accompanied her swaying where she sat. "You promised me years ago, Kara. You swore you'd stay away from them. From him. You swore you wouldn't—"

"They killed Dad." Kara kept her voice even and firm. It was hard talking about something they'd silently agreed never to address again. It had been the only way either of them could move forward. To get beyond the tragedy of not only losing Kara's father, but the violence surrounding how he'd been lost. "I'm sorry, but a promise I made weeks after he died when I was still a kid can't override the truth and reality of the situation now." It hurt to say, but it also felt good to finally be honest with her mother. She looked to Howell, who was watching her carefully. "I'm sorry if you think I lied, Mom. I'm more sorry that I kept this from you, but you can't sit here and say you're completely surprised."

Pamela pressed her lips into a thin, white line.

"Did you really think I just locked it all away and forgot about it?" She wasn't trying to be cold or accusing, simply honest. "I'm a prosecutor. The same as him. You had to know the Alessis would be an equally strong motivator all over again." She took a deep breath and let it out, along with the guilt and regret. "I'm also his daughter, his only child," she whispered. "What else would you expect of me?"

Pamela tried to pull her hand free, but Kara held on. "That doesn't explain what happened to you today." Pamela didn't aim the statement at Kara, but at Howell. "If she's telling me all this now, something's happened."

Howell looked between them, waited for Kara to nod ever so slightly in approval.

"There was an...incident after we spoke with the witness," he said far more carefully than Kara had expected. "She's okay. We both are. The details aren't impor—"

"Yes," Pamela snapped, her hand squeezing Kara's so hard that Kara flinched. "The details are quite important."

"It was a bomb, Mom." She wasn't about to let Howell take the hit on this one. "Social media is still running with the idea it was a gas leak, but it was a car bomb. Just like the one they left for Dad." Which meant she was close. Probably closer than she'd realized.

"It went off before we reached the vehicle." Howell's gaze dropped to her mother's hand, to the wedding set she continued to wear even after all these years.

Whatever color had been left in her mother's face drained. "A car bomb." The deadened tone sent a shiver up Kara's spine. "I suppose they figured since it worked once..." She trailed off.

"I'm okay, Mom." Kara shifted closer, slipped one arm

around Pamela's shoulders and tried to reassure her. "I'm okay."

"It's not enough they took my husband," Pamela whispered vehemently. "Now you've made it so that they're coming after you, too. I can't do this again." Pamela shook her head and in that moment she pulled herself free of Kara's hold. "Losing your father was almost insurmountable. You're the only reason I got through it. Now you're telling me I almost...that I might lose you, as well."

"You're not going to lose me," Kara insisted as her mother got to her feet and began to pace.

"You can't promise me that," Pamela accused with a ferocity Kara had rarely seen. "The Alessis don't stop until they get what they want. You know this, Kara." She swung back around, her eyes filled with absolute terror. "You. Know. This."

Kara couldn't argue. She wanted to be angry with Howell for making her tell the truth, but how could she be when he was right? Instead, she choked back the tears that so desperately wanted to escape.

This had to be out in the open so her mother could be prepared. More importantly, protected. That didn't mean Kara had any words that could come close to making the current situation better.

"Pamela." Howell's calm voice eased the anxiety twisting through Kara's entire body. "You're right. Promising you won't lose Kara is what my mother calls a spiderweb promise. Quickly made, seemingly strong, but ultimately easily breakable. But here's a promise I can make to you. If you can't believe Kara, then please believe I will do everything in my power to keep Kara protected and safe."

"And just how are you going to do that?" Pamela demanded. "Are you going to camp out on our front lawn and double-check her car every morning to make sure it doesn't blow up with her and my grandchildren inside?"

"Mom," Kara sighed, her patience slipping. "I don't think—"

"No, you don't think, do you?" Pamela moved away and turned to stare at the framed photo of the family on the mantel above the fireplace. One of the last pictures taken of the three of them—Pamela, Patrick, and Kara—coincidentally, at that same lodge. She took a deep breath, then another. "You haven't thought of anything but the Alessis since you were thirteen years old." She folded her arms in front of her. "Ridiculous of me to think otherwise. You're as reckless as he was. Your father never thought anything could happen to him, either. Times like this I wish you weren't his daughter."

It was only then, hearing her mother rail against the man they'd both adored, that she felt a sledgehammer of reality come down upon her. But that same sledgehammer had also broken through the last layer of grief the two of them had refused to share.

"You're right, Mom." It was oddly freeing, speaking about him like this. It was as if doing so hollowed out a space inside of her she hadn't realized was crammed full of grief. "I haven't stopped thinking of Dad's case since the day he died. He had Sal Alessi solid. He had his witness locked down to the point he had no doubt about a conviction. I've read the files. I know—"

"When?" Pamela gasped. "When did you read the files?"

Kara's gaze immediately shifted to Howell. She'd promised she'd be honest with her mother, but now was not the time to tell Pamela that Uncle James—the same Uncle James who had gotten her in to see the deputy director of the US Marshal Service—had finally agreed to her request to read her father's locked away files on Kara's eighteenth birthday.

"I might not have standing in this home, among your family, to make this assertion," Howell said as Kara desperately searched for a reasoned response, "but given your daughter's professional connections, I'd have been surprised if she hadn't read the files." He flinched, as if not completely convinced he'd said the right thing. "I haven't read them myself, Pamela, not yet, but hearing you two now, I'm going to make the assumption that your late husband underestimated how far the Alessis would go to protect themselves."

Kara looked to her mother, who stood with her back to them, spine straight and stiff.

"Kara isn't going to make that same mistake. That's why she came to the Marshals' office and it's why she's asked for my help. And yes, while it's true I'm following orders, I'm also a believer. She convinced me, Pamela. That this is something worth pursuing. Something important. Something that can't be left or forgotten. She also scares me because I know she's not going to stop. That's just how it is."

"I need to do this, Mom." Kara could barely speak with all the gratitude filling her. "Howell's right. They got past us today, but they won't ever again. I've also got something Dad didn't. I have Howell. And I've got his brother, Aiden, and a team of people willing to go as far as I need them to go to make this case. To get a guilty verdict. I just… *We* just need…time to make that happen."

She took a steeling breath. "And I need one other thing. I need you and the kids safe."

Pamela turned, slowly. Her eyes narrowed in suspicion. "That's why Lana and Eamon are here. You're afraid the Alessis might come after us."

"We can't rule it out," Howell said. "I know we only met this morning, Pamela, and that feels like ages ago. But as I said on the phone, I need you to trust me. This is what I do. This is the world I know and right now, the one thing I know for certain is that you and the kids need to be put somewhere you can't be found. My brother's already got a place set up. It might be for a few days, it could be for a few weeks, but it will be comfortable and most importantly safe."

"Mom, I know—"

"Don't!" Pamela spun on Kara. "I'll get there eventually, Kara, but don't push me. Contrary to what I implied earlier, I'm not foolish. Delusional, maybe. I let myself believe you'd put the Alessis out of your mind because I couldn't bear the thought of you picking up where your father left off. I can't pretend anymore, can I?" She shook her head as if to clear it. "I can't afford to."

"No," Howell, told her. "You can't."

"Okay." Pamela took a long, deep breath and when she let it out, she nodded. "Okay. Whatever you need us to do, we'll do. On one condition." She pinned Howell with a stare that made Kara shrink back a bit in her seat. "You make sure my daughter comes back to us. Alive. Unharmed. In one piece. You make me that promise, Marshal Howell McKenna, and I might have enough faith left to believe you."

"Once you and the kids are safe, Kara will be my only

priority," Howell said in a way that left Kara blinking in shock. The intensity in his voice, the steely determination, made her feel protected, valued and…cared for. "I've been doing this for more than a decade. I'm good at it. That's as close as I can come to a promise."

"Well." Pamela brushed away the tears that had begun to fill the corners of her eyes. "I guess I should thank you for not lying to me. How soon do we have to go?"

"That depends," Howell said. "How fast can you and the kids pack?"

Chapter 8

Howell stood in the back corner of Kara's white and slate-gray kitchen, half looking out into the backyard that was part dormant vegetable garden, part playground, half listening to Eamon and Aiden discuss their plans. He'd snagged one last cookie before Pamela packaged the rest of them up, earning himself a slightly less approving glance from Kara's mother.

Seems as if he was in the doghouse alongside her daughter for the time being. Not a bad place to be, all things considered.

The slightly rusted and sagging metal swing set was evidence of a childhood well lived and two kids who had lost some, if not most of their interest in such activities. Even from inside he could hear the strained whining of the swing moving in the chilly breeze.

He'd just taken the final bite of cookie when his cell phone rang. Eamon and Aiden paused, glancing over at him, but he held up a finger, pulled out his phone and stepped outside.

Deputy Director Coleson's name flashed on his screen. "Sir."

"I'm sorry I wasn't available to take your earlier call," Coleson said. "Fill me in on the explosion."

"Yes, sir." The frigid air felt almost cleansing as he paced along the patio. He gave his boss an abbreviated rundown of the morning's events, ending with, "We're putting Kara's family into protective custody right now."

"As much as I agree it's the right move, I'm not sure the Marshal Ser—"

"I've got it covered, sir." Howell didn't often cut his superiors off. "Minotaur Security is taking the lead. My brother's got a car coming for us in a little while. Kara and I are going to head into New York to track Juliet Unger's friend Jazz and that laptop."

"Guess it pays to have your brother be one of the best security consultants in the country," Coleson said slowly. "What about Juliet Unger? Where are we on the search for her?"

"No word on any sightings as of yet." And Howell had the strong suspicion they wouldn't until Juliet wanted to be found. "I'm going to make arrangements to see if we can get in to see Juliet's grandmother. She has dementia but maybe someone at the facility will have some information to impart."

"New York," Coleson murmured. "Okay, we've got three open safe houses—"

"Again, already taken care of, sir." His cheeks were beginning to go numb from the cold. The sun was beginning to set. Chances were it would be completely dark before he and Kara got on the road. "Appreciate the idea, but all our safe houses are monitored and our goal has always been to keep this limited to as few people as possible."

"The further you move off book, the less cover I can give you."

"Then it's a good thing I'm used to working alone."

He'd meant it to be a joke. Mostly. "I'll keep you in the loop, sir, but for the next few days I'd appreciate it if you could forget I exist."

"Tell your brother if I don't hear from you in a week, to expect a call from the director."

"Yes, sir." Howell glanced around as the back door opened. "Thanks." He disconnected and returned inside. "Boss is filled in," he told Aiden. "Eamon." He held out his hand to the former FBI agent. "Good to see you again."

Eamon Quinn was one of the few men Howell could look dead in the eye. He hadn't yet broken the FBI habit of wearing a suit jacket and tie, but the guy was settling in nicely at his post-retirement job at Minotaur. His posture and expression and demeanor had lightened to the point that he at least smiled a lot more than he used to. Howell wouldn't say this to very many people, but he'd admired Eamon's dedication to the Crimes Against Children task force within the agency. A dedication that had lasted far longer than that of most agents given its devastating emotional toll. Eamon had avoided burnout, but only barely.

"Sorry if this whole thing is messing with your downtime," Howell said as Eamon shook his head.

"Lana's been feeling a bit cooped up lately with all the office work back home," Eamon said easily. "Doing something different should recharge her battery. And mine." He glanced over his shoulder to the stairs where the distinctive sound of sibling arguing descended. "We'll take good care of them."

"I have no doubt."

"I'll have two additional teams trading off shifts in a car nearby at their safe house," Aiden told him.

Howell frowned. "You don't think that'll be, for want of a better word, overkill?"

"No such thing where the Alessis are concerned," Eamon said before Aiden could. "That family's been skittering under law enforcement's feet for decades. Personally, I appreciate the added backup."

Cautious and practical. Howell nodded his approval.

"Place is ready for you in New York. Bowery area," Aiden told Howell. "It's not my best or biggest offering, but it's the only one currently vacant and it's secure. My team's got it stocked and left a satellite phone for you with mine and Eamon's numbers programmed in. Don't use any other device to call either of us from here on."

"Got it."

"Hey, guys." Former Seattle PD detective Lana Quinn walked in. Her dark hair and eyes were offset by glistening olive skin that betrayed her Persian heritage. Like her husband, Eamon, her expression spoke of professionalism and responsibility and her easygoing smile calmed what nerves Howell had about the entire situation. "I think we're good to go. I've got the kids' suitcases down." She pointed to the stack of games on the counter. "Until we get our safe houses up to family standards, I'm going to grab these."

"I'll get Pamela's bag." Eamon headed upstairs.

Alone again with his brother, Howell's mind had finally begun remembering more practical things. "My go bag was in the SUV." Which meant his clothes and other necessities had been blown to bits along with the car.

"Wondered about that when you said your laptop was in there." Aiden nodded. "I'll have what you need waiting for you at the apartment."

They left the kitchen. Howell caught sight of Mia and Jonah standing at the top of the stairs, the sound of raised voices echoing from beyond them. Jonah hugged a giant stuffed sea creature and cast an uneasy look at his sister.

"Pamela and Kara are still working things out," Howell said to Aiden. "Hey, guys. Come on." He waved them down and murmured to Aiden, "Give me a few minutes with them?"

"You got it." Aiden walked out the front door.

"I've never heard Nana so mad," Mia said as she stopped on the bottom stair. "I thought we were going on an adventure."

"You are." Howell motioned for her to sit next to him, then held out his arm for Jonah to join them. "Nice squid."

"Octopus." Jonah pushed his glasses higher up his nose. "His name's Octavius."

"Of course it is." Howell chuckled. "Well, he's very cool. And in answer to your question, Mia, you are going on an adventure. Your Nana's just dealing with some other things that have upset her."

"Is this about Grandpa?" Mia turned those big eyes of hers on Howell. She might be barely double digits in age, but those wise all-seeing eyes of hers were almost unsettling. "They always get upset when they talk about Grandpa. He died a long time ago." She sighed and rested her chin on her knees. "We didn't get to meet him."

"I know." Howell placed a hand on her shoulder. "And yes, your grandpa has something to do with this, but everything is going to be okay."

"How come Mom isn't coming with us?" Jonah asked.

"Because she's working. Duh." Mia rolled her eyes.

"Believe me, I think she'd much rather go on this adventure with you," Howell assured both of them. "But yes, she and I have some work to do on one of her cases."

"Is it dangerous? Is that why you're sending us away?" Mia's question shattered all of Howell's resolution to keep the conversation with them lighthearted.

"Your mom needs to know you and your Nana are someplace safe. It'll help us do our jobs faster." It was as close to the truth as they were going to get. "I'm hoping it won't be for too long."

"You're going to take care of her, right?" Jonah asked, flipping two of Octavius's tentacles around. "Nana says Mom forgets to take care of herself sometimes. Especially when she's working."

"I will be sure to make certain she takes care of herself." The idea of "taking care" of Kara Gallagher was both exhilarating and terrifying. As if she'd ever let anyone get that close. That said...

He shook himself free of those thoughts. Work, he reminded himself. They were *working*, not doing anything... else.

He glanced up and back as Pamela reached the stairs. "All right. Let's get this show on the road."

Mia jumped to her feet as Howell walked up to take the larger suitcase from Kara's mother.

"Just so you know, I didn't leave you any cookies," Pamela said with a hint of concern in her eyes.

"Good thing," Howell said. "I've already eaten my weight in them today." He carried the bag out the front door, left it on the porch for Eamon to grab. "Eamon has a phone that we can call him on," he told Pamela while Kara hugged the kids. "As soon as this is over, as soon as we know it's safe for all of you, we'll let you know."

Pamela nodded, but there were still tears in her eyes. "Don't let anything happen to her, Howell." She grabbed his arm and held on tight. "Please."

"I'll do my best." Because he needed it as much as she did, he drew her close and hugged her.

"I hope this safe house has a good kitchen," Pamela murmured before she sniffled, patted his arm and walked out the door.

Kara was holding both kids tight against her when Howell turned. For the first time, he saw that reality had set in and that she was finally feeling the weight of her decision to pick up where her father left off.

She kissed Mia first, then Jonah. She set them back and touched a hand to each of their cheeks. "You take care of each other, okay? And your Nana. Mind Lana and Eamon. No arguments, yeah?"

"We'll try," Mia said with a cheeky grin at Howell who had to duck his chin to hide his smile. "How long will we have to stay there? What about school?"

"Awww, man," Jonah whined. "We're gonna miss school?"

Howell had never heard more disappointment come out of a child's mouth.

"I'll call your school tomorrow morning and let them know we've had a family emergency," Kara said. "Everything's going to be okay. I'll be back as soon as I can."

"That's what Howell said," Mia confirmed. "Bye." She hugged her mom again, then pushed Jonah ahead of her.

"It's not too late," Howell told her as they followed them onto the front porch. Regan gave him a wave before she climbed into Aiden's SUV. "You can still go with them. I can—"

"No. I started this," Kara whispered as she continued to keep a brave smile on her face. Jonah and Mia hopped into the back with Lana, while Pamela took shotgun in Eamon's car. Kara leaned against him, her head resting against his shoulder. Howell slipped his arm around her waist and squeezed. "It's up to me to finish it."

"Is it me?" Kara asked as she followed Howell into the third-floor apartment in a building located in the Lower East Side of New York City. "Or is this place smaller than Aiden's car?" She only had to turn to the left to find herself in the living room while in front of her the galley-style kitchen, modern with bright white paint and new appliances, definitely offered limited cooking space. Her mother would have called the space…challenging.

"By New York standards, I'd say it's practically palatial." Howell set her suitcase against the wall, flipped a light switch and walked over to the pair of large windows that were curtained by thin white fabric. With the arrival of night, there was no shaking the exhaustion that resulted from the eventual adrenaline drain.

"Good news." Howell leaned forward, turned his head as he peered outside. "Looks like we're not far from Chinatown. We definitely won't starve."

Even now her stomach wasn't anxious for anything close to food. Kara curled her toes in her boots. It had taken her twenty minutes in the shower to get the stink off of her skin and out of her hair. Being alone had also given her sufficient time to cry and purge most of the fear and pent-up anxiety she'd been struggling to keep in check since the car bomb went off. Aside from her vomiting in the restaurant bathroom, of course. She could feel the energy draining from her system, that buzz of desire for sleep. Endless, dreamless sleep.

Her heels clacked against the hardwood floor as she deposited her briefcase containing her laptop and files onto one of two chairs situated at a small round table set against the wall in the kitchen.

"All in all, not too bad." Howell's voice echoed through the apartment as Kara checked out the rest of the space. The bathroom was miniscule but serviceable. The apartment itself was bright and certainly didn't feel too claustrophobic. She stood in the doorway of what one could only laughingly call the bedroom.

"I feel like I've known you long enough to understand quiet isn't a good mood for you." Howell's voice behind her made her jump.

"There's only one bedroom." Only one bed. Her face flushed at the very notion and she suddenly felt as if she were caught in a zany 1930s romantic comedy of errors.

"Bedroom's yours," Howell said without hesitation. "Couch'll be fine for me. I've slept on a lot worse, believe me." That he said it with such ease made her think he knew about the bedroom situation well before they'd opened the front door. He retrieved her suitcase to set it inside the bedroom and then she followed him back to the living room.

On the narrow oak and glass coffee table sat a thick laptop that looked like it came from a war zone. She'd bet half her bank account it was bullet—and probably car bomb—proof. Howell pulled a duffel bag out from beside the sofa, unzipped it and quickly examined the contents. "Looks like Aiden's people thought of everything." He pulled out a pair of jeans, clean T-shirt, sweater, socks and sneakers, plus all the essentials. "I'm going to grab a shower then we can talk about what we do next." He tossed a brand-new jacket onto the counter by the door.

She wanted to say she hoped to take a nap, but how could she think about sleep given what Juliet was probably going through? "I don't think I have the brain capacity to cope with a strip club at the moment. So... Juliet's grandmother?"

"Sounds like a plan. Have at it. You can give me a rundown once I'm feeling human again."

Grateful to have something to focus on, she accepted the assignment as he closed the bathroom door behind him.

She still felt like she was going to jump out of her skin, but she could chalk that up to their car exploding only hours ago. Two of Aiden's agents had arrived at her house shortly after he and Lana and Eamon had departed with her family. They'd been handed the keys to a new SUV parked out front as well as the key and security code to the apartment building while Howell had accepted a new phone with instructions to only use his personal one in case of an emergency. The assigned parking space connected to this apartment was located in a structure only a block and a half from where they were staying. Kara had to admit, Aiden seemed to have thought about everything, right down to the kitchen supplies and well-stocked cabinets and fridge.

When the shower turned on in the bathroom, she quickly grabbed a bottle of water out of the fridge, grabbed a caffeine-laden pod from the drawer and set the coffee machine to the maximum size possible. She organized the files she'd brought with her and stacked neat folders around the computer she powered up. Phones and computers were good for most things, but there were times she thought better by reading off paper and writing things out.

Anxiety continued to ping inside of her and she wondered not for the first time how long it would take to feel normal again. Her computer blinked to life as she stifled a yawn. She had to widen her eyes to stop from drifting off and it was a good thing she did because the first image that came to mind was a rather intimate one featuring Marshal Howell McKenna. Naked. In the shower.

She covered her face with both hands, groaning as she willed her mind back on track. She needed to settle her mind, preferably on something completely opposite to the daydreams that the kisses they'd shared had triggered. Where another kiss like that might lead.

"Trouble," she muttered and shook herself back to reason. "It's only going to lead to trouble."

Passion and desire had absolutely no place in their current situation. It was only going to complicate their already fraught circumstances and distract them from what they needed to do.

On the one hand she was anxious to hole up and devise a foolproof plan to finding her witness before anything tragic happened. On the other…close quarters and Howell McKenna were going to prove challenging. Especially since she was now familiar with how it felt to be held in his arms.

"Stop it." Kara slowly sank into one of the bucket chairs at the kitchen table. But her overwhelmed mind was only capable of traveling on one of three tracks: One, Howell; which, given her level of attraction for him, should remain off limits. Two, Juliet. The only thing keeping Kara from completely panicking was remembering what Howell had said on the drive down from Connecticut. If the Alessis wanted Juliet dead, they'd have left her body in her room at the lodge. Third, numbers. Facts. Figures. Logic.

She'd have considered her family as fourth, but at least with them she felt relatively secure in the knowledge they may very well be the safest three individuals on the entire eastern seaboard.

The coffeemaker stopped sputtering and dripping and she immediately surrendered to the familiar and intoxicating aroma. Hot cup in hand, she returned to the table and, doing her best to empty her mind of anything other than what she could control, logged in to the dedicated Wi-Fi and clicked on her search engine.

Two minutes later she was asleep.

It took Howell a good long while to feel human again. Years of training and practice left him capable of going long periods without sleep, but the unfamiliar levels of worry he felt with this case were slowly eating away at his control. Protecting a witness was one thing and, in a lot of ways, it was predictable.

There was nothing predictable about this case. Or Kara Gallagher in particular.

He tugged on the clean shirt over damp skin, ran restless fingers through his wet hair and quickly tidied up the barely-there bathroom. It would do the job, but man… He shook his head. These New York apartments really skirted the edge of livability. It wasn't often he longed for his two-bedroom loft in Jersey. It had occurred to him, briefly at least, that they could have stayed there, but, if what he suspected about Juliet was true, his identity might put them in as much risk as Kara's. That meant his home wasn't safe for either of them.

The residual steam escaped the bathroom when he pulled open the door. He immediately smelled brewed coffee, which at the moment seemed like nirvana. The shower had helped clear his mind and he had a plan of action in place. The only problem was going to be...

Kara.

He stopped beside the kitchen table, dirty clothes stuffed under one arm, and looked down at her. Her computer screen was filled with a goofy image of Mia and Jonah hamming it up for the camera. An odd tug caught him in the center of his chest, as if he'd needed reminding of what was at stake.

"Kara." He touched a hand to her shoulder, kept his voice low.

She didn't move, simply remained where she was, head resting on her outstretched arm, all but splayed across the table as if she'd utterly surrendered to fatigue.

He pivoted, mind racing ahead of him as he realized his biggest problem might not be so big anymore. Howell quickly stashed his clothes in the second duffel bag that had been packed in the first and, standing over Kara, he stole the mug of coffee she'd brewed and took a long drink.

Straight black, no sugar. He smirked, appreciating the commonality.

Before he talked himself out of it, he carefully slipped one arm under her knees, the other behind her shoulders. He lifted her out of the chair.

She stirred, but only a little—a sign of how tired she was. But it was enough for her to turn her face into his shoulder and sigh in a way that had him wishing he were taking her into the bedroom for something other than sleep.

He could still smell that telltale hint of smoke, a reminder of just how close they'd both come to being blown into the afterlife. The warmth of her body sank into his as he carried her into the bedroom, taking care to avoid the rather narrow doorway.

He set her down on the mattress, carefully stretching her out, and she rolled over, arms reaching for something or someone who wasn't there. He wondered—was she thinking, dreaming of him?

He removed her shoes, a pair of ridiculously high brown ankle boots that matched the cozy knit sweater she wore. He'd noticed how the color brought out the gold and amber sparks in her eyes. He placed the shoes on the floor near her suitcase and covered her with the light blanket draped across the bottom of the bed. A faint smile showed on her lips and she curled into the throw.

Howell found himself standing over her, frowning at her as he contemplated exactly what space she'd begun to take up in his life. The sooner this case was over the better, he reminded himself. The more distance he put between them would be best for all of them. He was too much of a risk in every sense of the word. Even with his promotion, he'd be called in as a consultant at a moment's notice. And besides, Kara wasn't a solitary entity. He struggled at the best of times to maintain a solid relationship with his own kids—he did not want to add Mia and Jonah to that list of people to potentially disappoint. Alone was just...better.

For everyone.

He reached out and tucked her hair away from her face. The instant his hand touched her skin, she shifted, as if pushing herself into his hand. Even asleep she struck him as remarkable. Not only because she was one of the most beautiful women he'd ever encountered, but in sleep he could still see that steely determination and dedication he'd not so long ago found irritating.

Kara Gallagher was a woman of many talents, Howell thought as he stepped out of the room and closed the door. Not the least of which included being able to transfix him to the point of distraction.

It explained why he was feeling more than a little off-kilter.

A quick search of one of the cabinets revealed a not so healthy stash of his preferred snacks. Aiden always paid particular attention to the details. The chocolate-covered marshmallow cookies had always been a comfort food for him and something he kept on hand when he was puzzling out complicated cases.

He checked Kara's computer again, but she hadn't even gotten started before she'd crashed. Instead of doing a search that he could do later himself, he shifted his attention to her files. Not the summarized report she'd provided at the Marshals' office, but the full, unedited details.

Howell took a mental image of how she'd arranged her files, then picked them up and set them on the coffee table next to the secure laptop Aiden's people had left for him. No sooner had he powered the machine on than his new cell phone rang.

"Everything okay?" Howell answered as if he and his brother were already in the middle of a conversation.

"Pamela and the kids are doing fine," Aiden told him. "Took you long enough to open the computer."

"Let me guess. You had some kind of alarm set on it so you'd know?"

"Something like that," his brother said in a way that made Howell think that Aiden was grinning.

"Give me a sec." Howell retreated back to the kitchen for his coffee and plate—even though he could have demolished the entire package of cookies in one sitting—before settling in on the hopefully comfortable sofa. "Needed to clear my head before checking it out." He tapped the speaker button, sipped coffee and looked at the screen that was filled with folders. "Ready to get to it. What did you give me?"

"Everything my people could come up with on the Alessis. Reports, photographs, media mentions. Found some interesting information from other law enforcement agencies. Don't ask how."

Howell smirked. He knew better than to do that.

"I've also got you a direct communications portal to Jason Sutton. He's working on a deeper background check on Juliet. No use delaying the info by using me as a middleman. He'll keep me in the loop, though. He's already onto something hinky, though."

"Yeah?" Howell managed around a mouthful of cookie.

Aiden paused. "Did you go marshmallow or chocolate chip?"

Howell rolled his eyes. "Marshmallow." Although with his mouth full it sounded more like *marfallow*.

Aiden laughed and some of the tension eased. "You earned it after today. You might want to check with Kara about how far back she looked into Juliet. I'm betting it's not more than ten years because before then, things get a little wonky as to her existence."

Howell reached for his coffee as he tried to come up with any explanation other than what he suspected to be true. "So she's a fabrication." It made the most sense, so it didn't come as a complete surprise. The question was why? The other question was what was her interest in Kara?

There wasn't a good answer that he could think of, which only added to the pressure of needing a solution and fast.

"The social security number went active a little over fifteen years ago. Credit report shows some serious gaps in activity, but not enough to trigger a full-on investigation. Social media presence is sporadic at best, which to Jason is a serious red flag. She's on the grid just enough to establish a presence—"

"Or to pass a preliminary background check," Howell guessed.

"He's working on cross-referencing multiple databases, banking and cell phone records. He should have something more solid tomorrow. None of this surprises you, does it?"

"Nope." Howell glanced toward the bedroom in case Kara woke up and overheard them. He needed time to get this information fully formed in his mind so he knew how to present it to her. "What about the toothbrush Regan *borrowed*?" He winced at the term, the idea of stealing evidence not sitting entirely well with him. The fact that part of him was anxious and interested in results countered that niggling guilt. "Who are we running DNA and prints with?"

"Even with my connections, it's going take until tomorrow at least. Might be time to start thinking about investing in my own evidence lab. Hmm."

"Put a pin in that for now," Howell said. "Do we have confirmation on Juliet's college and work history?"

"Near as we can tell, everything Kara has on her is checking out. College graduation followed by about two years working part-time at a local bookkeeper's. Then there's a pretty big gap. More than three years before Briarwood. Working off the books at Velvet and Vice would fit that time frame."

"All under this false name." Howell blew out a long breath, rubbed his fingers across his forehead. He still couldn't comprehend the reason for the fake identity. "I was really hoping she'd lied about working at the club."

"Sorry," Aiden said as Howell typed in the website. "I know you aren't a fan of strip clubs."

"Gentlemen's club." As if the distinction actually mattered. "Any chance Jason—"

"Got a look at the current employee records?" Aiden snorted as if he'd been underestimated. "Happy to say they do keep some and that a few of their employees are on the up-and-up. There's one Jasmine Portola listed as a senior specialist hostess. Been working there eight years. Also of note is her address. It's the same as Juliet's, until Juliet moved to Connecticut to start work at Briarwood. My guess is that's the Jazz you're looking for."

Howell frowned. "Seems careless to make it that easy." And Juliet Unger did not come across as careless. "She left importance evidence against a crime family at an address she could be traced to?"

"Another question you get to answer when you catch up to Juliet."

"All right then." Howell checked the clock. His adrenaline level was already amped up. He wasn't going to sleep anytime soon. Might as well make the most of the time he had—he glanced again at the bedroom door—and Kara's being asleep. "If Jasmine isn't working tonight, I can try her at home."

"You taking Kara with you?" Aiden asked.

"I am not."

"Living dangerously, I see," Aiden teased. "Good luck."

"Thanks, bro."

"Happy to help get this case closed and locked up tight."

"Because I'm using one of your safe houses?" Howell teased.

"Because I want you and Kara away from the Alessis as soon as possible. Stay safe, Howell."

"I've got you on speed dial if I get into trouble."

Velvet and Vice sat in Upper Manhattan, surrounded by financial institutions, business firms and apartment buildings with doormen who made more money in a year than Howell had made his entire career. Howell paid his cab driver and pulled up the collar of his jacket against the cold night air.

From its outside appearance, one had to know what they were looking for to identify the place. There were no flashing neon signs reading Girls, Girls, Girls that sent strobing temptation into the night sky. Instead, an elegant black and gold plaque on the cement wall displayed the street number and name, as if beyond the heavy double doors made of glass, there was nothing more than a private cigar and port club. For the most part, it was. Didn't matter it was owned and operated by one of the most criminally connected families in the country.

The quick online search Howell ran before leaving the apartment hadn't pinged the place as anything more than being owned by the Alessis. Near as he could tell in the databases available to him, there were no current investigations. The last thing Howell wanted to do was hone in on someone else's show.

A club of this type was either sparkling clean when it came to solicitation and other...personal interactions—so law enforcement purposely stayed away—or the owners knew how to operate under the radar.

Howell tended to believe the latter.

It was the music that always set Howell on edge. Music that hit him square in the chest the instant he pulled open one of the doors. That deep, throbbing gut-pounding beat designed to keep an audience mesmerized to the point of losing track of the contents of their wallets.

The lobby was cast in a blue light, adding to that hypnotic feel, as he approached the welcome desk and the solitary woman who offered him a practiced, patient smile. A group of middle-aged men stood in the corner by the door, their discussion muted mostly by the music, but also by Howell's lack of interest.

"Good evening, sir." The hostess inclined her head in a way that made her long, straight black hair drape over one shoulder tattooed with an elegant floral bouquet. The silky black dress she wore spoke of domination and titillation, her heavily lined eyes coated with a cool detachment.

"Evening." Howell slouched a bit, put on his best "I'm a fish out of water" expression and slowed his speech to a bit of a drawl. He was well aware everything about him screamed cop. The aw-shucks attitude was the only other role he knew how to play. "I'm just in town for a couple of days. Friends of mine suggested this is the place for a distraction." He met her gaze. "I was told to ask for Jazz? Is she working tonight?"

"She is." Her eyes shifted to the double doors to her left. "You'll find Jazz just inside. Table six." She indicated the sign on the front of the desk that also displayed their strict Look, Don't Touch policy. "That'll be a hundred dollar cover charge."

"Ah, okay." He wished he could conjure up a blush but settled for ducking his head. "I don't suppose that includes a drink?"

"Drinks are extra and we require a two drink minimum."

He pulled out two fifty dollar bills and handed them over. Her nails were talon-like and painted a deep, blood red. "Think I can expense that?"

"Depends on your accountant," she said as if she'd heard it before. "Please. Enjoy yourself." She reached under the desk and the doors opened, immediately increasing the pounding of that bass tenfold. His ears instantly began to ache.

The blue of the lobby followed him inside. Four dancers on two stages were performing, each taking control of a dance pole that left them spinning, twirling and climbing beneath seizure inducing lights. Business was hopping and proving that it wasn't only New York that didn't sleep. Neither, it seemed, did Velvet and Vice's clientele. The music overwhelmed any conversation that might be taking place among the crowd of men lined up at the long bar against the back wall. Tables of varying heights and sizes blanketed the floor around the twin stages outlined by chairs for closer views and interactions.

Howell had to admit *classy* was a word he didn't often use in reference to strip clubs, but it fit this place perfectly with its velvet decor accenting the navy blue fabric with touches of crystal and gold. The dancers' costumes, which seemed to be little more than a collection of well-placed sparkles, left nothing to the imagination.

The female servers wore rhinestone-accented thin-strapped thigh-length dresses similar to the one worn by the lobby hostess. One step up from lingerie, Howell thought, which added to the upscale feel of the place. The place smelled clean, like pumped in oxygen combined with money.

That steep cover charge probably financed the upkeep and then some. He surveyed the patrons, noting the near professional attire. Other than the two male bartenders, the only other employees he spotted were women.

The heels they were wearing made him instantly think of Kara's shoes but he found them nowhere near as alluring. *Kara*. Just thinking about her reignited both his determination to get answers and his desire to return to the apartment.

Temptation thy name was Kara.

Discreet table numbers reflected onto the tabletops from custom lights overhead. Thankfully, he found table six just far enough away from the stage to feel somewhat comfortable. The two blondes performing on the first stage appeared to be mirroring one another. The dancer closest to him shifted her attention from the man sitting inches from her stiletto covered feet to Howell, a sly smile appearing on her full painted lips.

Practice kept his gaze steady as he sat and waited for his server to approach. Undercover had never been his forte. His sister Regan handled it beautifully and even treated it like some kind of drama class assignment. Howell, on the other hand, often felt the need for a hazmat shower afterward.

The woman who arrived was on the shorter side with big blue jaded eyes and platinum blond hair sparkling with glitter. If what she had on display had been gifted by nature rather than a cosmetic surgery genius, she was more than enough to make Howell believe in a higher power.

"What can I get you?" Her voice rang perfectly clear over the throbbing music.

"Jazz, I presume?"

Caution jumped into her eyes before she eyed the wallet he pulled out of his pocket. "For the right price, I can be anyone you want." The smile that curved her painted lips spoke of temptation and feigned interest.

He pulled out another fifty, held it out between two fingers but yanked it back when she reached for it. "Juliet sent me." It wasn't a lie. Exactly.

Jazz was good, but not fast enough to hide her doubt. Her smile widened as the caution in her eyes grew. She set her tray on the table and slipped up and into the stool across from him. Her hand covered his in what felt like a rehearsed action, her gaze shifting to the bar before returning to hers. "Juliet who?"

"The Juliet who asked for my help earlier today." He paused. "She's your roommate, isn't she?"

"Oh, *that* Juliet." She looked down at his hand—or

more specifically, the money he held. "Yeah, she comes and goes but trust me. She doesn't need help. With anything."

Of that, Howell had no doubt. Jazz's hold felt cool and rehearsed. Not at all as warm or tempting as simply being in the same room as Kara. "Juliet's in trouble, Jazz. She said she gave you something for safe keeping."

Her expression didn't change. She simply looked at him.

"What she gave you is dangerous."

"Let me guess." Jazz sighed dramatically and in a way that reminded him of a less talented Juliet in the acting department. "I suppose you're here to relieve me of my burden." She looked pointedly again at his wallet. "You want me to turn something I may or may not have over just because you're pretty and asked nicely?"

"Everything okay over here, Jazz?" A large, bulky man with spiked blond hair and tattoos covering his neck appeared at the table. Howell looked beyond him to the bar and instantly identified the well-dressed man sitting at the end of the bar nursing a drink. His dark-eyed stare was locked utterly and completely on Jazz.

Rafael Alessi.

He held a cut crystal glass in one hand and wore a tailored black suit, black shirt and stark silver tie in a way that would have identified him as criminally connected even if he hadn't been the son of Sal Alessi.

"Everything's fine, Karl," Jazz said easily, reaching out and slipping her fingers through Howell's even as she cast her gaze over her shoulder at Rafael. "Tell Rafi he can relax. We're just doing some negotiating, aren't we?" The smile she turned on Howell didn't come close to reaching her eyes. Rather, he could see her processing and working the possible angles with every blink of her heavily mascaraed eyes. "It's okay, really," she insisted to the bouncer without breaking eye contact with Howell. "He's harmless."

Karl looked at Howell who was smart enough to offer a shaky smile before he shifted his gaze away. The last thing he wanted to do was give off law enforcement vibes. Karl moved on to the next table where a pair of what looked like gullible college boys had stepped into a wonderland of look-don't-touch fantasy.

"Your boyfriend doesn't look too happy with me," Howell said, indicating Rafael.

"Rafi's rarely happy about anything. I hadn't seen Juliet in over a year," Jazz eased back into their conversation as easily as she'd slid onto her stool. "Best year of my life, if I'm honest. Trouble follows that girl around like a lost puppy. Then about six weeks ago, here she comes, out of the blue, using the key she never gave back and asked if she could have her old room for a bit."

"I take it you said yes."

"She offered me five grand in cash," Jazz scoffed. "Damned right I said yes, which is when she hit me up about keeping something safe for her. Like you, she said it was hot. That people would be looking for it. Should have known it came with strings," she muttered. "She bought me cheap, didn't she? Whatever she gave me is worth a lot more than five thousand." She scowled. "I knew I should have asked for more."

"She didn't lie, Jazz," Howell said. "Most of the people who want it aren't going to be nice about asking you for it." He resisted the urge to look back at Rafael Alessi. "If they ask at all."

"Like anyone's nice." Her words were almost lost in the music, but Howell could read lips well enough to get the gist. "I bet you're nice, though. Yeah, you strike me as a really nice guy." She sighed after smiling into his expressionless eyes. "You also strike me as taken."

"I—" Was he? "When was the last time you saw Juliet?"

She shrugged, her glitter-dusted skin sparkling against the lights. "Two, maybe three weeks ago. Said she had something to take care of, but she'd be back to collect her things. Tell me something..." She ran a finger down the back of his hand while she continued to hold it in her other. "Am I right in thinking there isn't a healthy way for me to cash in on this thing she left with me?"

"That's correct," Howell confirmed. "I'm your only safe solution, Jazz. Trust me, you want it out of your hands."

"Trust *you*." She snorted again, her fingers tightening around his. She narrowed her eyes, inclined her head. "I don't trust anyone. Especially a cop. You are one, aren't you? You sure come across as one."

"Afraid so." What was the point in lying if telling the truth would earn a modicum of good will?

She swore, eyes narrowing as she tried to tug her hand free. Howell held on.

"Cops are more trouble than Juliet." She glared at him even as Howell felt Rafael's eyes on him. On them.

"You hear about that explosion at the beach in Connecticut earlier today?" He could tell by the way she sat up straighter that she had. "Happened in the parking lot of the motel where Juliet's been staying. She hasn't been seen since."

Disbelief shone in her eyes. "Juliet's dead?"

"Unknown," Howell said. "Could be. And it could be she's dead because someone came looking for what she gave you."

"You're serious." Jazz blinked. "Huh. Guess she wasn't lying for a change. She never tells anyone the whole truth. Not in my experience at least."

Of that, Howell had no doubt. "I can give you two hundred in cash, now, another three when I have it in my hands. That's my offer." Howell stiffened his hand, hoping to get his point across. She stared at him for a good long while, long enough for him to wonder if there was something else behind her reluctance other than negotiating a higher price. "Are you in trouble, Jazz?"

"No more than anyone else." There was something sad in her voice. Resigned even. "I'm not some damsel in distress, Lawman. I'm excellent at what I do, I'm careful and I make a very good living at it. Not much more I can ask for than that." She smiled again. "Except for maybe that five hundred you offered."

Howell's radar must be off. He couldn't decide if he believed her or not. If it was merely bravado, she was good at it. If it was the truth…

"Fair warning," Howell said. "I found you the same day Juliet told me about you, Jazz. I did it through legal channels. Others won't have any firewalls and they'll move faster. Be careful, please. Juliet took more effort to protect what she asked you to hide, than she did protecting you."

"Yeah." Another smirk. "Sounds like her." This time she blew out a long, controlled breath, irritation flashing in her eyes. "You know what? This is stupid. In fact, I told Juliet this plan of hers against Sal was *stupid* years ago when she first came up with it." She paused, appeared to be considering her next words. "You've got yourself a deal. I'm going to assume you already have my address since you know Juliet lived with me." She slid off the stool, stroked a finger down his nose. He handed her two one hundred dollar bills that also included his card. To sweeten the deal he added the fifty he'd offered earlier.

"You get the rest when I get the item," he confirmed.

"I sleep until three, then come back here at six." She tucked the cash into her exposed cleavage. "See you anytime in between, Lawman."

He waited a beat, casually watching her walk to the bar where Rafael Alessi sat with his hand wrapped tight around his glass. Jazz stopped, nuzzled up to him, then gestured to Howell in a way that had Alessi's dark eyes landing on him like a ten-ton brick.

Howell played it cool, seemingly ignoring the attention as he pulled out another twenty, tossed it on the table and got out of his chair. The hair on the back of his neck stood at attention, that all too familiar, well-trained instinct kicking into action.

The Alessis were dangerous on any given night. He'd bet adding jealousy to the toxic mix could very well turn dangerous to deadly.

Howell made his way through the club, keeping an eye on the mirrored wall that showed Alessi signaling to bouncer Karl, along with another man. The music continued to pound to the point his head hurt and his ears ached.

He used the entry of a large group of barely legal, boisterous and well on their way to inebriated college boys to mask his exit, ducking his head in the hopes of disappearing into the crowd.

He offered a quick and forced friendly wave to the hostess in the lobby, ignoring the kerfuffle behind him as he pushed open the door.

Outside, the night had closed in. The street wasn't nearly as crowded now and he immediately turned left, scanning the area in front of him for...

Kurt's voice carried. A deep almost growling sound that made Howell's ears perk up. He had no idea what Jazz might have said to Rafael Alessi, but given his own conversation with her, Howell didn't believe for one second that she had any kind of verbal filter in place.

Were they coming after him? He kept his pace steady, shoved his hands into his pockets. A quarter block away, half block...there! That would work.

He quickly sidestepped into the tiled entryway of a hole-in-the-wall deli currently closed for refurbishment. Howell pivoted, angled himself in a way that he could see the front of the club through the angle of the window.

An SUV limo pulled to a slow stop. Kurt moved in, opened the door and stepped back as a middle-aged man wearing a finely tailored suit appeared. The man snapped his blazer closed, offered a quick nod of acknowledgement to Kurt and his cohort before he was escorted inside.

Howell let out a slow breath. Serious misjudgment on his part, enough that he felt like a first-year recruit. Unable to identify that odd sensation coursing through his system, he began to walk. It wasn't until he hit the next intersection and turned back to the apartment that he put a name to it: doubt.

He frowned, bent his head into the wind as he sped

up. He didn't *doubt* anything. It was a luxury he couldn't afford.

Believing he was being followed when he clearly wasn't could easily be laughed off, but the reverse could just as easily happen. Being off-kilter because his head was too filled with Kara, that could lead him to not seeing danger when it was right on their heels. And that, he told himself as he continued into the night, could get them killed.

Chapter 9

Kara startled awake. Her heart was pounding to the point she had to press a hand against her chest.

Where...where am I?

She stared blankly up at the stark white ceiling, confusion lifting gradually. The unfamiliar bed, the soft blanket she never would have bought for herself because one of her kids would have immediately stolen it. She curled her toes, trying to remember when she'd taken off her shoes.

Only when she spotted her suitcase by the bedroom door did the pieces fall back into place. She checked her watch, then groaned and pressed the heels of her hands to her eyes. 8:00 a.m.

Clearly yesterday had caught up with her and knocked her out. She hadn't slept in this late since before law school.

A gentle muffled rustle of activity had her kicking free of the blanket and dragging herself out of bed. She slid open the door and poked her head out. She quickly leaned back, needing a moment to process the intoxicating sight of Marshal Howell McKenna standing barefoot, wearing jeans and a T-shirt that made him look like a rugged cowboy from her favorite Montana cattle ranching TV show.

She caught herself fanning her face, something she had never, ever done before.

She clenched her fist, trying in vain to get herself centered and back on track. It wasn't like her to be distracted, especially by a man, but everything that had happened in the past day or so was new territory, wasn't it? When she stepped from the bedroom, she quickly turned her back on him and raced into the bathroom to get herself together. She washed her face and brushed her teeth. Tried to do something with her hair. Then stared at herself in the mirror with an unfamiliar dazed and anticipatory gleam in her eyes. She touched both hands to her cheeks, willed herself to calm down. It took a few deep breaths.

When she emerged, she did so with a tired smile and a racing heartbeat. "Morning." She offered an uncertain, almost shy wave she didn't remember ever giving anyone before now.

"Morning." His smile could have broken through the darkest of storms. She could feel the cage she'd built around her heart begin to weaken. "Sorry if I woke you."

Howell stood at the kitchen counter. He was cracking eggs into a mixing bowl. The aroma of fried bacon and onions and peppers cooking on the stove wafted into her nose and she nearly swooned. Seemed her stomach had finally recovered.

"It's okay." Hugging her arms around herself, she joined him at the counter and looked longingly at the coffee machine. She placed a new pod inside and retrieved a clean mug. "I can't believe I slept so long."

"You were definitely out." He cracked another egg and plopped it into the bowl. "Hungry?"

She frowned.

"What?"

"Nothing. It's just..." She offered an apologetic smile. "I'm sorry you went to all this trouble, but I hate eggs."

"Ah." He shook his head and started beating up the bowl's contents with a fork. "That's because you haven't had *my* eggs. You're going to love these. Trust me."

"You can trust me to gag on them," she mumbled as her coffee filled. "But I'll give them a shot."

"Good to hear."

Obviously, he was a morning person. Kara caught sight of two healthy slices of sourdough bread peeking up out of the toaster and instantly embraced them as her backup breakfast plan. She cast a quick glance to the files stacked up by her laptop. They were almost, *almost* the way she'd left them. "Read anything interesting?"

"Huh?" Howell looked over his shoulder and didn't seem the least bit concerned when she gestured to her files.

"Oh, yeah. Just thought I should catch up." There was no apology to be seen or heard. "I think we're mostly on the same page now where Juliet is concerned."

Juliet. Reality slapped her completely awake. "I still can't help but think she's dead." She hadn't meant to say it—didn't even realize she'd been thinking it. Now that she'd done both... "I screwed up. Completely miscalculated everything. And now she's—"

"She's not dead." Howell set the bowl aside and faced her, crossing his arms over his chest in such a way that exposed muscular biceps and forearms that until now she hadn't realized were so well...defined. She heated from the inside out. "Kara?" He leaned forward to catch her stare with his gaze. "You okay?"

Not remotely. "How can you be so certain?" She distracted herself by retrieving her coffee and drinking it far too fast. Her mouth and tongue immediately protested. When he turned to her again, it was with complete resolve and sincerity on his handsome face.

"I just am. But it's also something I look forward to proving." He stepped closer, close enough that the warmth of his body seeped into hers. She lifted her chin as he rested his hands on her shoulders.

Her eyes fluttered closed. Her hands came up, gripping his upper arms as if she could brand him with her desire. Her entire body began to hum as he dipped his head to brush his mouth against hers. Softly at first, then more firmly. His tongue stroked hers, dancing and twirling to the point of erasing all doubt and thought from her mind.

When he ended the kiss, she moaned softly and tilted her head to show him that she wanted more. His lips found hers again. This man, this marshal, was doing the impossible. She had to remind herself to kiss him back. To take as much as he was offering and to demand more than he planned to give. She rose up on her toes as his hands cupped the sides of her face, thumbs stroking her cheeks as the kiss took her toward an entirely new and different timeline that left her longing for release.

He set her back down, lifted his mouth from hers. She could feel the warmth of his breath on her face as she met his gaze. "If..." Her voice cracked and he smiled. She cleared her throat. "If that was your way of trying to help me clear my mind, I can assure you it did not work." She wasn't entirely sure she'd ever think clearly again.

"Thought I'd get a real kiss on the record, Ms. Prosecutor." He kissed the tip of her nose. "One that didn't have anything to do with annoying your ex. This one was all me." He pressed his mouth to hers briefly. "And you."

The feelings she'd banked so long ago, embers she'd let die, were stoked back to life. Every cell in her body felt recharged and ready to go. She licked her lips, determined to keep the taste of him in her memory.

"What ex?" she asked with a slow smile that had him chuckling.

"Excellent response. And now that we've got that settled..." He slowly, very slowly released her and took a step back. "Breakfast."

Like she was supposed to do something as mundane as eat after a kiss like that?

"There's something I need to tell you," he said as he emptied the bowl of eggs into a pan on the stove and began to stir them. "And I'm going to lead with the fact you were never going to go with me in the first place, so don't argue about how I went off without you."

Feeling daring and more than a little curious, she walked up behind him and, touching a hand against his right arm, snuck around the other side to grab a piece of bacon. It felt good, touching him. Knowing he wanted her to. Feeling that strength and confidence and recognizing that when he smiled at her, he meant it. "So kissing me was a kind of Novocain for a verbal procedure?"

He shook his head, caught her hand and, his eyes glued to hers, bit off part of the bacon for himself. "You do have a way with words. I went to Velvet and Vice last night. To meet with Juliet's friend, Jazz."

She wasn't entirely sure what she'd been expecting. She waited for the irritation to form, for the frustration over being left out of her investigation to surface, but it was only a mild sort of annoyance that turned up. "Did you get the drive?"

He arched a brow. "That's all you've got?"

"For now." Truth be told, the idea of going into a gentlemen's club hadn't been on the top of her to-do list. "Depends on what you say next."

"Obviously she didn't have it on her, but I made arrangements to get it later this afternoon before she heads back to work."

"So I get to go this time?" She blinked overly innocent eyes at him.

"There it is." He shook his head, returned all his focus to their breakfast. "Believe me when I say you would have stuck out like..." He hesitated. "Let's just say you would have stood out."

"I'm choosing to take that as a compliment."

He reached over and pressed the toaster lever down. "Go get comfortable on the sofa while I finish this up."

Before she sat, she caught sight of a yellow legal pad, the top sheet of which was covered in notes written in a firm blocky cursive. He'd written down fragments of his conversation with Jazz, noted that Rafael Alessi had been in the club. "What's this mean?" She picked up the tablet and sat back on the sofa. "Jazz said Juliet's been planning something for years? Did she mean what's happening now?"

"I think now is a part of whatever it is." Howell leaned back to meet her curious gaze. "Aiden called last night. Kids and your mom are doing great by the way."

She smiled, unsurprised. "I haven't been worried, actually. Aiden instills faith."

"Good to hear. He suggested I ask you how far back you went with your check of Juliet."

"Ten years." She didn't have to think about it. "Standard background checks tend to be seven. I always hedge my bets." She sipped more coffee. "I don't like surprises."

"Well, you're about to get one. Juliet Unger's a false identity."

The coffee tasted bitter as it slide down her throat. "How do you know?"

"Preliminary results from the deep dive Aiden's doing into her. We'll have something more solid later when we talk to Jason, but yeah. Whoever your witness is, her name isn't Juliet."

Howell buttered the toast before switching off the burner that had cooked the eggs, then he ducked into the refrigerator and pulled out a chunk of cheese he immediately started shredding on a grater.

Cold realization blanketed her like ice. "I just walked into it, didn't I?"

"Walked into what?"

"Whatever it is she's doing. She could have said the sky was purple with green dots and I'd have believed her because she had the evidence that would put Alessi away."

"You two do seem to share that particular...tunnel vision."

Kara barely heard him. "All I saw was the possibility of finally making Sal Alessi pay for killing my father. That's what she saw. I avoided everything else, including her real motivations, whatever they were or are." She'd been played and that did not sit well with her. "I just went with whatever she told me because someone was finally telling me what I wanted to hear." He stood before her, a plate in each hand. "Really?" she asked when he offered her one. "You aren't going to say I told you so?"

"No," he said quietly. "I'm going to say let's eat."

"Admit it," Kara said as she scooped another mouthful of eggs into her mouth. "There's some kind of special foodie magic in these, isn't there?"

Howell watched from where he sat beside her on the sofa, more than a little amused. He was on his third cup of morning coffee that sat steaming beside his empty plate on the table. The sun streamed through the curtains, both warming and filling the apartment with hope and more than a little anticipation.

Anticipation born of his need to kiss her again.

The very idea had his lips curving in a secretive, promising smile.

In all honesty it could have been raining kittens and poodles outside and he'd still have thought it a beautiful winter day. That kiss they'd shared at her house yesterday hadn't been a fluke but a promise of something he'd never anticipated experiencing. A connection. One he couldn't imagine severing anytime soon if at all.

Her comment lightened his heavy heart despite the somewhat surly tone in which she said it. "It's more like you're starving and not thinking much about what you're eating." That and the half a pound of cheese he'd topped it off with. He'd take the reluctant compliment, though. "I'd like to ask you something."

"About the case?" She bit into her toast. Butter dribbled down her chin and she swiped at it with a finger, then stuck her finger in her mouth. Their gazes met and everything inside of him turned to molten desire. The amusement in her eyes confirmed it wasn't one sided. If he hadn't made tentative plans for the day and they were without a number of mysteries to solve, he might have suggested spending their afternoon in the bedroom.

"Not about the case." He forced himself to look away and reach for his coffee as a distraction. "I'd like for you to tell me about your dad."

He saw it immediately. The curtain of grief dropped instantly. She tried to hide it, to shift in her seat as she set her plate aside. Finally, she loosened up, curled her legs under her and settled into the sofa. Her luxurious dark hair shimmered in the sunshine, eyes filling with an acceptance he could only imagine came with pain. "What do you want to know?"

"Everything." Patrick Hewitt had been the defining factor of Kara's life. But all Howell knew was that his death had transformed her into this amazing, exciting, headstrong woman sitting beside him. A woman who had shifted everything for him. Howell recognized his life wasn't going to be the same ever again. "What did you call him?"

"Daddy." She smirked, leaning into the word as she rested her elbow on the back of the excruciatingly uncomfortable sofa. "I was a daddy's girl from day one. I have this, I don't know if it's a memory or a feeling or just something I want to be true." She tilted her head, a ghost of a smile playing across her lush lips. "I remember being little. Maybe even still a baby. And feeling him lifting me into his arms. I can imagine his smile and hear his laughter and he looked at me with such…" She pressed a hand against her chest as if it suddenly hurt. "Love. I could feel how much he loved me. That never went away. Until he died."

"It doesn't take much to become a father," Howell agreed. "But it takes everything to be a dad." He was one of the lucky ones. His father was a tremendous man worthy of Howell's love and respect, but mostly, he was a good, kind man that Howell was fortunate enough to still have with him. One thing he'd worked hard on with his own kids after the divorce was to make certain that Zoe and Logan always, no matter what, knew they could count on him to be there for them. He couldn't always be available in the moment, but the same could be said of any parent. The older they got, the more difficult that was to make happen. All the more reason he really wanted out of the field.

Tears glistened in her eyes and she nodded. "Yeah." Her voice broke and she swiped away the solitary tear that trickled down her cheek. "My dad had a rule. Work was work, home was home. Up until the last few years of his life, he didn't even have a home office. That changed, of course." She managed a wan smile. "I always told myself that's how I'd be with my kids." What light there was in her eyes faded. "Sometimes I think Garrett wasn't wrong. Sometimes I think he's right to call me out on—"

"Garrett wouldn't be right if he told you rain was wet." Howell cut her off immediately, refusing to let her go down that road. "He really did a number on you, didn't he? Garrett. Coming at you about your work, about your ability as a mother. As a woman." He had to couch his frustration. The idea anyone, especially someone lucky enough to have won her heart, could have turned around and used those emotions as a weapon against her? "Your ex-husband is an insecure boy who never learned how to be a decent man."

He expected laughter. He expected something other than the blank, processing stare she gave him. Something shimmered there, but he wouldn't let himself believe it was anything more than appreciation for the sentiment.

"Regan was right," she finally said. "She said you were the most honorable person she'd ever met. I'd say they broke the mold with you, but they never even had one, did they? It's just who you are."

"I'm a McKenna," Howell admitted. His sister's compliments meant more to him than he could express. "It's how we're all made. But I asked about your father, not your ex-husband."

"Daddy was happy. Focused," she added with a quick shrug. "Brilliant. He could count cards and was a nightmare to play gin rummy with."

Howell laughed at that.

"He always said he wanted to spend a week in Vegas so we could get a new house. Not sure that would have paid off. Mom always said it was more luck than math."

"I noticed she still wears her wedding ring."

"She still thinks of herself as married," Kara explained, touching the charm at her throat. "She'll never take it off. She gave me his ring, even suggested I wear it on a chain, but I can't do that. So I bought myself this instead. Maybe someday I'll be able to wear his ring, when I can finally think of him as being at rest." She swiped at more tears.

So that was it. Not just revenge. Not just finishing the job Patrick Hewitt had started.

Kara wanted her father to be at peace, knowing the fight he'd started had finally ended on the terms he'd set.

"He was a terrible cook. The morning he…died…" She cleared her throat. "That morning he'd gotten up early to cook breakfast. Eggs. The only thing he could make edible. That was the last…" she broke off, lifting her suddenly understanding eyes to Howell's. "Since that day they've always turned my stomach. The smell… It always smells like ash to me. Ash and fire." Recognition dawned. "It wasn't the eggs," she whispered, her eyes going wide with acceptance before she laughed. "All these years, it was never eggs that I hated."

"It was the memory," Howell confirmed. "And no, before you ask, I had no idea about your issues with chicken productivity. It's one of the few things I can cook without ruining."

"And here I thought your sister was the shrink in the family." She pushed forward, slid across the sofa toward him.

It was the most natural thing in the world for Howell to open his arms and draw her in, holding her as she curled into him. When her arms slipped around him, she buried her face in his chest in a way that spoke of instant comfort and safety. It was, Howell thought, one of the most perfect moments of his life.

"He was a good man," she whispered. "I wish you could have known him."

"I do in a way." He pressed his lips against the top of her head. "I know him through you." He tilted his head and pressed a light kiss against her mouth. "And so do your children. Whatever else happens, he'd be proud of you, Kara. That should be enough."

"It should be," she whispered. "It's not. But it will be. Soon."

It was, Howell realized, her way of reminding him that there wasn't any moving forward emotionally—together or alone—until she could put her father's murder and Sal Alessi's conviction behind her. "We've got time before we meet Jazz." Howell kept his arms around her, not willing to relinquish holding her for the moment. "Computers and files aren't going to get us anywhere for the time being, but a care facility might."

"Care..." Kara sat up, braced her hand on his chest as she looked at him. "Care facility. Juliet's grandmother?" She shook her head. "But she has dementia. She won't be able to tell us anything."

"Probably not," Howell agreed and felt strangely abandoned when she moved out of his hold. "But maybe the staff or other residents can. Visiting hours start at ten."

"Sounds like a plan to me."

Kara and Howell walked side by side down the short hallway to the reception desk at Brookside Court Senior Care in Midtown Manhattan. With its large glass entryway and neutral design that spoke of homey comfort, the place didn't remind Kara of any of the long-term care facilities she'd ever encountered. A security desk sat in a recessed section of wall, tucked out of the way, but close enough for someone there to watch over the entrance of the facility. The uniformed officer in the chair gave them a nod of acknowledgement as they passed.

"Am I the only one wondering," Kara said, "how, even with her, um, dancer earnings, Juliet is able to afford this place?"

"You are not," Howell said. "But remember, we've

reached a point where everything Juliet told you, told us, should be taken with a grain of salt."

True. Kara scowled. Juliet had lied about a lot of little things which, given Kara's math skills, added up to something a lot bigger. She couldn't believe anything of what she'd been told up until now, including what might be on that laptop and hard drive she and Howell had yet to get their hands on.

A pair of young women in colorful scrubs walked past, offered warm smiles of welcome. The air was filled with the aroma of baked apples and an overworked heating system.

With hues of dark red, brown and gold, the lower level of the five-story building offered large and clear directories to their dining room, community meeting room and various activity areas. The wall to the right of the reception desk was filled with numerous resident photos. Kara veered off in that direction while Howell spoke to the receptionist.

Whoever had taken the photos clearly had a talent for bringing out the residents' personalities. Kara could practically hear laughter behind the smiles and found herself touched by the emotion on their faces. Although not everyone looked happy, and a few looked really annoyed, the display was a testament to the facility's dedication to its residents and patients.

"We've got a problem." Howell's voice in her ear made Kara shiver. "They don't have a resident with the last name of Unger."

Kara flinched. "I don't recall Juliet mentioning her grandmother's last name, actually." She'd just taken what Juliet had told her on faith. She'd never stop being mad about that. That she'd simply accepted her words. And because certain things had checked out, she'd assumed everything else would, too.

She scanned the photos, skimming the names, paying attention to the women. "Estelle," she murmured as she made quick work of the display. "Estelle... This one, maybe?" She pointed to a woman with short silver hair and a wide toothy smile. Her chubby cheeks and round face resembled Mrs. Claus with a serious twinkle in her eye. "Hang on," she told Howell. "I've got this." She led Howell back to the clerk. "I'm so sorry. My husband's horrible with names. We were hoping to speak with someone about Esty. We're friends of the family."

"Oh!" The young woman with plaited dark hair touched a hand to her throat. Her name badge identified her as Nancy Klingman. "Esty's one of our favorite residents. How nice. She has visitors."

"Her granddaughter comes by to visit fairly regularly, I understand," Kara commented, but the woman frowned and shook her head.

"I haven't known Esty to have anyone come for quite some time." Suspicion marred Nancy's brow. "Are you certain it's Esty you want to see?"

No, Kara thought. She wasn't certain. But there wasn't any other name that came close to Estelle. "We're in town for the day," Kara explained. "We thought we'd drop in and check on her. Speak with her doctors, see how she's doing."

"Well, I can tell you, she's a spitfire as always," Nancy waved off any concern. "Woman has a talent for putting a smile on everyone's face. I think she's playing bunco at the moment in the solarium. Would you like me to show you the way?"

"That'd be great, thanks, Nancy." Howell touched Kara's arm and she turned puzzled eyes on him. He shrugged and the two of them followed their guide through the large lobby. "I'm thinking dementia and spitfire don't necessarily go together," he murmured and upped Kara's irritation at their currently confusing situation.

Juliet's well-crafted story had just tipped out of the truth realm and landed straight in fiction.

"She probably assumed you'd take her at her word that her grandmother wouldn't be of any help."

"Then I'm not the only one who's made mistakes," Kara said. Her concern for Juliet's safety was quickly eroding and turning into anger. She did not like being used. No matter the reason or rationale. And right now, she was feeling like a severely weathered doormat. "So Esty's pretty active, is she?" she asked Nancy.

"Oh my, yes. Everyone loves her. She leads several of our craft classes. Knitting, crocheting. She used to teach high school art back in the day from what I heard." Nancy stopped at a set of paneled glass doors and pushed one open. Inside the room, more glass walls overlooked beautifully manicured gardens on three sides. Outside, winter coated the city. It was like a reverse snow globe in which the residents lived. "Esty, you have company." Nancy touched a hand to the older woman's shoulder.

"I do?" Esty, looking exactly as she did in her picture, shifted around in her chair, her face splitting into one of the widest smiles that Kara had ever seen. "Hello. I don't know you, do I?" Esty cast a side-eyed glance at the receptionist. "Some days I have trouble recalling the friends I've made."

"Hello, Esty." Kara walked over and crouched down, grabbed the arm of the chair for balance. "Juliet asked us to come by and check up on you."

"Juliet." Esty rolled her eyes and hooted. "Girl's playing games again, isn't she?" Esty cackled and accepted the handful of dice one of her fellow bunco players scooped toward her. "So dramatic. Always so dramatic. Ah, farts." She scowled at the unlucky roll. "Sixes always give me the gip. Roll for me, Florence," she said to the woman beside her. "I'm not passing up on company." She lifted her chin and caught sight of Howell. "Especially, handsome company. What's your name?"

"Howell, ma'am."

"Ma'am. Now that's got a nice ring to it. I prefer 'your ladyship,' however." She winked and Kara laughed, pushing to her feet when Esty moved her chair. "You can stop eavesdropping, Nancy. I can take care of them from here. We'll go back to my room for a private chat."

"If you say so, Esty." Nancy smiled, clearly not offended by Esty's comment. "Please make sure she doesn't talk you into a cigarette," she murmured to Kara as she passed her. "She just got off oxygen and we're trying to keep it that way."

"Understood," Kara agreed as Howell followed Esty's encouragement to grab the chair's handles and wheel her out. "I'm Kara, Esty. Has Juliet ever mentioned me?" Esty eyed her, a confused look on her face. Had Kara misspoken?

"Not here." Esty pointed to the door. "Turn right, then down the hall. Room 117. Shhhh." She put her finger against her lips as Howell navigated the corridor. "Door's unlocked," she told Kara when they arrived at her room. "Go ahead."

Kara didn't dare disobey. There was something commanding and almost officious about the older woman despite her congeniality.

Esty's one-bedroom apartment was fairly spacious and included a small kitchenette, a sitting room with a big-screen TV, comfortable easy chairs with a lift mechanism and a bedroom with a state of the art hospital bed and all-access bathroom. Kara took a quick tour while Howell helped Esty out of her wheelchair and into the plush chair by the window.

"Now." Esty pointed to the crocheted afghan on the arm of the sofa. Howell retrieved it and draped it over her legs. "You've done this before," she teased him.

"A few times," Howell confirmed.

"Your girl there is a curious one," Esty said, then raised her voice. "One might even say nosy!"

Kara's cheeks went hot, but before she could respond, she spotted the collection of framed photographs on the top of an antique writing desk. All of the pictures were of young people from various eras, some going back as far as the seventies given the attire. The tint had faded in some images, but it was the picture in the center that caught her attention.

"Yep, that's her," Esty said. "She's gone and got herself into trouble again, hasn't she?" Esty *tsk*ed and shook her head. "I love that girl to death, but she never met a situation she couldn't exploit. Smart as anything, especially with numbers and computers. Got herself a good job working them." She watched Kara closely. "You're not really friends with her, are you?"

It wasn't an accusation per say. More like a resigned observation.

"I'm a lawyer," Kara said, deciding at the last minute to abandon their planned story. If Howell disagreed, he didn't show it. Trust, she thought. He trusted her to do this her way. "Juliet's been helping me out on an important case."

Esty looked at Howell. "If she's a lawyer, what does that make you?"

"I'm a US marshal, ma'am."

"A marshal." Esty sat up straighter, beaming from ear to ear. "Well, I'll be. I thought they only had those on TV these days."

"We're a real thing, Esty." He pulled out his badge to show her. "We're having trouble locating Juliet and we're hoping you might be able to help us out."

"First thing you should know is that Juliet's made up. It's a persona she created when she was a girl, after her mother died. A coping mechanism. Trying to become something, someone else. Fierce imagination she had from the second she landed on my doorstep. Poor thing. Sixteen years old and you'd have thought she carried the entire world on her shoulders. Never trusted anyone. Well, eventually she trusted me. And Billy, too. He was one of my other fosters. Always happy to do her bidding." She shook her head. "Giselle makes really good use of people."

Kara sank onto the sofa beside Howell. "She came to live with you when she was sixteen?"

"That's right. Put on the electric kettle for tea, dear,

would you?" Esty pointed toward the kitchen. "I've got some cookies left over from Christmas. Don't tell the nurses, though. They aren't on my diet. I was the sixth, no, seventh foster home she was assigned. And the last. Until she was eighteen. Then, like they always do, she left."

Kara nudged Howell, hoping he got the message to keep Esty talking while she went into the kitchenette.

"We won't tell a soul about the cookies," Howell assured her. "Those pictures on the desk." He pointed to the ones Kara had been looking at. "Are those all your foster kids?"

"Some of them." Esty's pride was evident. Kara filled the kettle and tapped the button to start it heating. "Had about thirty or so over the years. Never had children of my own. Never married. Never found someone who could put up with me. But I had love. Plenty of that." She tapped her heart. "And for most of those kids, that's exactly what they needed. Love and rational discipline. An environment to thrive in. That was always my goal."

"That's something to be proud of," Howell assured her.

"I've got more pictures there." She pointed to the old-fashioned album on the small coffee table. "Take a look if you like. Might be some in there of…Juliet."

Something about the way she continued to say the name didn't sit right with Kara. "Why do you think she chose Juliet as her name?"

Howell picked up the album and began going through the pages.

"Like I said," Esty stated. "It was always about the drama with her. Don't get me wrong, she's taken good care of me. Not many of my kids are still around, but she and Billy, they're special. Put me in this place when I got sick a few years back. She told me I never had to worry about being alone again and she was right. You look confused, honey." Esty frowned at Kara. "Oh, of course. I didn't answer your question, did I? Juliet was one of her mother's favorite characters. Last time I saw her she was using Camille, from that Greer Garson movie. Have you seen it?"

"No," Kara admitted. She hadn't seen a movie that wasn't animated or featured a superhero in years.

"I have," Howell said as he flipped through pages. "She dies from tuberculosis in the arms of her lover, correct?"

"Man knows his cinema," Esty declared. "Before her mother died, they would read and watch all these tragic stories. *Romeo and Juliet. Camille. King Lear. The Scarlet Letter.*" Disapproval shone in Esty's eyes. "Terrible thing to do to a child—focus them on sadness and death. Those heroines became Giselle's way of coping. She'd change her name and hope to change her situation." Her mouth twisted. "Guess she never stopped pretending if you two are looking for her. A US marshal?" Esty shook her head in dismay. "What's she gone and done now?"

Giselle. Kara's gaze shifted to Howell's. He nodded encouragingly.

"Ah, Giselle's agreed to testify in a trial for me." Kara heard the kettle shut off and went back to the kitchenette. She picked up a mug and held it in the air for Esty to see. "What kind of tea would you like?"

"That lemon ginger. Should be right there in the front jar. Has a bit of a kick to it."

Kara made quick work of the tea, then walked away to let it steep a bit. "I need to find her, Esty. I need to talk to her, but I can't do that without her real name."

"Yeah, figured as much." Esty pursed her lips. "I'm going to tell you something, Kara. It's important and I need you to believe me."

"Okay." Kara sat back down on the sofa.

"You can't put that girl under oath. She won't tell the truth about anything. Not if there's a chance to lie. It's just how she's made, you know? It's not all her fault, mind you. It is unfortunate. In my day, we'd say she'd been born under a bad sign."

Kara returned to the kitchen on shaky legs. Esty wasn't wrong and Kara could feel the case slipping out of her grasp. However, some things were falling into place. Giselle's fractured history. Her pretending and lies. But other questions were presenting themselves. Questions she thought they'd already answered.

She pressed a hand flat against her suddenly nauseated stomach.

"What do you take in your tea, Esty?" She managed to choke out.

"Just one spoon of sugar, please." She pressed a finger to her lips. "Our secret. It's in that jar marked flour. I like hiding things from the nurses," she told an amused Howell. "Although they found all my cigarettes. Don't suppose you…?"

"Neither of us smoke, I'm afraid," Howell said. "Do you have any ideas as to where we might find Giselle, Esty?"

"That girl could always vanish like smoke," Esty said.

"Then maybe you could tell us everything you remember about Giselle from when she came to live with you."

"Pffft!" Esty picked up her tea. "Don't have to tell you. You can read it yourself. File cabinet in my closet. I've

got all the kids' files in there. Legally I was supposed to destroy them after they left my care, but in some instances, those files are the only things that show they ever existed." She shook her head. "I'll take care of them until my dying day. Go on." She shooed Kara into the bedroom. "You've been wanting to snoop. Takes one to know one."

Kara smiled, her heart tipping. "Yes, ma'am."

"Let me see that badge again," Esty ordered Howell as Kara headed for Esty's bedroom. She could smell an overwhelming scent of lavender and...detergent. There were more pictures on the dresser and a beautiful painting over the bed. The small closet had two doors that opened out. Inside Kara found a tall filing cabinet. She pulled the top drawer open.

The files weren't particularly organized as far as Kara could see. By year, maybe? She took a deep breath and dived in, flipping through dozens of names. Giselle, finally! She yanked on the folder and flipped it open, scanning the then twelve-year-old's intake report that placed her in the New York foster care system.

The anticipation of finally getting some answers left her trembling so it was hard to focus on the information in front of her, but she forced herself to skim the key points. Hands trembling, she drew her finger down, processing. Moving on. Processing...

Father, no details listed. Mother, deceased, suicide. Hanged. Found by then twelve year-old daughter Giselle. Her last name?

Kara gasped.

Her heartbeat began to race and she slapped the file shut, hugged it against her chest as she returned to the living room. The instant Howell saw her, he slowly rose to his feet.

"You found something."

She nodded, her entire body shaking. "We need to go. I'm sorry, Esty. I need to take this file with me."

"Just promise to bring it back," Esty ordered. "And next time stay for tea. Do me a favor, Marshal?" She said as Howell joined Kara at the door. "Tell Giselle I love her. That I always loved her, but maybe it's time for her to stop pretending."

Kara's heart broke. She could see the pain in Esty's eyes. Pain that a mother felt when a child disappointed them.

"I'll do that, Esty," Howell said. "I give you my word."

Chapter 10

Despite his impatient curiosity, Howell waited until they were back on the street before he asked any questions. "What is it? What did you find?" He slowed his pace to match hers.

Kara hugged two folders against her chest. "It's..." There was sheer panic in her eyes. Shock. Not unlike what he'd seen in those moments after the car bomb exploded. "It fills in some of the blanks."

Howell scanned the area for someplace to go. He didn't want to be out in the open and he didn't know this part of the city enough to feel comfortable wandering around. He hailed a cab and when one pulled up, he had to steer Kara to the door. Before he climbed into the back seat, he checked the area, looking for anything out of the ordinary or, more importantly, anyone focused on them.

Once inside, he gave the driver the cross street to where the apartment was, then kept his voice low when he spoke to Kara. "Let me see."

He pried the file out of her cold hands and flipped it open.

"Giselle's mother was named Angela Santoro," she said dazedly while Howell skimmed the reports.

"Obviously that means something to you."

"Yes."

Howell turned his head and looked at her, waiting for her to go on.

"Angela Santoro was the primary witness against Sal Alessi in my father's case." Her voice sounded detached, distant. "She died three months after my father did."

"Alessi killed her?" Howell didn't find anything in the file to indicate that. All he saw was the intake report and the various listings of foster parents Giselle had gone through in her six years in the system.

"No. Not directly, anyway. Angela committed suicide," Kara whispered. "Giselle found her." She clenched her fists. "The case collapsed after my father was killed. Whatever deal she'd made for protection for her and her child must have died with him."

Howell closed the folder, stared out the window for a moment at the slow moving traffic. "So, Giselle is what? Reliving her mother's last months by offering to testify against Alessi? That would mean." He shook his head to get the ideas in order. "That would mean she's been planning this for...years."

"And she cast me in a supporting role," Kara said. She turned in her seat, the panic finally dimming behind the determination Howell knew Kara thrived on. "You were right, back in the hotel room. She's always known exactly who I am. Who my father was. She knew I wouldn't, couldn't, say no to this case."

Howell winced. The first rule of a con: know your mark. And he was beginning to see that that is exactly what Kara had been to Juli—Giselle. It was obvious the woman had it in for Alessi. Had she targeted Kara as a co-conspirator?

Or as a way to get revenge on a man she clearly had issues with?

"She put herself into Alessi's employ." Kara sounded as if she were working it all out in her head. "First, at the club, where I bet she knew exactly who Albert Mercer was. She played him until she got what she really wanted, which was a job that would give her access to the Alessi's business records."

"Hold on, Ms. Prosecutor." Howell couldn't stay quiet any longer. "That's a lot of supposition on your part. You can't know any of this is true."

"Yes, I can," she said calmly. Too calmly. "Because it's exactly what I would have done in her place."

It was—Howell realized as the shock wave slid over him—the last thing he ever expected her to say. "No, it's not."

"Yes. It is." She didn't look apologetic or contrite, simply...honest as she kept her voice low. "You said it yourself. You even questioned my motives. Was I out for justice or payback? I didn't see half of what was in front of me. What does that tell you?"

"You told me you knew where to draw the line and I believed you." Mostly.

"But that means I know where the line is." There was a bit of defeat in her gaze now, but also a clarity that made him shiver. "I don't think this has anything to do with bringing Sal Alessi to justice. This is about avenging her mother's death."

The cell Aiden gave him dinged, alerting Howell to a text message from his brother. He glanced at the screen. "They've got security footage from the convenience store across the street from Tidal Cove," he told Kara. "He wants us to take a look at it."

"Why?" Kara asked. "What does it show?"

Howell texted back, asking for more details, but Aiden remained adamant.

"He says we need to see it for ourselves."

"Awesome," Kara muttered. "That doesn't sound ominous at all."

The open laptop on the coffee table was dinging when they opened the door to the apartment.

Despite the warmth, Kara couldn't help but shiver against the morning chill that clung to her.

Had there ever been a time, Kara wondered, when her head hadn't been spinning? Not just with the facts of the Sal Alessi case, but in general. With life stuff and the kids and work and...

She couldn't recall the last time she'd simply tuned out and relaxed. She followed as if in a fog. For the first time in her life, she couldn't help but wish for a moment or a collection of them to turn off her brain and just...live.

From the moment her father had died, whatever switch had activated her had never been turned off. And if it had been that way for her...

Kara hung up her jacket and purse on the hook by the door.

If it had been that way for her, she could barely begin to fathom how Giselle Santoro felt.

To survive what she'd been through—her mother's suicide, her time in foster care—clinging to imaginary personas to help preserve her sanity as she moved through life alone...

Even as Kara's anger simmered, there was sympathy. And more than a little understanding.

She heard Howell exchanging pleasantries with whoever was on the other end of the call. A call she wasn't particularly looking forward to hearing about considering the overload of information she was already struggling to process.

Caffeine would help, she told herself as she set two mugs to brewing. She needed to get her thoughts under control. There was no walking away from this, whatever this was. There was only getting through it and, once she was through it, she wanted it all over and done.

When this was over, she didn't want to give one more thought to Sal Alessi or anyone connected to him for the rest of her life.

"Kara." Howell held out a hand. She looked at it for a good long moment. The second she took it, she knew it was the final step into the unknown. But she also knew that whatever they were walking into, it had to be done together.

She was grateful and relieved not to be alone. This man, this marshal who not so long ago had resented and barely tolerated her, had become something more. Something important. Something special.

Someone she did not want to walk away from anytime soon.

Funny. She blinked at the sudden awareness. That idea didn't make her feel the least bit weak or less than. Howell McKenna's presence in her life made her feel, for want of a better word, invincible.

"Coffee." She pointed to the machine and turned away before he could tell her whether he wanted any. It would give her the needed time to process and accept that the woman she'd pinned all her hopes on to bring Sal Alessi to account for his crimes had been using her for her own purpose.

Chances were that that alone tainted Kara's case to the point of blowing it up as effectively as that bomb had destroyed Howell's SUV. Even if and when they got their hands on the evidence on that laptop, what possible way could Kara get it admitted into court?

Hence, the spinning thoughts.

When she carried the filled mugs over to the sofa, she forced herself to meet Howell's gaze. She expected sympathy, even pity, and a condescending it'll-be-okay expression to be painted on his handsome face. Instead, what she saw was the determination, anger and resolve she was only now beginning to rebuild within herself.

The affection she felt for him in that moment sank through her and warmed her to the point that she couldn't imagine anyone mattering as much to her as he did right now. Was that...was it possible she was finally, truly, authentically falling in love?

The idea had her lowering herself onto the sofa beside him. When she handed him his mug, he took it and slid his other arm around her waist, his hand resting on her hip as he settled closer.

Not alone, she thought and resisted the urge to sink into him. She never wanted to be alone again.

"Okay?" he asked as she turned her attention to the thirty-something man with close-cropped brown hair looking at them through the computer screen. "Kara, this is Jason Sutton."

"Aiden's hacker." Kara was instantly reminded of a

certain shield-wielding superhero her daughter was particularly fascinated with. "Nice to meet you."

"Thanks. You, too."

"Jason's wife, Kyla, is a prosecutor in Sacramento," Howell said. "I bet you two have a lot in common."

"I'd love to meet her sometime," Kara said without thinking. She wondered, for a panicked moment, if Howell would read more into that than she intended.

"We'll have to make that happen," Jason said easily. He gave off very laid-back vibes. Behind him, bookcases were filled with various psychology textbooks and a multitude of framed photographs, including quite a few of toddlers and infants.

The Sacramento contingent of Aiden's company, Kara thought, were a close-knit group to be sure.

"So, the video footage we've got from after the car bomb went off. Let me share the screen so you can watch." Jason clicked a few keys on the keyboard and Howell's laptop filled with a grainy black-and-white image while Jason was relegated to a small box in the top right corner. "Keep your eye on the 2009 Ford parked at the edge of the screen."

Kara followed his finger to where he pointed—almost completely out of sight of the camera. The smoke and impact of the explosion hit, plumes of smoke, dust and fog bursting across the screen. Kara didn't blink. Instead, she watched as an all-too-familiar figure raced out of the side exit of the lodge, a bag hitched over her shoulder.

Giselle ran to the car and climbed inside, clearly of her own volition.

Just before the car drove off, the driver turned and stuck his head out the window to check for traffic.

The silence pressed in on Kara along with the cold realization that their suspicions about Giselle and her motives had just taken a dive off one ginormous cliff. There was no processing the churning in her stomach, in her chest, in her head. There was only what played out on the screen.

"Hang on." Kara leaned over so she could see the action more clearly. "Can you play that last bit back? And freeze it on the driver's face?"

"Sure." Jason tapped quickly on his keyboard.

"You aren't seeing things, Kara," Howell said quietly. It should have irritated her that he read her so easily—that he knew what she was thinking. Instead, it felt as if she didn't have to explain or excuse anything. "It's him."

The bomber? Yeah, she knew. There was no mistaking his face from the beach. But that wasn't what she was looking for.

"Play it one more time, Jason, please," she asked. "From before the explosion."

The video reran, then played once more.

Howell's arm tightened. "Kara, it isn't going—"

"She doesn't flinch." Kara still couldn't fathom Giselle, not from any angle. "She was already on her way outside when the bomb went off. And she didn't flinch when it exploded." She looked to Howell, wanting him to tell her she was wrong; knowing he couldn't. "She knew it was coming because she was in on it." And had even probably planned it.

"Yes."

He said it so simply, so without question, that she sagged a little. "You already considered this," she whispered.

"I assumed she used the explosion as a distraction to

disappear," Howell confirmed. "And to finish whatever actual plan she has against Alessi."

"But how do I—?"

"It was the same kind of bomb," he told her. "The one at the lodge, it was the exact same kind as the one used to kill your father."

Kara shook her head, not understanding. "You're sure?"

"Yes. There was…" He hesitated. "Yes. This was about setting up Alessi for the attempt on your life, Kara. I can't say whether she meant for you to die in that explosion or not, but it put Sal Alessi at the top of the suspect list. This is about making Alessi pay, if not for her mother's death, then for your father's. And…yours."

Kara felt like she was in a daze. She couldn't quite grasp the truth of it, not nearly as easily or completely as Howell obviously had.

"And you didn't think you could tell me any of this before now?" It wasn't an accusation. Exactly.

"I wanted more proof before I suggested the idea to you," Howell admitted. "Between the forensic results on the bomb, the video clearly showing she knew about it, other evidence we found at the scene, along with the information we have about Giselle's past, I'm convinced. It was time."

It hurt, to be thought of in that way. But could she honestly blame him? "You were worried my dedication to the case would make me dismiss your suspicions." There was a distance between heart and voice that she couldn't quite bridge.

"Yes."

She wanted to hate him for that; she wanted to be angry

and offended but she couldn't be, could she? Because he'd done what any prosecutor would have expected. He'd waited for evidence of his theory before springing it on her. Had trust been an issue?

"I had it all in my head," Howell said. "That was enough. Until now. Jason, what's the status on locating the bomber?"

"Detective Hale is on it. BOLO has been issued for both of them. Took it wide up and down the East Coast."

"Don't think they appreciated Giselle and her boyfriend setting off a bomb in their jurisdiction. Did you by chance run the plates?" Howell asked as he picked up his coffee and drank.

Jason scoffed. "I might be out of practice, but I'm still good. Plates won't help you. They were reported stolen forty-eight hours ago from a truck parked in a shopping center. And before you ask, the car they used was found abandoned a little over an hour ago just outside Jersey. It wasn't only wiped clean of prints, Howell. It was torched. There's nothing left."

Great, Kara thought. Another dead end.

"Okay, then let's get into the background check you ran on Juliet or, rather, Giselle," Howell said. "He's got access to more databases than you do," he told Kara.

"Excellent," Kara said. "Whatever it takes."

"Keep in mind, please," Howell glared at the screen. "That it would really suck if, at the end of this conversation, I had to arrest you, Jason. Or my brother," he muttered under his breath.

"Noted and agreed." Jason typed on his keyboard. "Suffice it to say... Yeah. Prints are confirmed as belonging to Juliet Unger."

"Hang on." Kara got up and retrieved the file she'd built on Juli—Giselle. "Read what you've found out, Jason? Background information, please," she called as she headed back to the sofa, sorting through papers.

He did and Kara read furiously, double-checking each bit of data. "It all matches," Kara confirmed. "Schools, degree, employment records. Arrest record. It's all the same. Given how far you've gone back, that means Giselle began building Juliet's persona when she was...what? Eighteen?"

"I think it started earlier than that," Jason said. "Juliet started popping up on social media when she was sixteen. From then on, Giselle gradually disappeared and Juliet took her place."

"Made infiltrating Alessi's businesses easier," Howell said. "This wasn't something she did for you, Kara. You were just the last part of a plan she put in place years ago. First, the strip club, then the construction company. Not even crime families like them are going to do a deep dive like we just did. They don't have the patience."

"Maybe." Still, Kara wondered how long she'd been in Giselle Santoro's sights.

"As far as the DNA on the toothbrush Regan, um, *found*," Jason said. "That's going to take some time." He typed furiously, eyes darting back and forth. "But print results just came in. Running them through my program now. Seeing what hits we get."

"Law enforcement databases, right?" Howell asked.

"Sure." Jason shrugged without looking at them. "We'll start there."

Kara felt a headache pressing against the backs of her eyes.

"Hang in there." Howell drew her closer and pressed his lips against her temple. "We're going to figure this out."

"Everything that's popping up connects to Juliet Unger," Jason told them. "I mean, I can cast a wider net," Jason added, "but it's going to take me some time and I'm going to need to know where to look."

Kara lowered her head into her hand, squeezed her eyes shut. What were they missing? What was the piece that would…

"Foster records." Howell sat up straighter. "Jason, we need to run her prints through the foster databases. And maybe facial rec for our bomber, too. Billy," he said to Kara as she caught on. "Esty said Billy always did Giselle's bidding. How much you want to bet that's our guy?"

"You might want to steer Detective Hale in Billy's foster care direction," Jason suggested. "Keep at least part of this admissible in court."

"Agreed," Kara said. "Also, it could give us some leverage down the road."

"On it." Howell pulled out his cell and began to text the detective in charge of the bombing in Connecticut.

"Most states keep records of the kids in the system at least thirty years after they're discharged from the program," Kara told Jason. "Let's go back that far, Jason."

"Which states are we looking at?" Jason asked. "I'm going to start with Jersey since that's where they abandoned the car."

"Connecticut." Kara said. "Check Connecticut, too."

"It'll be New York." Certainty rang in Howell's voice and he hit send on the text. "Everything about her says New York. It's where her grandmother—foster mother—

is, it's where she worked for Alessi and it's where she lived with Jazz."

Kara wanted him to be wrong, but even as she hoped, she could feel the entirety of the last few weeks' worth of work crumbling around her. Not only that, but the idea she'd been tricked or used...

She could feel her focus shifting away from the man she'd wanted punished all her life and toward a woman who wanted the same thing for not dissimilar reasons.

"No way—" Jason sat back in his chair, eyes wide with surprise. "You were right, Howell. The prints popped up in New York. She went into the system a little over twenty years ago and they belong to..." He squinted at the screen. "There she is. Hello, Giselle. Only..." He frowned, leaned closer. "What is this?"

"What's what?" Kara ignored the exhaustion that was beginning to overtake her.

"There's a strange notation in Giselle's foster records." He cringed. "Close your eyes, Howell. You never saw me do this." He shook his head. "Oh, man, if I end up back in prison for this—"

"Prison?" Kara looked at Howell who shrugged.

"I'll explain later," Howell said, a wry smile on his face. "What? Hang on." Jason's eyes went wide. "So these files were sealed by an order of the court. There was a petition made to the court shortly after Angela Santoro's death. It went through family court and was approved in, wow, four days."

"That's unheard of," Kara said, unable to ignore the sinking feeling. "Family court doesn't work that fast. Ever."

"Unless it's paid to. What kind of petition, Jason?" Howell demanded. "Filed by whom?"

"It was filed on behalf of Sal Alessi and it was a request to..." Jason sat back in his chair. "No wonder she's so messed up. Alessi petitioned the court to have his name removed from Giselle Santoro's birth certificate. Guys—"

"That's it." Kara 's entire body went cold. "That's what we've been missing." She met Howell's intense gaze. "Sal Alessi is Giselle's father."

Chapter 11

Howell had hoped, after putting Kara on a satellite call with her mother and children, that he'd see the spark he'd come to love reignite in her eyes. Instead, he watched her now, standing in front of the window, staring out at the February sky, looking as gloomy as the clouds overhead.

It was a lot for anyone in her position to take. The truth about Giselle Santoro's parentage, the straight line that linked Kara to Giselle via their shared tragedies, the meticulous deception Giselle had run on Kara by pushing buttons only she could understand the impact of, had all manifested into a tension Howell wasn't certain he—or anyone else—could break through. Didn't mean he wasn't going to try.

He got far too close to her before she realized he was there. She turned, looking at him over her shoulder, those ghosts heavy behind her eyes.

"Here." He held out the glass containing two fingers of the scotch he'd found in the cabinet over the fridge. "Drink. It's a McKenna family cure-all."

That she didn't hesitate and downed the drink in two large gulps without choking was either the most impressive thing he'd ever witnessed or the sexiest.

Again, he thought. Both could be true.

She set the glass down on the coffee table with a thunk. Only then did he see the gauzy bag she held in her hand. It took him a minute to remember where he'd seen it before.

"Giselle gave you that back in the hotel room."

"Yep." She wiggled the bracelet free, dropped it into her palm. "Should have been my first big sign something was off."

"A beaded bracelet?" Howell set his own glass down beside hers and took it. "Why?" He turned the bag over and over again, looking for something he clearly didn't understand. "Is it some kind of code? The colors? The pattern?"

"It says Mia," Kara said flatly and there, finally, was the fire he longed to see catch once more.

"Well, sure." He still didn't understand. "That is her name."

"I never told her my daughter's name." Kara's smile was tight and cool and barely controlled. "I never tell anyone because she doesn't belong anywhere in that world. Well, I guess I told you, didn't I?" She threw both hands up in the air in frustration. "Always the exception, aren't you? That...that *woman*." Her voice dropped low, her tone full of anger as she clenched the bracelet. "That woman handed me a red flag I should have seen right from the start. She knew precisely what she was doing and why she was doing it and it didn't stop her. It's bad enough she used me, but she tried to use my kid. My kid, Howell."

The pained expression on her face undid him. He stepped forward, wrapped his arms around her tightly and never wanted to let her go. She burrowed into him. Sobs of frustration left her trembling. Howell willed her pain to go away, to take it on himself, but there was nothing to be done other than what he'd already chosen to do.

"I have rage," she whispered. "So much rage. I don't know what to do with it. I don't want it and yet it just… sits there." Her breath emerged on another sob. "This is why you work alone, isn't it? If you don't let anyone in, if you don't trust, then you can't feel…this."

"The flip side is the risk that I'll stop feeling anything at all," he admitted as he eased his hold and set her back so he could look at her. He held her face in his hands and stroked his thumbs down the sides of her cheeks that contained no trace of the tears he expected to find.

Her hands gently clasped his wrists, holding him in place as she stared up at him. Her dark eyes shimmered with the only thing he ever wanted to see in their depths: hope. And promise.

He dipped his head and waited, wanting her to make the next move, if there was one. Slowly, she rose up on her toes and closed the distance between them. She captured his mouth with such heat and possession that he knew he'd never forget this moment. Not for the rest of his life. His body reacted instantly, welcoming her nearness and setting him ablaze from the inside out, top to bottom.

She dived in, pressed his mouth open with hers, demanding, invading, devouring him to the point he lost his breath. The taste of her had intensified from this morning. It wasn't a hesitancy this time, or a shyness or timidity, but a full-on desire she seemed to be not only surrendering to but embracing.

She moved closer, pressed her body so completely against his that he went hard immediately. Her touch, her passion, sent him off the charts as he continued to let her take what she needed, however far she wanted to go with it.

The promise of what might happen flooded his senses, but he still held on to reality by the barest thread. Her arms encircled his neck, keeping him against her, and she shifted herself in a way that drove any thought other than her straight out of his head.

He had to breathe, to hold on to whatever trace of reason he still had and took his mouth from hers.

The whimper she offered in response nearly had him delving back into her. Her breathing was as ragged and pent-up as his and he pressed his forehead to hers. It was agony to say the words, but he needed her to believe he had no expectations for what might come after this stolen moment.

"This doesn't have to mean anything," he murmured in a tone he didn't recognize.

Her eyes flashed. "It already does."

"I just meant." He almost lost control right then and there. "If you need this—"

"I do." Her hands fisted in his hair and brought his head back toward hers as she rose up on her toes. The scent of her—wildflowers and spice—sank into his senses and threatened to undo him once and for all. "I do need this. I need you." She kissed him again and nearly sent him toppling over the brink. "And for the record." Another kiss. A deeper kiss. A longer, soul-scorching kiss that came close to ending him. "I don't think once is going to be nearly enough." She sank down, just enough to put an inch between their swollen lips. "If that's okay with you?"

It was a challenge he had no trouble accepting.

He caught her mouth once more, so focused on the way

her tongue engaged with his that he almost didn't notice the frantic moving of her fingers as she grabbed at the hem of his shirt. He dipped slightly, slipped an arm securely around her waist and turned her from the window, urging her toward the bedroom.

She clearly had other ideas and tugged, enticed and tempted him every which way as they moved through the apartment, until he'd pressed her against the wall beside the front door. He braced his hands on either side of her, struggling for breath, staring into the endless depths of her brown eyes.

Those hands of hers were magic as they yanked up his shirt—pulled it free from his pants—before drawing it over his head. She sucked in a ragged breath as her palms flattened against his bare chest and moved restlessly over every inch of him, the heat of her touch seared every thought from his mind. Except for one.

The thought of her.

The backs of her fingers brushed his waist as she slipped her hand beneath the waistband of his jeans. He fused his mouth to hers, catching her groan in his mouth.

"If you keep that up," he whispered. "We're going to end up doing this on the floor."

She smiled, a seductive gleam glittering in her eyes. "Nothing wrong with that."

Oh, but there was. Intense he could take, but he wanted her comfortable. More importantly he wanted her writhing beneath him on a bed that she could sink her hands into.

She unbuttoned his jeans before he realized it, slid the zipper down and slipped her hand inside.

"Commando," she breathed and dropped her head back. "Just when I didn't think you could get any sexier."

When she touched him, he went harder than he'd ever gone in his life.

"Floor?" she teased.

He couldn't form words and instead scooped her into his arms. He carried her into the bedroom, set her down amidst the blankets she'd crawled out of this morning. She immediately shifted to her knees, reaching for him again, but he held up a hand and backed out of the room.

"You have got to be kidding me!" she called out as he ducked into the bathroom. Less than a minute later he was back with the box of condoms he'd found in the vanity drawer. She covered her mouth with her hand, amusement filling her eyes. "Your brother really does think of everything."

"Now is not the time to talk about my brother. And you are far too overdressed." He stepped forward and captured the hem of her sweater in both hands. In one fluid move, he lifted the top over her head and tossed it aside. "Front clasp." He released her bra with a quick flick of his fingers. "Practical. Completely unsurprising."

"I'll work on surprising you in other ways then."

He pushed the straps down her arms and sent the bra in the same general direction as her sweater. Before he kissed her again—and he could not wait to kiss her again—he took a moment to glance down at her rosy, peaked nipples that begged for his attention.

"You keep looking at me like that and this will be over before we even get started." Her breathy promise had him reaching out for her. A gentle caress that soon had her repeating his name and swaying toward him. "Please, Howell. Please."

Her hands skimmed up his bare arms, her short nails

scraping to the point that she gave him chills. "Please what?" he asked as the warm air of the apartment hit his skin and she returned her attention to his jeans.

"Please stop being so damned considerate." She tugged down the denim and drew him forward. Seconds later, they were lying in a heap that neither was willing to leave.

It was a dance of tangled limbs and laughter, zippers and fabric falling away beneath determined hands and desperate bodies longing for release.

When she lay there, beneath him, wearing only a pair of thin cotton panties, he held her hips in his hands and ducked his head. His tongue dipped into her navel and she drove her fingers into his hair, gasping in a way that made him feel more alive than he could ever remember feeling before. Lower, lower, he trailed his tongue to where the remaining fabric separated them.

With his fingertips he slipped her panties down. When he uncovered that part of her, he instantly replaced the soft material with his mouth.

She cried out the instant his lips touched her. He didn't stop kissing and laving as she orgasmed and thrashed beneath him. The charge he felt was like a bolt of electricity he couldn't control and didn't want to. Her moans of pleasure spurred him on as he teased and aroused the gentle folds.

"No fair," she whispered. She tried to catch her breath. "We should have done that together."

"Don't worry." He pressed his lips against her thigh and felt her tremble again. "We will."

Her arm flailed out and it wasn't until she smacked him in the head with the condom box that he realized what she was doing. They laughed and he rose up.

Together they ripped the box open. Packages of condoms went flying, but he trapped one before it almost fell off the bed.

"No." She put her hand over his and took the foil square from him. "Let me."

Never in his life did he think the most excruciating experience he'd ever have would be to watch Kara Gallagher slowly, patiently, tear open that piece of foil and pluck out the condom. She shifted, presumably for a better angle, and wrapped her hand around his steely length. Again, her touch had him struggling for control, but he refused to let go. Not yet. Not until he was inside her.

"Proceed with caution," he said through gritted teeth.

The light in her eyes shifted to that of a temptress. The efficiency with which she covered him both astonished and impressed, but it was when she lay back on the bed and opened herself to him that he realized he'd been fooling himself into thinking there would be any walking away from her.

She was, he knew in that moment, the only woman he would ever feel this way about for the rest of his life.

She was, he accepted as he lowered himself and pressed into her, the woman who had captured him—heart and soul.

"Slower," she whispered and arched her back, the tips of her breasts brushing against his chest as he moved over her completely. Her breathing went rough as she spread herself wider, her hand skimming against his length as he eased himself in. "I want to feel every inch of you." She lifted her mouth to his just as he entered her.

Whatever plans he'd had to extend their pleasure evaporated as soon as she wrapped her legs around him. She lifted her hips, rotating slowly at first as he began to thrust. Mere seconds passed and her fingers were clawing at his back, the pressure building. Pressure that he needed to release, although he held on to it, reveled in it, for as long as he could.

The happy, satisfied sighs she offered sounded like music to him. His hands swept into her soft hair as he ground his mouth against hers. He could feel her pulse hammering along with his, could feel her body begin to tense as she peaked. When she tightened around him and cocooned him in her arms, he finally gave in and the release they shared sent them both into a rapture reserved only for those who give themselves over completely to the other person.

It was, ungentlemanly, Howell thought, a few minutes later, to remain splayed over a woman after such pleasure. He felt her fingers entwined in his hair, her touch so gentle against his skin, that, near as he could tell, he was as close to a heavenly moment as he could have ever imagined.

"I'm curious," she murmured. He lifted his head. "No. Don't move. Not yet." She tightened her legs around him and stroked a finger down the bridge of his nose. "Was that you controlled or uncontrolled?"

He smiled, trying not to laugh, but how could he not when she made him so happy. "A little bit in between."

"Huh." She tilted her head to the side, trailed fingers over his shoulders to his chest. Her gentle touch was like silk to the point that he would either purr or hiss next. He wasn't sure which. She pressed her lips to his and when he opened his mouth to her, she pushed him over and onto his back.

He would have protested, but she reached over for a

new condom, which meant he was entirely focused on something else before she straddled him. Her soft, sensual beauty partnered with the determined look of desire on her face quickly robbed him of any coherent thought.

"I think I'll take control this time," she said as he held on to her hips. "That okay with you?" She began to rock, trance-like, in a rhythm that had him surrendering completely.

"More than okay," he managed to say and she upped the tempo. "I'm totally and utterly in your hands."

"Two things New York does better than anyone else." Kara stabbed chopsticks into the container of vegetable chow mein. "Chinese food and delivery." Sitting cross-legged on the bed beside Howell may be her favorite new activity in the universe. Well. Second favorite. She had her next bite almost to her mouth when she caught Howell looking at her. "What?" How was it, even after everything they'd just shared, the man could make her blush with a glance. Not that she wasn't looking at him in the same ravenous way, although sustenance was currently taking priority. "What's wrong?" She swiped a finger under her lips in case she had food stuck on her face.

His smile was easy, almost teasing, and incredibly sexy. Almost as sexy as the solitary sheet resting low on his torso. "Just thinking that that shirt never looks this good on me."

She glanced down at his T-shirt, which she'd grabbed off the floor when she'd gone to retrieve their phones so they could order dinner. They were on countdown mode before heading out to meet with Jazz and—hopefully—get their hands on Giselle's laptop.

Kara grinned. "Didn't think it was appropriate to collect our dinner naked." The fact they'd blown straight through the afternoon wrapped in each others' arms had been a bit...surprising. And exhilarating.

"It's New York," Howell said as he popped open another take-out container. "Delivery people have seen it all. Oh, good. Kung pao. You okay? With...this?"

"Yeah." She smiled into her food, determined to get over any timidity that might remain. "Sure, I'm okay with this. With us. You?" Part of her worried what would happen if she got the answer she didn't want to hear. "I imagine the last place you ever imagined us ending up after that day in court last year was here."

"You'd think." He leaned over, dipped his chopsticks into her container and pinned his gaze to hers. "Or we admit it was inevitable. We fit well together. In more ways than one."

She nodded, tucked her hair behind her ear. "Yes, we do."

Howell chewed and swallowed. Honking from the street below interrupted what he was about to say next. A beat passed before he spoke again. "To be honest, it's kind of hard to picture you ever fitting well with your ex."

Kara stuck her chopsticks in her mouth and simply stared at him. "He is what he is." She shrugged. "And what he was for me was a lesson well learned." She inclined her head to look at him from a different perspective. "I know what—and who—I want now."

"I appreciate that." He pried open the container of pot stickers and plucked up a dumpling.

"I've spent too much time resenting and despising him, Howell." And wishing he could change when it was clear

Garrett could not. "Right now, I'm happier than I've been in a very long time and I'm going to enjoy every second of it." She leaned forward just as he did and pressed a kiss against his lips. "Garrett is as good as he's ever going to be, Howell. I'm ready to move on."

"You mean move on with me, right?" Howell's feigned seriousness only made her laugh again.

"I meant what I said earlier, despite my foggy brain," she added. "This means something to me." It must. She hadn't been with anyone since her divorce. "I think... I think I'd really like to see where we can go from here." Seeing as she was already half in love with him, what other direction was she going to go? "I like who I am when I'm with you, Howell. More importantly, I like you." More than liked. She...she ducked her head in case he saw the truth. "That's a good way to start a relationship, don't you think?" How she wished she'd thought this out more before saying anything.

"Friendship is the best way to start something. That lasts," he agreed. "Nice to know we're on the same page. Now." He grabbed the chow mein out of her distracted hand. "My turn."

Never in her life had she been with someone who made her smile as much as Howell McKenna. Falling into bed with him may very well have pushed her over the boundaries of what she'd always wanted, always hoped, she could be. Happy.

A cell phone rang.

"Yours or mine?" she asked automatically, then rolled her eyes at his frown. "Right. Mine's on lockdown. I forgot. You find it?" They shifted around the food containers and wrinkled sheets.

"Got it." He told her. "McKenna."

Kara distracted herself by poking through the two other containers, one that had way too many vegetables in it for her liking and the other—

"Detectives are on scene?"

Howell's tone had her head snapping up. "What?"

He frowned. "Yeah, no I appreciate the call." He checked his watch. "We'll be there shortly. Thanks." Quitting the call, he said, "We need to go. Now."

"What?" Kara repeated as he kicked out of bed and leaned down for his jeans.

"That was the NYPD calling about Jazz."

"Giselle's friend from the club. What about her?" Even as she asked she could feel the dread circling the room like a specter. "Howell? Is she okay?"

"No." Howell pulled up his pants. "She's dead."

She wasn't your witness.

It didn't matter how many times Howell reminded himself of that fact, it didn't help lessen the guilt. He took his charges seriously and despite Jazz being only tangentially related to the case, it still put her under his purview. Frustration and failure were part of the job. But even after all these years, they weren't any easier to process. Or accept.

"This isn't your fault," Kara said as they exited the cab in front of the cordoned off apartment building about six blocks south of Velvet and Vice.

"Now is not the time to be reading my mind." He slid a loose arm around her waist, wanting—no, *needing*—to remind himself she was safe. He pulled out his ID and badge as they approached the front door. Yellow crime scene tape kept onlookers sequestered a good ten feet on either side of the building's entrance. After identifying himself and mentioning the officer's name who had called, they made their way inside and up to the fourth floor. "You doing okay?" Maybe if he could concentrate on Kara for a little while he could regain his focus.

"I should be asking you that question." She covered his hand with hers, gave it a quick squeeze before they stepped away from one another. "You aren't responsible for this, Howell."

"We'll soon see, won't we?" he muttered. There was no doubt about which direction to walk upon leaving the elevator. The hallway was lined with uniformed officers and, three doors to the left, a woman in a dark suit with an old-fashioned leather-bound flip notebook walked out of the apartment of record for Jasmine Portola. "Detective Fuller? I'm US Marshal Howell McKenna. Appreciate the call."

"Sorry it had to be made. Detective Macy Fuller." She offered her hand to Kara. "And you are…?"

"Kara Gallagher from the federal prosecutor's office in Connecticut." Kara's all-business tone helped shift Howell back to professional mode. "Jazz was a potential witness in a case I'm currently building against Sal Alessi. Marshal McKenna is working with me."

It took all the effort Howell had not to react. Would have been nice if she'd given him some warning before she went public with the case. She may as well be declaring open war against the Alessis. The smell of cordite permeated the air along with that strong, all-too-familiar stench of metal that always accompanied large amounts of blood.

"Sal Alessi?" Detective Fuller let out a low whistle.

Her blond hair was streaked with silver and pulled away from her face in a loose knot. "Well, I guess that helps explain several things. Come on in." She inclined her head for them to follow. "Victim was shot point blank with a Glock 17. Through and through. Pulling the slug out of the wood now." She gestured to the spot where the polished bookcase had splintered.

Jazz was on her back in the middle of her living room floor. Blood spatters coated the bookcases, books and furniture from where the bullet had exited her back. Her head was turned, her right arm stretched out and a finger pointed toward the window.

The area rug beneath her was soaked with blood.

"No sign of a break-in," Detective Fuller said. "It's looking like whoever did this was let in."

"Or they had a key," Howell said, recalling what Jazz had said about Giselle simply turning up out of the blue and letting herself into the apartment.

"No roommate on record according to the building manager," Detective Fuller said. "Owner is listed as Rafael Alessi. He's also registered as the owner of this…" She turned and accepted a plastic evidence bag containing a gun from a uniform. "Glock nineteen. Recently fired. Serial numbers clear as day. Always nice when they don't clean up after themselves. Never known an Alessi to be this careless."

"Motive?" Kara asked.

"Definitely personal. Place isn't ransacked, so they got what they came for." She motioned to Jazz's body. "Only person I'm looking at is Rafael Alessi."

Probably, Howell thought, because someone wanted it that way. "Rafael will have an alibi." Howell wandered the room, taking in the stylish and elegant decor that spoke of lots of money, which Jazz didn't have. High-end furnishings. Leather sofa, bronze floor lamps. A faux brick fireplace that harkened back to the year the building had been constructed. Floor-to-ceiling bookcases filled with pristine collectible books that had clearly never been read. Place looked more like a college professor lived here than a mobster's girlfriend. "Wouldn't hurt to bring him in for questioning, though."

"Agreed," Detective Fuller said. "I'm heading over to Velvet and Vice as soon as we're done here." She paused. "Anything you two can tell me about your case?"

"Only that Jazz was in possession of evidence we need to locate as soon as possible," Kara said.

"It was supposed to be here," Howell added. "We'd made arrangements for me to pick it up later this afternoon. Mind if we take a look around the rest of the place?"

"Knock yourself out," Detective Fuller said. "Just don't get in the way of my guys. If you find anything—"

"We'll let you know," Kara assured her.

"When you run prints on the weapon," Howell said, "include those of a Billy Atherton. He's the primary suspect in that bombing at the Tidal Cove Lodge in Connecticut. Detective Hale is running that investigation."

"Good to know." Detective Fuller made some notes. "Appreciate the info. Happy searching."

Howell drew Kara out of the living room and into the galley-style kitchen. "You know telling her about the Alessis is going to put the case on full blast, don't you?"

"Yes." She folded her arms over her chest and had the same determined expression on her face as Mia had the other day when she'd been looking at Howell's badge.

"It's dawned on me that I've been playing by Giselle's rules from the start. She set me up, Howell, for whatever twisted game of revenge she's got going. I don't like being a tool or a pawn, and right now, I'm feeling like both. I told her we had to keep this quiet for fear of alerting the Alessis. She's banking on me sticking to that plan, which means I need to stop doing whatever she expects of me."

"So you're turning yourself into bait instead?"

"I'm only bait if someone takes it." It was clear she'd given this a lot of thought, although when that might have happened he couldn't fathom considering how they'd spent a good portion of the afternoon. "Unpredictability is the way we beat her. I'm done being used. That ends," she declared. "It ends now."

Howell had to give her credit. She was convincing. If not a little terrifying. "I retain the right to pull you back if you go too far."

She shrugged and smirked. "At this point, it's your primary job. Let's get to work."

Chapter 12

"There's nothing here." Kara stood with her back to the now covered body. Only the dead woman's finger stuck out from beneath the sheet as the lab techs finished up processing the scene.

"Sure doesn't seem to be," Howell confirmed as he yanked off the gloves he'd gotten from one of the techs. "At least not in the rooms I checked. No extra fake air vents—"

"Fake air vents?" Kara frowned at him over her shoulder.

"Makes for a good hiding place," Howell told her. "More than three in a large room tends to be a sign. This one only has two." He pointed to each one.

She wandered to the window and touched her own gloved hand to the antique radiator. She crouched, then ran her fingers over the polished metal.

"What are you looking for?" Howell asked as he examined the books on the shelves.

"I saw this in a TV show once. Wondering if anyone turned this into a hiding place." But no, there weren't any hinges or loose fittings.

"Not big enough for a laptop," Howell reminded her.

"Right." She stood up so fast she sent the floor lamp

crashing to the ground. The metal shade clanged against the floor when it bounced near Jazz's body. "Oh, geez." She immediately reached for the lamp, then stopped. Stepping back, she craned her neck and looked down. "Howell?"

"Yeah?"

"Is she...pointing at something?" It was a reach for sure.

Howell came over, followed the line from Jazz's protruding finger across the floor to the wall. She crouched beside him as he moved his hands over the wood paneling on the wall and floor.

"I don't... Hang on." He pivoted, pressed a finger into a notch in the wall.

Click.

A floorboard popped up where the lamp had stood.

Kara stood up, grabbed the lamp and turned it. Howell pulled up the slat of wood. She shined the light into the hole.

"Looks like a laptop to me." Howell grinned up at her. "Good catch, Ms. Prosecutor."

"Jazz is the one who did it," she whispered. "What do we do now?"

Across the room, where Kara had left her bag by the door, her cell phone rang.

"Go ahead," Howell encouraged her as he waved to one of the officers. "I've got this."

She retrieved her phone and answered it without looking at the screen.

"You found it."

Kara spun around, frantic eyes landing on Howell. "Giselle."

Howell motioned for the tech person to take some photos before he came to her side. Kara immediately tapped open an app and began to record the conversation.

"I wondered if you'd ever look beyond your own desire for revenge to go deeper into my background." Giselle's voice was monotone and matter-of-fact. "I made a bet with myself, you know. That you'd be so focused on *him*, so determined to make a case against Sal, that you wouldn't pay much attention to me. Guess I lost."

"By *him*, you mean your father." Only now were things finally making sense to Kara. "The father who denied you all those years ago. The father you planned to frame for my murder."

"Do you know what it's like to be erased, Kara?"

The question came across as practiced, as if Giselle had been waiting to be able to utter the words. The fact she didn't deny Kara's accusation about the car bomb sat heavy on Kara's heart. *Negligible.* The word rang loudly in her ears.

"Do you have any idea what it's like for your presence, your very existence, to be erased. On purpose?"

"I don't, no."

"Of course not. Because after your father was killed, you still had your mother. You weren't left alone. You weren't denied."

"No," Kara said quietly and reached for Howell's hand. "I wasn't. Was I supposed to die, Giselle? Was that the plan? Then why the pretense with your so-called evidence?"

"I didn't want to kill you," Giselle said with exaggerated patience. "I was hedging my bets. Alive or dead you could put him in prison. Either you got a guilty verdict by prosecuting him with the evidence I gave you or I framed him for your murder."

"As simple as that." She'd said it so calmly, so rationally Kara almost, *almost*, understood.

"Even now," Giselle scoffed. "You're standing there with that do-gooder marshal and my evidence. The evidence I left for you."

"Evidence I can't use against him, Giselle. Not now. You've tainted it." It and everything else Giselle had given her would be deemed inadmissible. Against Sal Alessi, at least.

But against Giselle? Hope sprung back to life inside of Kara.

"I gifted you everything you've ever wanted," Giselle said. "And you couldn't see it through. Now you've stopped looking at him and you've started hunting me. After everything I've done for you. For us! I want him to pay for what he's done as much as you do. Why can't you see that?"

Kara heard the echo of a siren screaming down the street in the background of Giselle's cell.

Kara stiffened, her gaze immediately landing on the pair of windows on the other side of the room. She tugged her hand free, walked around the sofa and looked out across the street, into windows and down at the shadowed, late-afternoon sidewalks.

"Oh, Kara. You're so close," Giselle's tone turned simpering. "Look up."

Kara felt Howell move in behind her as she lifted her chin.

There, standing at the ledge on top of the building, a solitary figure with blond hair blowing in the icy winter wind.

She covered the phone with her hand. "She's on the roof," she whispered. "Across the street."

Howell didn't say a word as he backed up, then turned and raced out of the apartment.

"I'll be gone before he gets here," Giselle said. "I'd say you've been useful, Kara, but you've disappointed me. Even more so than Jazz. I was wrong. I assumed we wanted the same thing."

"We probably do," Kara agreed. "I'm just not willing to break the law to do it." The siren roared louder. "I'm done, Giselle. There isn't going to be a case against Sal." The admission of it stung more than she expected. More than she wanted it to.

"Yes," Giselle scoffed. "I've comprehended that much. In which case, I'm going to need the laptop back."

Kara looked over her shoulder to where Jazz lay dead. "I take it she refused to give it to you." Kara strode off, racing down the stairs to catch up with Howell. Farther below, in the lobby, she could hear him yelling for backup. "Whatever Jazz chose to do or not, she didn't deserve to die for it."

"She betrayed me," Giselle snapped. "She was supposed to be my friend but all she wanted was money. She told me since the police were involved, she figured she'd earn a bigger commission. Said she was done until I paid her off. So I did. With Rafael's gun. I gave her grief when he gave that to her a few years ago. I warned her it would only get her hurt."

Kara sped down the stairs, amazed she was doing so well in the sky-high booted heels she wore. "You knew where she kept the weapon."

"Using my own half brother's gun to set him up for

murder was pretty inspired, I have to say. I did that on impulse, mind you. I can think pretty well on my feet."

Kara made it to the last set of stairs. Her legs were burning, but she could feel the cold air blasting from the street. "What is it you want, Giselle?"

"I want what I've always wanted. What my mother wanted." Giselle's voice started to cut in and out. Footsteps echoed on the other end of the call. She was on the move. "I want to be seen. I want to be accepted. I want my birthright. And I'll get it. With your help," she said on a laugh, the distinctive sound of a metal stairway releasing and crashing to the ground blasting through the call. "I want that laptop back and you're going to give it to me."

"Or what? You're a wanted suspect, Giselle. There's nothing you can do—"

"How safe are you going to feel, Kara, if you have something I will do anything, including killing my so-called friend, to retrieve?" She paused long enough for a chill to race down Kara's spine. "How safe do you think your mother and Mia and Jonah will be?"

Kara skidded to a halt on the sidewalk, her knees going weak.

"You're going to bring me the laptop, Kara. I'll let you know where. And when."

The call went dead.

Kare could see a pair of uniformed officers hurrying toward the apartment building across the street. She caught sight of Howell already exiting the front doors empty handed.

"Alley!" Kara yelled as she dodged cars, holding out her hands in an almost futile attempt for clear passage. "Howell, she's on the fire escape in the alley!"

Howell shifted directions, but Kara was already sprinting for the side of the building, her adrenaline pumping. There! She could see the fire escape clearly now and the figure quickly descending to the final ladder. But nothing happened. Something metal banged and banged again, and it took Kara a moment to realize the final ladder hadn't released.

Giselle threw herself over the railing, then dropped to the ground, rolling twice before she got back to her feet. She dived into the car parked at the rear of the alley. Kara had assumed it was empty.

The engine rumbled to life.

Kara kept running, only to stop abruptly and grab hold of a large green garbage dumpster on wheels. She tried to push it into the path of the car, but it was too heavy.

Tires screeched. Headlights flashed. Kara dropped her phone and pushed harder as the car accelerated and headed right for her.

Howell grabbed her from behind and spun her out of the way as the car crashed into the dumpster, sending it careening into the wall.

For the second time in as many days, Kara found herself thrown to the ground—broken concrete beneath her—with Howell on top, shielding her. The impact had again driven the air from her lungs.

Howell released her immediately, leaped to his feet and pivoted with his weapon drawn. He fired once and shattered the back window. The car screeched away, sirens rising and giving immediate chase.

She got to her feet.

"What were you thinking?" He spun on her so fast he made her dizzy. "*This* isn't part of your job!" He bent down and picked up her cell that had somehow, miraculously, survived the drop.

"I was keeping her distracted," Kara defended herself. "I thought." Only now was she able to catch her breath. "Did you get a plate?"

"I got the plate. And it won't do us any good. With the back window blown out they'll ditch the car right away."

"Good." Kara braced her hands on her thighs and looked up at him. "Let's see how she does with her plan now."

"What plan do you have exactly?" Howell asked Kara as they stood in the observation room at NYPD's homicide division. The coffee they each sipped could have doubled as toxic sludge and could, Howell surmised, be used as a nasty interrogation device. One sip of this crap would get anyone talking. Howell looked through the one-way glass to the man and woman sitting on one side of the scarred metal table, Rafael and Elena Alessi.

He'd almost, almost, gotten the white-hot memory of seeing that car barreling toward Kara out of his head. Chances were it would be a while before it was completely purged. Once again, he'd come within a thread's thickness of losing her. Two times was enough.

There would not be a third.

They'd been given a surprising amount of grace and courtesy. No doubt facilitated by Kara's boss as well as Howell's—he'd called in the last of his favors with Deputy Director Coleson. He knew his superior was willing to go to bat for him but asking him to buy into whatever plan Kara had was asking a bit too much.

Or so Howell assumed. It wasn't as if she'd filled him in on everything yet.

"Did you listen to my conversation with Giselle?" Kara asked him in that calm, controlled voice he recognized from when she'd questioned him in court. "Did you hear what she said?"

"I heard the words, and I heard her threaten your family, but I'm betting you heard something more."

"She thinks we're the same," Kara murmured as if surprised he hadn't yet seen the connection. "She gifted me with evidence I could use to avenge my father's murder while she went after what she wanted."

"She wants to take her rightful place in the Alessi family," Howell said. "Not to put too fine a point on it, but I don't see that as being the same."

"The enemy of my enemy is my friend." Kara turned calm eyes on him. "She's not done using me yet and even if she was, I still need her."

He should have known the bluster about her giving up the case against Alessi was a ruse.

"The encryption code for the laptop." So far the only thing they knew about the laptop was that it had a failsafe with a massive encryption-coded password that could only be accessed via a USB drive, which was nowhere to be found. "You think she has it."

"Of course she has it. It's her safety net." She took another drink of coffee and winced. "Wow, this is terrible." She set the cup down. "I was wrong earlier when I said I was done letting her use me. I think we're about to go another round."

Howell's stomach dropped straight to the tips of his toes. "You aren't serious."

"She threatened my family." It was, Howell thought, the first time he heard ice in her voice. "You already know there isn't any other way to play this, Howell. I'm part of it. She made me a part of this the second she learned about what happened to my father. I know what it's like to live in that space, to see only the revenge you need, that you think is going make you whole again."

"I thought you said you wanted justice, not revenge," Howell reminded her.

She faced him, a small, understanding smile curving her lips. "It should worry me how you saw through me on that front. It was how I felt. But it's not anymore. Sal Alessi isn't my main target right now. It's Giselle I want. For killing Jazz. For threatening my kids. For setting all this into motion. For not caring who else got hurt. And because if we get her to cooperate, I can still use her testimony against Sal." Her smile widened but didn't come close to reaching her eyes. "Are you in?"

Like he was going to walk away from her, now or ever. "Did you have any doubt?"

"No." She stepped closer to him, rested a hand on his chest and lifted her lips to his. "I have absolutely no doubts where you're concerned. Trust me, okay?" Her gaze lingered on his mouth. "Just a little bit longer."

He rested a hand on her hip and together they turned when the door opened.

Detective Hale from Connecticut and Detective Fuller from New York walked in together, their expressions pinched but resigned.

"We've been instructed to give you first crack at Rafael Alessi," Detective Fuller stated. "But we'd like to go in with you if you don't mind."

"That's fine," Kara said. "I need Howell out here. We'll have to have Aiden on this," she told him when he frowned at her. "Details to come. Wish me luck."

He caught her hand in his for a brief moment and squeezed. "Always."

"Hello, Elena." Kara followed Detective Fuller into the interview room. She carried only one file folder, which she kept a tight grip on. Behind her, Detective Hale slid into the room silently and took up a position by the door. "Nice to see you again."

"Kara." Elena rose to her full five-foot-seven height and extended her hand. As usual she was dressed impeccably in a tailored black skirt and sharp turquoise blouse. The blazer she wore was nipped in at the sides, while her long dark hair with the razor-sharp cut hung down her back. "It's been a while. Isn't this out of your jurisdiction?"

"Remains to be seen," Kara admitted. "Please." She motioned to Elena's chair. "Sit. We have some things to discuss."

Elena placed a hand on her brother's arm. "My client won't be speaking."

"Of course." Kara nodded. "Understandable. I'm so sorry for your loss, Rafael." Like his sister, Rafael Alessi was dark-haired and keen-eyed and in as full fashion-forward mode as a man with his means and wealth could afford. But it was his eyes—red-rimmed, swollen and shocked—that seeped into her and for a moment, she felt more than a kick of sympathy. "I've been told Jazz was a lovely young woman. I know how difficult it is to lose someone you love."

"I didn't kill her."

"Rafael." Elena's one word of warning had Rafael sinking down in his chair. As if grief were going to swallow him whole, Kara thought. "My client has an alibi for the time of Jazz's death." She reached into the briefcase at her feet and pulled out a solitary piece of paper. "This is a list of everyone who can attest to his whereabouts at the time in question." She pushed the paper across the table. "We're here to be cooperative and I hope that is understood moving forward."

"His prints were on the murder weapon," Detective Fuller stated.

"I gave it—" Rafael choked.

Elena's hand tightened on Rafael's arm, this time digging in her talon-like nails. "The gun was a gift from my client to a woman he cared about. For her protection. And he's agreed to a paraffin test to confirm he hasn't shot a weapon in a number of weeks. Is there anything else?"

"Yes, actually." Detective Hale stepped forward and opened his own file folder. "This is a communications circuit. Do you recognize what this is for, Mr. Alessi?"

"Uh." Rafael glanced at his sister, who gave an almost dismissive shrug of her shoulder. "Yes. We use circuits like that in demolition at Briarwood. They set off explosives."

"This particular circuit was found in the rubble of a car bomb that exploded at the Tidal Cove Lodge in Connecticut recently," Kara said. "Its serial number matches a batch that was delivered to Briarwood construction more than seven months ago."

"I don't see how—" Elena began.

Kara cut her off with a sharp wave of her hand. "Who signs for supplies at Briarwood Construction, Rafael?"

"Um." He looked scattered for a moment. "Albert Mercer most of the time. He's the one usually in the office. Either him or one of his assistants. Oh, wait. That woman who was stealing from us. Julie something. Juliet Unger!" He sat up, suddenly firm in his convictions. "She took over approving deliveries to take on more responsibilities."

"Would you have records of those signatures?" Kara asked.

"We can certainly get them to you," Elena confirmed. "Is that all?"

"No." Kara crossed her legs and opened her file. "Does the name Angela Santoro mean anything to you?"

"No," Rafael said immediately, but recognition flashed in Elena's lips tightened into a thin line.

"I believe Angela Santoro has been deceased for quite some time," the younger Alessi sibling stated. "And I don't know what she would have to do with anything currently."

"You'd think that," Kara said with a nod and ticked off the box of Elena being aware of her father's history with Angela. "And I understand why hearing her name might make you a bit fidgety, Elena. After all, there was some suspicion your father had something to do with her death all those years ago."

"That's a lie," Elena said sharply. "Angela Santoro hanged herself. It was ruled a suicide." Her eyes narrowed on Kara. "Are you so desperate to blame our family for what happened to your father that you're going to dig up the memory of a dead woman?"

It wasn't quite the reaction she'd anticipated, but then

Kara had begun to accept expectations no longer played a starring role in her job. "I know who's to blame for my father's death." Kara passed a glance to Rafael, who looked a bit confused by the exchange. "I might not ever be able to prove your father ordered my father's death, but that's not why I'm here right now. I'm here because someone's trying to frame Rafael for Jazz's murder." Her gaze flicked to Elena. "We've recently been presented with evidence of fraud, money laundering and racketeering in regards to your family businesses. The duplicate sets of books Albert Mercer has been keeping for you for the past three decades?" She smiled as recognition rose on Elena's face. "I have them. And the same person who gave me that evidence is the one responsible for killing Jazz and setting you up, Rafael."

She opened the file, set it on the table and turned it to face them.

Elena and Rafael leaned forward to look at the picture of Giselle Santoro.

"This is her!" Rafael poked a finger against the image. "That's Juliet from the office."

"She does look familiar." Elena shook her head. "But I can't say from where."

"Maybe this will help." She slid Giselle's picture aside to expose the one of Angela Santoro. "Does it help, Elena?"

Elena swallowed so hard Kara heard it.

"But." Elena glanced between the photos of the two women who looked so similar they could have been twins. "I don't—"

"Her name isn't Juliet Unger," Kara told the siblings.

"It's Giselle Santoro. She's Angela Santoro's daughter." She waited a beat. "She's your baby sister."

As far as payoffs went, Kara put it in her top five professional accomplishments. Just seeing the shock on Elena's face as she was presented with something she could never have prepared for... Well, it wasn't going to get much better than that.

"What does this mean?" Rafael demanded. "Elena? Did you..." He balked. "Did you *know* about Giselle?"

"I'm his lawyer," Elena said quietly. "Of course I knew. But I echo my brother's question. What does this mean?"

Kara had been hoping they'd ask. "It means your little sister is a chip off the old block. She got your father's tenacity and single-mindedness when it comes to getting back at the people who have wronged her in some way. You two, I'm guessing, are two and three on her list. Guess who's number one?"

Elena's eyes sparked, not with anger, but with panic. "She's going after our father."

"She is. Here's the thing." Kara leaned forward and rested her arms on the table. "I can stop her. But I need your help."

Elena turned her head. "What kind of help?"

"A phone call." Kara motioned to the cell phone sitting near Elena's hand. "I want you to call your father and set up a meeting. You're going to tell him it's necessary to keep your business records safe. You're going to tell him who I am, who my father was and that I have an offer to put to him. One that will make him quite happy. Understood?"

"If I don't?"

Kara shrugged. "It's entirely your choice. But I can

promise you, arranging this meeting is the only chance you've got at keeping your father alive. Personally, I'd be fine if you say no." She offered a quick smile. "I don't think Giselle is going to be so kind as to make it quick. Something to consider."

Elena touched her phone and yet still hesitated.

"Make the call," Rafael whispered desperately. "She's a psychopath. She murdered Jazz. There's no telling what she's going to do to him."

Eventually, Elena lifted her phone to dial. "Dad? It's me. Yes, I'm with him now. I think there's a deal to be made with one of the prosecutors. Kara Gallagher. She wants to meet with you." She lifted her eyes to Kara's. "Yes, that Kara Gallagher. You meet with her, this case against Rafael can go away."

She didn't flinch as she listened, then nodded. "Okay. Two hours. She'll be there. Bye, Dad." She set her phone on the table face down. "There's an estate in Great Neck. Off Kings Point Road. Security code is seven-eight-two-four. Please..." Elena's tone softened. "Don't let her hurt him."

Kara simply blinked. "I'll do my best."

She stood up, left the file and pictures where they were—along with the two detectives—and departed the room. Howell pulled open the door to the observation area before she reached it and handed her her cell phone.

Kara kept her eyes on his, taking strength and comfort from his steady gaze as she dialed. "Giselle? I've got a counter offer for you. I'm ready to deal."

"I do not like this."

"I heard you the first three times you said it," Kara told Howell as Aiden futzed around with the signal from the surveillance wire he'd hooked her up with. The space in the classic dark gray van—marked as a power repair company right down to matching the logo of the local service—was almost as claustrophobic as a clam shell. Close quarters for sure with its bank of equipment and screens and...who knew what else. All Kara knew was that Aiden had come through the second Howell called.

Cutting it close on time, though. They'd needed another person to drive so that Kara could get wired up.

"You're going to be in the same room with two killers," Howell reminded her as she fixed him with a stony stare. It was, she had realized a little over ninety minutes ago, the only way she'd get through this. By pushing forward and putting her faith not only in the man she loved, but in his family as well.

"I've got the signal from the in-home security camera system." Regan McKenna swiveled in one of the small chairs in front of the computer screens. "Do me a favor and try to keep Alessi in the front of the house. Easier access if this goes sideways." She flashed a quick smile. "Not that it's going to."

Kara could hear Howell gnashing his teeth.

"Hey." Kara reached out, caught his hand. "I can't focus if I think you're out here worrying. I know what I need to do. I know what's at stake. I'm good, Howell. I need for you to be, too."

His jaw tensed.

Aiden rolled his eyes. "That's his not-ever-going-to-happen expression," he told Kara. "Just accept it and move on. Okay." He sat back, tapped a few buttons. "Talk normally."

Kara swallowed hard and cleared her throat. "Would it help if I told you I love you?"

Regan snort laughed. Aiden grinned.

Howell glared. "That's not funny."

"It's kind of funny," Kara admitted, then leaned forward and grabbed his face for a quick kiss. "It's also true. Something else to stew on while I'm in there. It'll be over in a little bit," she promised him. "I have no intention of getting myself killed. Not only because I've got a future in mind with you but because if I did, you'd have to tell my mother and let's face it, I care about you too much to let that happen."

"She really does make a good argument," Regan said. "Question, Kara. How do you feel about obligatory once-a-month Sunday dinners with the family?"

The idea warmed her and removed at least some of the chill threatening to make her tremble in fear. "Like it's something to try."

"Great." Regan grabbed her cell phone and started to text. "For the record, I'm locking this down before you leave the van. Another thing to keep you alive and motivated. Our mother's wrath if you have to cancel on account of death."

"It's nice to know your sense of humor is a genetic trait," Kara told Howell. "Let me go," she whispered when his hands tightened around her arms. "I'll be fine. I know how to make a closing argument, remember? Trust me, Howell. Please."

It wasn't that she wasn't scared. She was petrified, to be honest. But she had to take this last step out of the past if she had any hope of a future with him. The next few minutes could very well dictate the rest of her life. So yeah. She took a deep breath. She knew what was at stake.

"Go," Howell said. "Just know if one thing goes wrong, I've got the code and I'm coming in."

"I'm counting on it." She kissed him again, then squeezed through the siblings to the back door. The second she got a breath of fresh air, reality hit.

"Here she comes." Aiden's voice echoed in her ear. "Blue Volvo pulling up about fifty yards from the security gate. Looks like you're on, Kara."

"Got it." She started walking, hands deep in the pockets of her jacket, head down against the wind. Daylight was beginning to fade, but if they did this right, by the time the sun set, they should all be home. "Is she alone?" she asked quietly.

"Near as I can tell," Aiden confirmed.

Kara's heels clacked against the frozen cement. She walked past the iron gates of the estate that Sal Alessi called home, hurrying to close the gap to Giselle Santoro's car. Giselle got out, looking, Kara thought, so much like her deceased mother she may as well have been her ghost. Her hair was back to black, which meant the blond hair had either been a very good wig or she'd spent part of the day with a bottle of dye. There was an air of elegance about her now, reminiscent of Elena at her most professional.

"He's expecting me," Kara said as Giselle approached. "Do you have the encryption drive?"

"Yes. Did you come alone?"

"That was the deal."

Giselle scanned the area, her gaze skimming right over the van. "No US marshal hanging around?"

"I left him at the police station with your brother."

Kara thought that might get her attention and keep it away from Kara's backup.

Giselle stalked past her, leaving Kara to catch up at the gate. "What's the code?"

Kara ignored her and elbowed her out of the way to enter the numbers Elena had given her. She couldn't be seen to be a pushover. When the gate clicked and slid open, she followed Giselle inside the property, hoping that Aiden was as good as he'd promised and that they could make quick work of that gate if necessary.

Kara's heart pounded so hard she could barely hear herself think. They walked along the cobblestone drive to the front door. Kara reached out, pressed the latch. The door swung open.

"Looks like you're finally home, Giselle," Kara said with a tight smile.

Giselle frowned at her. "Not yet I'm not." She shoved inside, leaving Kara to follow once more.

The sound of a motorized wheelchair whizzed in the air a moment before Sal Alessi made an appearance from around a curved marble hallway. He was a shell of his former self, Kara realized. At least fifty pounds lighter, he barely resembled the photographs she'd spent most of her life obsessing over.

She expected the waves of hatred, of loathing, of anger to come flooding through her, but instead, all she felt was pity. And more than a little satisfaction in the knowledge his life's work was about to end.

The light from the overhead chandelier had him shielding his eyes as he looked at her.

"I'll say this for you," Sal Alessi's raspy voice echoed in the vaulted room. "You got your father's single-mindedness."

"Among other things," Kara said. "I'm not here to talk about my father."

"No?" Sal cackled. "Then what is it you're hoping I'll give you in exchange for my son's freedom?"

"How about another daughter?" She'd wondered exactly how she'd broach the subject. Too late.

"Yesss, Kara," Aiden's voice came through the earpiece she wore.

It seemed to be only now that Sal realized they weren't alone. Maybe that was because Giselle had taken a bit of a walk around the entry hall and had now stepped out from the enormous floral arrangement in the center of a circular table.

Sal pushed the lever on his chair forward and zoomed closer. He stopped a mere inch from Giselle.

Kara watched as recognition crossed his sallow features. His silver-gray eyes narrowed without any affection or emotion.

"Hi, Dad." Giselle tilted her head, kept her hands in her pockets. "I'm home."

Sal looked to Kara, then back to Giselle. "What kind of crap is this? What's she doing here?" Sal pointed a shaky finger at Giselle and turned his chair away from her. "This is between you and me, counselor."

"Believe me," Kara said slowly, "she has a vested interest in how this conversation goes. She's the one who framed your son for murder." She caught sight of an elegant sitting room even as she heard Aiden and Howell exchanging commentary in the van. "Shall we?" She didn't wait for permission. She simply walked into the room. "Are we alone?" Kara faced him again when he whizzed in.

"Staff'll be back in three hours. That's how long you've got to explain yourself." He zoomed past her to the empty space between an end table and brocade sofa. Antique furniture filled most of the space that included a baby grande piano covered in framed family photographs. Photographs depicting Elena and Rafael and their mother at various stages in their lives. All stages of their lives.

It was the photographs that drew Giselle across the room.

Kara waited, somewhat impatiently, for Giselle's emotions to get the better of her. But they didn't surface. Not when she stood there staring at the family she'd been denied. And not when she faced the father who had turned away from her.

"This is what you wanted," Kara reminded her. "Now give me the drive."

Giselle ignored her and sat in the seat across from her father. "What I want, I don't have. Yet." She narrowed her gaze. "Do you even know what I've done?" Sal looked uncomfortable. "The lengths I went to. The time it took. I infiltrated two of your businesses, hacked into your server, offloaded evidence that can send you and my brother and sister to prison for the rest of their lives."

"What about it?" Sal scoffed.

Giselle crossed her legs with more elegance than Kara believed was possible. "Do you know why I did all that? It was to prove myself to you. To prove I'm a true Alessi. That I'm worthy of your attention. Of a place in this family. And now, I've brought you the only lawyer with the guts to try to take you down."

Kara watched, as if in slow motion, as Giselle pulled a gun out of her pocket.

"Just say the word, Dad." Giselle released the safety. "Just say the word and I'll end her right now. I'll prove to you that I'm the only child you've got who's willing to go all the way. To do whatever it takes. Just say the word, tell me you made a mistake and that you accept me. Acknowledge me as your daughter and I'll finish the job."

Kara could hear the frantic activity coming from the van, and Howell in particular, as she stood in the middle of the sitting room, frozen in place.

She held her breath, unable to stare at anything other than the barrel of the gun pointed right at her. Her chest tightened and she had to remind herself to breathe.

"Well, Dad?" Giselle asked. "What do you say?"

Kara swallowed hard, wanting nothing more than to close her eyes so she wouldn't sense the shot coming. Instead, she jumped when Sal Alessi burst out laughing.

Had Kara's heart not already been steeled against Giselle's pain, she would have felt more than sympathy for the other woman. She'd have understood completely if she'd turned the gun on her father.

"Go ahead and shoot her," Sal stated. "She makes no difference to me. Elena's always had a specific word for you, hasn't she, Ms. Gallagher?"

She tried to speak, had to cough and clear her throat. "Negligible," Kara croaked, finally. "She says I'm negligible."

Giselle flinched.

"You trying to turn her into some kind of weapon against me shows me just how stupid you are and how unfit you are to be a true Alessi. A legitimate Alessi!" He pounded a hand against his frail chest. "You're just like your mother. Useless. And pathetic. Scrambling for any crumbs of affection I might toss her way." He wheeled closer to Giselle. "I got two for one when I ordered Patrick Hewitt's death. I'm just grateful your mother saved me the cash it would have cost to kill her next."

Kara held her breath even as a wave of grief crashed inside of her. Tears prickled the backs of her eyes, tears she couldn't hide when Giselle looked in her direction.

"Did you get what you wanted?" Giselle asked as she lowered her gun. "I saw the truck outside," she added at Kara's sudden shock that must have shown on her face. "I saw how you and the marshal are together. There's no way he'd have let you do this alone." The resignation and sadness in her expression left Kara shaking. "You've always been loved. By your father, by your mother, your children. And now him."

The gun dangled at her side as Kara listened to Aiden, Howell and Regan scrambling at the entrance to the house. Kara stepped toward Giselle, who had gotten to her feet. For an instant she feared Giselle was going to turn the gun on herself.

Instead, she aimed it at her father's chest.

"Don't!" Kara leaped forward as the sound of footsteps pounded. "Giselle, don't. Don't let him win."

"He won the moment he signed me away." There was no emotion on her face now. Only detached resolve. "No one's ever wanted me."

"Esty loves you," Kara said. "She loves you so much and she told us to tell you that it's time to stop pretending. It's time to let Juliet go and figure out who Giselle Santoro, Giselle *Alessi*, truly is." She took another step, so close, so close to touching the gun. "I promise she loves you, Giselle. Don't break her heart this way." The gun wavered.

"You're a coward just like your mother!" Sal spat. "Go ahead! End me! It'll be a mercy. A gift."

Kara looked at him. "You're a fool." Not just a fool. "You're dying."

The front door burst open and Howell, Aiden and Regan ran into the sitting room.

"You're suffering," Giselle whispered in awe.

"No!" Kara stopped Howell from getting closer. "No, I've got this. Giselle?" It was the first time she'd spoken the woman's name with compassion. And understanding. She looked at Aiden and Regan as they started to circle around, silently pleaded with them to back off and give her a chance. "You came to me because you thought we were the same. Maybe we are. We both want revenge." She looked to Howell, whose brow betrayed his concern. "And we both want justice. Let him live. Give me the evidence. I'll make the case go as fast as I can. Together, we can do what you wanted. We can make him pay for taking away the people we love."

"Don't listen to her," Sal argued almost desperately.

"It's not just him you'll take down, Giselle. It's the entire family. The entire syndicate. You can destroy everything he's built. There has to be some satisfaction in that." Wasn't there?

Giselle looked at Kara, then at Howell. And then back to her father.

She took one step and...held out the gun for Howell to take. Out of her other pocket, she produced the USB drive. "The encryption code for the laptop. It contains the entirety of the Alessi business operations. Both sets of books and records of every false company they created to launder their money."

Howell handed the gun over to Aiden before he moved in to lock cuffs around Giselle's wrists.

"Where's Billy?" Kara asked Giselle.

"Gone." She blinked as if coming out of a daze. "He took off after nearly running you down in the alley. He... left me." Her eyes shone with acceptance. "Everyone always leaves me." She stumbled as Howell waited next to her. "Don't you ever leave her," she told him.

"I don't plan to," Howell assured her.

Giselle stopped in front of Kara, a look of peace having finally settled behind her eyes. "There's one other silver lining to this." Her lips curved and that spark of evil that was all Alessi shone through. "I'm going to prison as an Alessi. There will be power there," she said, tossing the comment over her shoulder at her father. "And I'm going to wield every single ounce of it."

Kara slowly sank into a nearby chair. Aiden was on his cell, speaking to the New York cops, arranging for them to collect Sal Alessi on yet-to-be determined charges. The old man sagged in his wheelchair, sobbing, his shoulders shaking as he covered his face.

It was, Kara thought, the last bit of weight that needed to be lifted from her shoulders, weight she'd been carrying for twenty-one years. When she breathed, it didn't hurt. It didn't ache. She felt...free.

It was past midnight before they exited the apartment elevator.

Howell had to keep looking over his shoulder to make sure Kara hadn't fallen asleep while walking behind him.

"Aiden said your mom and the kids should be back at the house no later than ten in the morning," he told her as he unlocked the door and guided her inside. He closed and locked the door behind them.

"That's what Mom said when I talked to her." Kara offered him a sleepy smile. "I can't believe it's over. I can't believe I finally got to tell her..." Tears pooled in her eyes. "It's all really over. Sal Alessi's going to go to prison for the rest of his life. However long that is," she added on a sob.

Howell wrapped her in his arms, held on as tight as he could for fear she'd slip away. "You did it." He pressed his lips to her forehead as she clung to him. "Or you will have as soon as you earn that guilty verdict."

"Mmm." She stepped away from him, retreated into the kitchen and opened the fridge.

Concern he hadn't expected landed in his chest. "What's mmm? I haven't learned that one yet."

Kara handed him a bottle of water and kept one for herself. "I'm going to talk to my boss after my head clears, but I think it's best if I turn the prosecution of the case over to someone else. It's a conflict of interest and..."

"And?" he pressed when her voice faded.

"I don't want to turn into Giselle." Pity shone in her eyes. "She's lived her entire life obsessing about revenge, about a man who couldn't care if she lived or breathed. That can't be me. I need to let this go. Whatever happens... happens. I've done enough."

Howell simply stared at her. He didn't want to argue with her, didn't want to try to change her mind, but he also knew how important this case was to her. "You're sure?"

"I want... No," she said with certainty, "the Alessis are going down and Giselle wants nothing more than to be the reason why. I'm fine with that. In fact..." She took a deep breath and released it. "It's one of only two things I want."

"What's the other thing?"

She moved him toward the sofa and pushed him down. When she landed beside him, she immediately curled into him in a way that said more about her trust in him than words ever could.

"I want my kids to get to know you better," she said. "And I'd like to meet your children. If that's okay with you."

He ran light fingers down her arm. "More than okay."

"We'll figure out the living arrangements," she said on a yawn. "I know you're hoping on that promotion."

"We'll see." There were other options available, ones that until now he hadn't been tempted by. Funny how falling in love with Kara had opened his mind up to all kinds of possibilities. "You happy where you are?"

She sighed. "We'll see."

"Kara?" He could feel her softly sliding into sleep.

"Mmm-hmm." She snuggled against him.

"I love you, too."

"Yeah." Even without looking at her, he knew she was smiling. "I know." She shifted slightly, wrapped her arms around him and rested her head on his chest. "Wake me in about an hour and we can discuss that further."

He kissed her temple and, leaning his head back, closed his eyes, finally feeling for the first time in his life utterly and wholly content.

* * * * *

For more romantic adventures from Anna J. Stewart and Harlequin Romantic Suspense, visit www.Harlequin.com today!

Get up to 4 Free Books!

We'll send you 2 free books from each series you try PLUS a free Mystery Gift.

FREE Value Over **$25**

Both the **Harlequin Intrigue®** and **Harlequin® Romantic Suspense** series feature compelling novels filled with heart-racing action-packed romance that will keep you on the edge of your seat.

YES! Please send me 2 FREE novels from the Harlequin Intrigue or Harlequin Romantic Suspense series and my FREE gift (gift is worth about $10 retail). After receiving them, if I don't wish to receive any more books, I can return the shipping statement marked "cancel." If I don't cancel, I will receive 6 brand-new Harlequin Intrigue Larger-Print books every month and be billed just $7.19 each in the U.S. or $7.99 each in Canada, or 4 brand-new Harlequin Romantic Suspense books every month and be billed just $6.39 each in the U.S. or $7.19 each in Canada, a savings of 20% off the cover price. It's quite a bargain! Shipping and handling is just 50¢ per book in the U.S. and $1.25 per book in Canada.* I understand that accepting the 2 free books and gift places me under no obligation to buy anything. I can always return a shipment and cancel at any time by calling the number below. The free books and gift are mine to keep no matter what I decide.

Choose one: ☐ **Harlequin Intrigue Larger-Print** (199/399 BPA G36Y) ☐ **Harlequin Romantic Suspense** (240/340 BPA G36Y) ☐ **Or Try Both!** (199/399 & 240/340 BPA G36Z)

Name (please print)

Address   Apt. #

City   State/Province   Zip/Postal Code

Email: Please check this box ☐ if you would like to receive newsletters and promotional emails from Harlequin Enterprises ULC and its affiliates. You can unsubscribe anytime.

Mail to the Harlequin Reader Service:
IN U.S.A.: P.O. Box 1341, Buffalo, NY 14240-8531
IN CANADA: P.O. Box 603, Fort Erie, Ontario L2A 5X3

Want to explore our other series or interested in ebooks? **Visit www.ReaderService.com or call 1-800-873-8635.**

---

*Terms and prices subject to change without notice. Prices do not include sales taxes, which will be charged (if applicable) based on your state or country of residence. Canadian residents will be charged applicable taxes. Offer not valid in Quebec. This offer is limited to one order per household. Books received may not be as shown. Not valid for current subscribers to the Harlequin Intrigue or Harlequin Romantic Suspense series. All orders subject to approval. Credit or debit balances in a customer's account(s) may be offset by any other outstanding balance owed by or to the customer. Please allow 4 to 6 weeks for delivery. Offer available while quantities last.

Your Privacy—Your information is being collected by Harlequin Enterprises ULC, operating as Harlequin Reader Service. For a complete summary of the information we collect, how we use this information and to whom it is disclosed, please visit our privacy notice located at https://corporate.harlequin.com/privacy-notice. Notice to California Residents – Under California law, you have specific rights to control and access your data. For more information on these rights and how to exercise them, visit https://corporate.harlequin.com/california-privacy. For additional information for residents of other U.S. states that provide their residents with certain rights with respect to personal data, visit https://corporate.harlequin.com/other-state-residents-privacy-rights/.

HIHRS25